KATHA

Other titles in the series

KATHA

SHORT STORIES BY INDIAN WOMEN

Edited by
Urvashi Butalia

TELEGRAM
London San Francisco Beirut

British Library Cataloguing-in-Publication Data
A catalogue record for this book is available from the British Library

ISBN: 978-1-84659-030-6

This edition published 2007 by Telegram Books

A full CIP record for this book is available from the British Library.
A full CIP record for this book is available from the Library of Congress.

Manufactured in Lebanon

TELEGRAM
26 Westbourne Grove, London W2 5RH
825 Page Street, Suite 203, Berkeley, California 94710
Tabet Building, Mneimneh Street, Hamra, Beirut
www.telegrambooks.com

Contents

URVASHI BUTALIA

Introduction

Today, it's become almost fashionable to say that women's writing no longer inhabits the margins of the literary world. Yet it wasn't so long ago that women found it difficult to be published. Certainly this was the case a little over a quarter of a century ago, when we set up Kali for Women, India's first feminist publishing house. At the time, feminist publishing was alive and well all over the world – in the UK, the USA, in Australia, Thailand, Japan, Chile, Germany, France, Finland and more – and it was the commitment and energy of feminist publishers that put women's writing on the international literary map. In Kali, in the mid-eighties, I recall that when we set out to publish a volume of short stories by Indian women writers, the task of locating authors was not easy. Existing anthologies had little to offer, and most women writing in their own languages in India were not known outside the language group or area. Many saw their own writing as somehow inferior, and preferred to keep it in the background in deference to the work of their writer husbands, or other writers. And finally, when we did manage to put a couple of anthologies together, despite the fact that they contained excellent writing, they passed virtually unnoticed. A larger project (that eventually resulted in a two-volume book: *Women Writing in India: 600 BC to the Present Day*), begun some years later and covering many different genres of writing, excavated other writers, other work and brought to public attention the wealth of writing by women that lay in obscure libraries or that had been written but not published for lack of attention and attributed importance on the part of the publishing world. Together, the work of feminist scholars and feminist publishers represented the first steps towards the remaking of the canon of writing, and questioned how these canons were made, and indeed who made them.

There's a story in this collection that, in some ways, best describes the kinds of silences that had for long surrounded women and women's writing. The protagonist of 'The Story of a Poem' by Chandrika B. is a housewife and also secretly a poet. It is this that provides the oxygen in her life. Whenever the urge to write takes her, she struggles to find time in the little moments of freedom she has between household work, between her daily tasks of sweeping and swabbing and washing and cleaning. One day, her husband and children leave the house, he to go to work and the children to go to school. She quickly finishes her morning chores and goes in for a shower. While there, the first few lines of a new poem come to her. She runs out to pen them down before they go out of her head. Standing naked and dripping by the dining table, she writes her lines. Later, involved in housework, she thinks of another few lines, rushes to where her piece of paper lies, and writes them down. Then, between this and that, other lines are added. As evening falls and the light begins to fade she writes the last few lines and, just then, hears her family returning. Immediately, she picks up the paper with the by-now-complete poem and shreds it to bits, throwing it into the bin. The author now tells the reader that if she wishes to read the whole poem, the only way to do so is to piece it together from the story!

Were Chandrika's protagonist to be writing today, however, it's likely that she would not have had to destroy her poem, although it's more difficult to guess whether or not she would still have had to hide it from her husband. It wouldn't be wrong to say that the growth of women's movements all over the world, and the work of women publishers, have helped to create an enabling environment in which women can have the confidence to write, and to know that they will be read. And this, in turn, has created an interest within the publishing world, both alternative and mainstream, in the market that exists for such writing. Thus there is a growing awareness that women's writing is no longer something that merely inhabits a niche, but rather something that has a place in the mainstream – and perhaps the evidence of this lies in the disappearance of feminist publishers from much of the world's literary map. Whether in India or elsewhere, there is no doubt that in recent years some of the most successful authors have been women, and that many of these have been published by mainstream presses.

This anthology puts together the work of a variety of Indian women writers. They come from different parts of the country, write in different languages, and choose different genres. And yet, the stories included here do not even begin to touch the tip of the iceberg of what is available in India. With at least eighteen official languages – that is, languages that have over a million speakers each – and several more waiting to join the list, with a rich oral culture and thousands of dialects, and with a storytelling tradition that is part of every household and community, India offers a wealth of literatures and genres and there is no way a collection such as this can even hope to represent them. Nonetheless the stories included here offer us at least one glimpse of the range of women's writing: the work of writers included here spans a half-century of writing, with the oldest of the writers being in her seventies and the youngest in her twenties.

Should women's writing be defined by their gender? Or, to put it another way, do women write their gender? These continue to be troubled questions to which there are no easy answers. Years ago, when women's writing was marginalized, such questions were easy to answer, for, clearly, the reason why such writing remained peripheral was precisely because of the gender of its writers. However, once women began to emerge into the mainstream literary world, many of them no longer wanted to be defined by their gender. Instead they wished to be seen as writers. This is as it should be, and there can be any number of arguments about whether or not it is right to put writers within the covers of a single book simply because they belong to a particular gender. Would an anthology of men writers, for example, have the same meaning?

And yet, it is important to note that such a yoking together of a group of writers is not entirely meaningless. In some ways it enables the reader to get a broad picture not only of the wealth of form and genre that characterizes writing by women, but it also provides a view of the changes that have taken place in such writing, in terms of both the subjects that women choose to write about and their preferred ways of writing about these. Thus the story itself is redefined – for some writers it becomes a long narrative with a beginning, middle and end, a plot, a structure; for others a fable, or a retelling of one; for others an email exchange, and so on. Similarly, the range of subjects that women now cover has broadened and expanded. One of the things that was believed to characterize women's writing was also what helped to somehow label it as a 'lesser' form of writing, and this was the supposed preoccupation of women with the narrow world of the domestic sphere. But this is no longer true: women write about all kinds of issues, they choose all kinds of genres. The old taboos are being broken and new forms are being created.

This collection does not pretend to be representative, for there is no way that within the covers of a single book one can represent the complex reality that is India. But it does offer a variety – in terms of age, language, subject and so on. It also does not limit itself geographically, touching on writers living in India and in the diaspora – for Indians are today everywhere. Perhaps the one claim that we can make here is that in putting together the work of a handful of women writers from India, this anthology signals the many riches that still remain unexplored and the wealth of writing that exists in the vast subcontinent that is modern India.

Glossary

adivasis	tribals
amla	citrus fruit believed to have medicinal properties
anchals	the part of a sari used to cover the head and breast
angan	courtyard
apsara	a divine dancer
azaan	Muslim call to prayer
bahanji / ben	sister
bas	enough
bhajans	devotional songs
bhakti	a form of devotion, in which the disciple communicates directly with his or her god
bihugeet/ biyanaam	song to mark the festival Bihu
buwa	medicine man
chaiwalla	man selling tea
chandlo/ mangalsutra	necklace worn to signal marital status
churidar-kameez	long shirt worn over tight trousers
dacoity	highway robbery
Devdas	a Bollywood film
dholak	drum
dupatta	a long scarf
gamosa	a small scarf usually draped over the shoulder
ghagra	a loose-flowing long skirt
ghungroos	bells worn when dancing

gurudwara	a Sikh temple
hakim	a traditional doctor
haveli	large traditional house
huzoor, huzooran,	
huzoorain	all terms of respect, meaning 'sir' or 'madam'; also means 'yes', as in 'yessir'
Jatayu	a mythical bird in the Hindu Pantheon, with the power to fly long distances
Kabir dohas	couplets composed by the poet Kabir
khuda hafiz	God be with you
kirya	ceremony performed a few days after a person's death
kumkum	mark on forehead to signal marital status; also worn for fashion
lalas	senior men, could be shop owners or just village elders; sometimes also used in a derogatory way
mahajan	a moneylender
Maharaj	a term of respect or status
mekhela-sadors	wrap worn in northeast India
mela	fair
namaaz	Muslim prayer
nikah	Muslim marriage
panchayati	concerning the panchayat, or village governance cell
pandal	an enclosure where events take place
pandas, pandits	priests
pujas, yagnas,	
havans puja	prayer, larger public prayer, and the sacred, or ritual fire, central to many prayers and sacrifices
purana	ancient epic
randis	prostitutes
rudalis	women who mourn for the dead
sarai	shelter
sardars	bosses, chiefs
shradh	a death ceremony
sindoor	vermilion powder put in the parting of a woman's hair to indicate marital status
vaids, hakims	traditional doctors or healers
Yudhistira	a character from the Mahabharata
zamindars	landowners

MARIJA SRES

How Kava Deceived Kavi and Defeated Her

As told by Jivabhai M. Katara

Kava and Kavi slowly recovered after the deluge, and started discovering their new surroundings together. With every passing day they felt more and more at ease with each other. But Kudrat's companion Deva said to himself: 'Let's complicate the relationship between them. Let's see who is the better of the two.' Actually, Deva being male favoured Kava over Kavi. So he organized a running competition or *spardha* for them.

Kavi was a very vibrant girl with a great sense of fun, and she knew she could outmatch the boy any day. So they ran a race, and she was far ahead of him and won.

But Deva had put it into Kava's mind that he must be better than the girl, and not to settle for defeat. He made Kava feel that it was bad to come second, and that he, Kava, would end up serving Kavi, when it should be the other way round. If not by strength, then Kava must win by trickery.

Kava stayed awake the whole night thinking what to do. Suddenly he saw something shining there on the ground. He picked it up. It was a pair of silver earrings. Oh, how smooth the ornaments felt to the touch, and how they sparkled in his hand. So he said: 'Right. This will distract her, and I'll win the next race.' And he dropped off to sleep happily. Little did he guess that the earrings had been placed there by Deva as part of his plot to boost Kava at Kavi's expense.

In the morning he went to Kavi, and suggested they run again. As they came to the starting line, Kava produced the silver earrings and dangled them in front of Kavi. 'Will you wear these in the race?' he asked. Kavi took them with delight, and as she struggled to put them on, the race began, and Kava ran far ahead. But Kavi was not slow either. Quickly, she snapped the earrings on and, running, outstripped Kava, and completed the race long before he came to the finishing line. Kava had lost again, in spite of his trick.

Kava was upset, but instead of losing heart, he determined to use more trickery.

The next morning, Kava presented Kavi with a nose-ring and bangles. Kavi was happy again to put them on, and while she did so, once again Kava started running. The ornaments did tend to slow Kavi a bit, but without much effort she caught up with Kava, and outstripped him once again.

Again, Kava spent the first part of the night planning Kavi's defeat, instead of making love to her. She felt sad for a while at his inattention, but when in the morning he ornamented her with a beautiful necklace which gleamed in silver against her darkish skin, she smiled again. Kavi wore it proudly, together with all the other ornaments he had given day by day, so that she almost forgot about the context, as she preened herself in the mirror. Deva reminded her that she had still to beat Kava that day, and so she ran, but with difficulty, so that they reached the finishing line almost at the same time, and it was agreed that she had won by a hair's breadth.

The last day of the spardha dawned, and Kava surprised Kavi with new jewellery. Although she knew that wearing these ornaments tended to slow her down, Kavi could not resist their beauty, and the way they enhanced her looks. She knew that the heavenly beings who were watching the competition envied her good looks, as well as her prowess in running.

That morning Kava came to her with yet another piece of jewellery. 'You must wear this breastplate,' he insisted. 'It's been made specially for you.' Kavi put on the breastplate of gold studded with precious stones, and was thrilled. And then Kava knelt down and added a pair of golden anklets, which tinkled with little bells each time she moved her feet. 'But they are too heavy,' Kavi protested. 'Nonsense,' said Kava. 'Imagine how the wind will carry the jhanjhar of your bells when you run!' And so she was persuaded to wear those as well.

Well, no one looked more gorgeous than Kavi all decked in her finery. But as Kava knew (and as Deva had planned) all these ornaments slowly but surely weighed her down. She was no longer as lithe and speedy as a gazelle.

The race started. It was the final race of the spardha, and whoever won would be declared the final victor. Once again Kavi simply flew along the track. Kava ran swiftly too, but he was always behind her. But as they ran in the heat of the sun Kavi felt pulled down by the weight of her jewellery, and her limbs could not move as easily as they had earlier. She felt tired and constrained. In a little while Kava caught up with her, and then overtook her. He increased the space between them, and never again did Kavi make up the distance. The race was won by Kava.

'I have won, and defeated you,' Kava crowed proudly. Kavi accepted with a smile. And Kava claimed the first place henceforward, whereas before Kavi and Kava had always walked side by side together. Ever since, men have used gifts, little and big, to distract women, and to make them do their bidding. Women, like Kavi, are happy to receive gifts, not realizing that like this they often lose their freedom. This is how even now the Dungri Garasiya tribe pays for the bride a *dapu*, a bride price, which shows how a woman becomes a man's property.

Rudali

In Tahad village, ganjus and dushads were in the majority. Sanichari was a ganju by caste. Like the other villagers, her life was lived in desperate poverty. Her mother-in-law used to say it was because Sanichari was suffering. At that time, Sanichari was a young daughter-in-law; she wasn't free to speak up. Her mother-in-law died when Sanichari was still young. She was never able to answer back. Sometimes the old woman's words came back to Sanichari. To herself she would say, 'Huh! Because I was born on and named after a Saturday, that made me an unlucky daughter-in-law! You were born on a Monday – was your life any happier? Somri, Budhua, Moongri, Bishri – do any of them have happier lives?'

When her mother-in-law died Sanichari didn't cry. At the time, her husband and his brother, both the old woman's sons, were in jail because of malik-mahajan Ramavatar Singh. Enraged at the loss of some wheat, he had had all the young dushad and ganju males of the village locked up. Her mother-in-law died in great pain, of dropsy, lying in her own excrement, crying out, over and over, 'Food, give me food!' It was pouring that night. Sanichari and her sister-in-law together lowered the old woman into the ground. If the rites weren't carried out before the night was over, they would have to bear the cost of the repentance rites for keeping the corpse in the house overnight. And there wasn't even a cupful of grain in the house! So Sanichari was forced to go from neighbour to neighbour in the pouring rain. Dragging the neighbours home with her, and handling all the arrangements for the cremation, she was so busy that there was no time to cry. So what if there wasn't? The old woman had given her so much trouble that even if Sanichari had tried to cry she wouldn't have been able to wring out any tears.

The old woman couldn't stand being alone while she was alive. She couldn't stand being alone after her death either. Within three years the brother-in-law and his wife were dead too. At that time Ramavatar Singh had started a hue and cry about throwing the dushads and ganjus out of the village. Terrified of being driven out, Sanichari was on tenterhooks. There was no crying over those deaths either. Was one to weep or to worry about how to burn the corpses and feed the neighbours cheaply at the shradh? In this village, everyone was unhappy. They understood suffering. So they were content with being fed just sour curd, sugar and coarse, parched rice. Everyone understood the fact that Sanichari and her husband didn't shed any tears – how is it possible to weep when you've borne three deaths in as many years? Their grief must have hardened into stone within them! To herself, Sanichari had sighed with relief. Was it possible to feed so many mouths on the meagre scrapings they brought home after labouring on the malik's field? Two dead, just as well. At least their own stomachs would be full.

She had never thought, however, that she wouldn't cry at her husband's death. And yet, such was her destiny, that this was just what happened. At the time her only son, Budhua, was six. Leaving the little child at home, Sanichari laboured hard for the sake of a little security in her household. She would go off to the malik's house where she would split wood, gather fodder for the cows and, in harvest season, work alongside her husband in the fields. A piece of land had been left to her husband's brother by her father-in-law;

together the couple had built a little hut on it. She had painted designs and pictures on the walls. Budhua's father wanted to fence in their angan, and grow chillies and vegetables. She had plans to raise a calf she would get from the malik's wife. It was all fixed. Her husband said, 'Come, let's visit the Baisakhi mela at Thori. We can offer worship to Shiva as well. After all, we've managed to save up seven rupees.'

The mela was a grand affair. The Shiva idol was being bathed in pots and pots of milk donated by the rich. This milk had been collecting in large tanks over the past few days. It gave off a sour stink and was thick with buzzing flies. People were paying the pandas money to drink glasses of this milk and promptly falling sick with cholera. Many died. Including Budhua's father. It was during British rule. Government officials were dragging the victims off to the hospital tents. There were only five tents. There were sixty to seventy patients. The tents were cordoned off with barbed wire. Sanichari and her son sat and waited beyond the barbed wire. They learnt that Budhua's father had died. The government officers didn't give her any time to shed tears. They burned the corpses quickly. They dragged Sanichari and Budhua off for a vaccination against the disease. The pain of the injections made them yowl. Still crying, she washed off the sindoor from her head in the shallow Kuruda River, broke her bangles, and returned to the village. They were new shellac bangles. She had just bought them at the fair. The panda of the Shiva temple at Tohri demanded that she make ritual offerings there before returning to her village, since her husband had died there ...

*

Bikhni was a childhood playmate. Everyone called her Kalikambli Bikhni because she always wore a ghagra made out of a black quilt. Carrying a bundle on her shoulder, she was striding along hastily. Not noticing Sanichari, she bumped into her.

'What the hell? Are you blind?'

'It's your father who is blind.'

'What did you say?'

'You heard me all right.'

A fine fight was brewing. Sanichari was all set to enjoy herself. A good set-to cleared the brain, got rid of a lot of undergrowth. That's why Dhatua's mother literally quarrelled with the crows – quarrelling kept both mind and body in fine fettle, the blood coursing through your veins like bullets from a gun. But as they glared at each other, Bikhni asked: 'Hey, aren't you Sanichari?'

'Who're you?'

'Bikhni, Kalikambli Bikhni.'

'Bikhni?'

'Yes!'

'But you were married off in Lohardaga.'

'I've been living in Jujubhatu for many years.'

'Jujubhatu? And I've been in Tahad, just half a day's walk from you! How come we never met?'

'Come, let's sit down somewhere.'

They settled down in the shade of a peepul tree. They eyed each other closely, before each relaxed in the realization that the other was no better off than herself. Like Sanichari, Bikhni's wrists, throat and forehead sported no jewellery other than blue tattoo marks; both wore pieces of cork in their ears instead of earrings, and their hair was rough and ungroomed. Sanichari handed Bikhni a bidi.

'Did you come to the market?'

'No, I came to look for my grandson.'

Sanichari told her about Haroa, about herself, about everything. Bikhni listened, then said, 'Is there no caring left in this world? Or is it our fate, yours and mine?'

Sanichari laughed bitterly: 'No husband, no son: wherever my grandson is, may he be safe.'

Bikhni said, 'I had a son after three daughters. Their father died long ago, I was the one who brought him up. I began to take in calves for rearing, and gradually I managed four cows, and two she-goats of my own. I got my son married, and I fed the whole village on dahi-chivda-gur after taking a loan from the mahajan.'

'Then?'

'Now the mahajan is about to claim my house by way of repayment, and my son is moving in with his in-laws.'

Bikhni spat while saying this. She said, 'His father-in-law has no sons. My son will live there along with his brother-in-law as his servant. I told him, let's sell the cows and repay the debt to the mahajan but my son took the cows and calves away to his in-laws. But I am Bikhni, after all. I've just sold my two goats in this market-place. My son doesn't know. Bas, I've got twenty rupees in the tank, and I'm off.'

'Where will you go now?'

'Who knows? Your son's no more, mine's as good as dead. Perhaps I'll go to Daltonganj, or Bokharo or Gomo. Beg at some station.'

Sanichari heaved a sigh. She said, 'Come with me. My two-roomed hut is empty. Each room has a platform to sleep on. Budhua built them. The vegetable patch still yields okra, eggplant, chillies.'

'And when my money runs out?'

'We'll face that when it happens. Your money is yours. Sanichari can still earn enough to subsist on.'

'Then let's go. Tell me, is there a water problem in your village?'

'There's the river. And the panchayati well, though that water's bitter.'

'Just a minute.'

Bikhni went to the market and returned after a short while. She said, 'I've bought some medicine for lice. We'll mix it with kerosene and massage it in, then wash our hair. Lice can worry you more than the most worrying thoughts.'

Walking along, Bikhni said, 'My granddaughter will probably cry for me. She's used to sleeping beside me.'

Sanichari said, 'Only for a few days. Then she'll forget.'

Bikhni was delighted with Sanichari's house. Right then and there she sprinkled the place with water and washed it down. She went off to the river and fetched a pot of water. She said, 'There's no need to light the stove tonight. I have some roti and achar with me.'

Bikhni loved housework. Within a couple of days, she had put a fresh coat of mud and dung on the floor of the house and compound, washed Sanichari's and her own clothes thoroughly, and aired all the mats and quilts. At home, she had withdrawn more and more from the housework as her daughter-in-law took the reins into her own hands. This was out of hurt pride, but her daughter-in-law thought she was lazy. Managing a household is addictive. It can set even someone as unhappy as Bikhni to dreaming unrealistic dreams. There was no knowing how long she'd be there – this was Sanichari's house. One day Bikhni began to dig and tend the vegetable patch. She said, 'With a little effort we will get lots of vegetables.'

The lice medicine killed the creatures in Sanichari's hair. After sleeping comfortably she realized that her sleepless nights had been caused by the lice, not by mental anguish. No matter how griefstricken one is, a work-worn body is bound to sleep well.

For some days the two of them ate off Bikhni's money. When that ran out, Sanichari felt as if the sky had fallen on her head ...

*

... Then she told Bikhni, 'Come, let's go to see Dulan. He's a crafty old rogue, but he has a sharp mind. He's sure to show us a way.'

After hearing them out, Dulan said, 'As long as there's a way of earning, why should anyone die of starvation?'

'What kind of earning?'

'Budhua's mother! Do ready-made ways of earning exist? They may exist for malik-mahajans, but do they exist for dushads and ganjus? We have to make our own opportunities. How much money did your friend bring with her?'

'Twenty rupees.'

'Tw-en-ty whole rupees!'

'Yes, but we've spent eighteen rupees on food.'

'If it was me, I'd have seen Mahabirji in my dreams long before the money ran out.'

'What on earth are you talking about, Latua's father?'

'Why? Can't you follow me?'

'No, what do you mean?'

'Before my money ran out, I would pick up a nice stone from the banks of the Kuruda River. I'd anoint it with oil and sindoor and proclaim that Mahabirji had come to me in my dreams.'

'But I don't even dream!'

'Arre, once you find Mahabirji, you'll have no shortage of dreams.'

'Hai baba!'

'Everyone knows you. It won't work if you try it. But your friend is new here, we'd all believe her. Then you could present yourself and Mahabirji at the Tohri market-place. Collect offerings from the devout.'

'Hanky-panky with a god? As it is, Mahabirji's monkey followers don't leave any fruit on my trees!'

'It's trickery if you consider it trickery. Not otherwise. You have a sinner's mind, so you think it's trickery.'

'How's that? Eh, Latua's father?'

'Because ... let me explain.'

'Go ahead.'

'Lachman's mother has rheumatism, doesn't she?'

'Yes, she does.'

'Well, she gave me ten rupees to bring her some holy oil from Chas. I didn't even go to Chas, just took her some oil from home after a few days. And it wasn't trickery because I didn't consider it to be. She massaged herself with the oil yesterday, and today she walked on her own two feet to the fields to shit. You know what they say – if your mind is pure, the Ganga flows even through wood.

Look here, Budhua's ma, there's no bigger god than one's belly. For the belly's sake, everything is permissible. Ramji Maharaj said so.'

Dulan's wife spoke up: 'Even when the old man lifts a pumpkin from the malik's field, he claims it's on Ramji Maharaj's advice!'

Bikhni said, 'We're in trouble. How can you help? Give us old women some advice.'

'Bhairab Singh of Barohi village has just died.'

'Yes, his son killed him.'

'So what? In rich families the son kills the mother, the mother the son. Forget about who killed him. Amongst us, when someone dies, we all mourn. Amongst the rich, family members are too busy trying to find the keys to the safe. They forget all about tears. Our malik has ordered a fancy funeral. The funeral procession will be tomorrow afternoon. They need rudalis to wail over the corpse. They've got hold of two whores. In the households of the masters, whores weep for the dead. These two were probably Bhairab Singh's whores at one time, now they're wizened crows. They'll be no good. The two of you go, wail, cry, accompany the corpse. You'll get money, rice. On the day of the kirya ceremony you'll get clothes and food.'

Sanichari felt an earthquake within. She exploded. 'Cry? Me? Don't you know I can't shed tears? These two eyes of mine are scorched!'

Dulan spoke in a cold, expressionless tone. 'Budhua's ma, I'm not asking you to shed the tears you couldn't shed for Budhua. These tears are your livelihood – you'll see, just as you cut wheat and plough land, you'll be able to shed these tears.'

'But will they take us?'

'What am I here for? If they don't get good rudalis, Bhairab's honour will suffer. The malik-mahajan demands honour even when he's a corpse. Bhairab's father and his generation kept whores too, but they looked after them. When they died, the whores mourned for them out of genuine affection and gratitude. But the Bhairab, Daitari, Makhan, Lachman Singhs of this world treat their labourers and whores alike – they tread them into the mud. So the randis don't make convincing rudalis. What vicious bastards that lot are! The worst is Gambhir Singh. He kept a whore, had a daughter by her. As long as the whore was alive, he kept the child in comfort. When the mother died, he told the girl: "A whore's daughter is a whore – practise your profession and support yourself."'

'Chhi, chhi!'

'That girl is now rotting in Tohri, in the randi bazaar. From a five-rupee whore, she's down to a five-paise whore. Budhua's wife is there too. She's in the same state.'

'Who wants to hear about her?'

Dulan said, 'Wear black clothing.'

'That's what we wear in any case.'

Dulan took them along. On the way, Bikhni said, 'If this kind of work comes along from time to time, and if we find jobs working the malik's fields or breaking stones, we'll be able to get along.'

Sanichari said, 'Won't there be talk in the village?'

'So let them talk!'

Bhairab Singh's accounts-keeper Bachhanlal knew Dulan. Lachman had put him in charge of the funeral arrangements, and it was no easy job. At the moment, he was preoccupied with how he could pass off two shovels, a clothes rack and some brass utensils he needed for his own home as part of the funeral requirements. As soon as he saw the two women he said, 'You'll get three rupees each.'

Dulan said, 'Such an important person is dead, and the rate for mourning him is only three rupees? At least five per head, huzoor.'

'Why?'

'They'll do such a good job, you'll want to give them a tip. Lachman Singh has ordered that ten, twenty are spent, whatever it takes, he wants some good rudalis. Two hundred rupees have been budgeted for this.'

Bachhanlal sighed, wondering how Dulan knew so much.

'Okay, five rupees each. Go sit outside.'

'And they're to get rice as well.'

'They'll get wheat.'

'Give them rice, huzoor.'

'Okay.'

'And feed them well – they can't mourn convincingly on an empty stomach.'

'Dulan! How many bastards died to give birth to you? Go, wait outside. They'll get fed.'

Bhairab Singh's second wife ordered that the rudalis should be served generously with a snack of chivda and gur. Prasad's father hadn't left them lacking in anything.

As she filled her stomach on the chivda and gur, Sanichari thought that perhaps her tears had been reserved for the time when she would have to feed herself by selling them.

At first the randis paid no attention to the two old village women. But Sanichari and Bikhni wailed so loudly, and sang such well-chosen phrases in praise of Bhairab Singh, that the market-place randis had to admit defeat. Sanichari and Bikhni wailed all the way to the cremation ground and all the way back. Each of them earned five rupees and two and a half sers of rice. Bachhan told them, 'You must come back for the kirya ceremony.'

'We'll definitely come, huzoor.'

At the kirya, they got clothes and feasted on puri, kachauri and besan laddus. They packed their potions to take home. Sanichari shared some with Dulan's wife. Dulan listened to all their news. He cursed. 'That bastard Bachhan was allotted two hundred rupees for this job, and he got away with spending only twenty.'

'That kind of thing is bound to happen, Latua's father.'

'Tell your friend to keep her ears open on her trips to the market. All the shops belong to the landlords and moneylenders. Tell her to find out who's ill, who's dying ... otherwise we won't get information in time. And she should tell them that she can arrange for more rudalis.'

'How?'

'Go to Tohri. The randi bazaar.'

'My God!'

'Will your friend go?'

Bikhni said, 'Yes, I'll go.'

Dulan said, 'Do you think we always had so many whores? It's these Rajput malik-mahajans who have created so many randis.'

His wife said, 'The whores have always been there.'

'No, they haven't. Not here. All the evil things have been brought in by *them*.'

'They've also been here forever.'

'No. Earlier, when the area was under the Raja of Chhotanagpur, it was mostly jungle and hilly land and adivasis lived there. This was a long, long time ago. The Kols in the district town talk about it.'

The tale Dulan told them was very significant: it explained clearly how the ruthless Rajputs infiltrated this remote area of tribals, and from zamindars, gradually built themselves up to the status of jotedars and moneylenders and established themselves as the masters of the area. The Rajputs were warriors in the army of the Raja of Chhotanagpur. About two hundred years ago, in protest against the cruel oppression practised against them, the Kol tribals revolted. The Raja immediately sent his army to put down the uprising. Even after the rebellion was suppressed, the Rajput warriors' aggression was not sated. They went on a rampage, killing innocent tribals and burning down villages. So Harda and Donka Munda started sharpening their arrows, and a fresh tribal uprising was imminent. Then the Raja sent his Rajput sardars into the sparsely populated Tahad region. He told them, 'Take as much land as is covered by throwing your swords in the air. Start at sunrise, and carry on till sundown. There are seven of you, claim as much land as you can in this way, then live off it.'

That's how the Rajputs settled in Tahad, and how they come to be masters of this region. From century to century their holdings and power increased. Even now they take possession of land, not by throwing swords in the air, but by shooting bullets at people and flinging flaming torches at settlements. Once they were all related, and though the blood ties have thinned, they all claim the same status and honour.

The lower castes live in settlements of decrepit mud huts roofed with battered earthen tiles. The tribal settlements look equally poor. In the midst of these are the towering mansions of the maliks, but they have certain things in common. Except for salt, kerosene and postcards, they don't need to buy anything. They have elephants, horses, livestock, illegitimate children, kept women, venereal disease and a philosophy that he who owns the gun owns the land. They all worship household deities, who repay them amply – after all, in the name of the deities, they hold acres which are exempt from taxes and reforms. Of course, there are differences between them – Aaitari Singh has six toes, Banwari Singh's wife carries the blood of a low caste gwala in her veins, Nathuni Singh has a stuffed tiger in his house.

After reminding them of all this he told them – 'These people need rudalis to prop up their honour. Now I've shown you the way, fight on.'

Sanichari and Bikhni nodded. For them nothing had ever come easy. Just the daily struggle for a little maize gruel and salt was exhausting. Through motherhood and widowhood they were tied to the moneylender, while those people spent huge sums of money on death ceremonies, just to gain prestige. Let some of that money come into Sanichari's home!

So Sanichari and Bikhni fought on. Everything in this life is a battle. Bikhni was not a woman of this village, but she became part of its life surprisingly easily. At sowing and harvest times, she laboured in Lachman's fields, at other times she visited the market and the shops near the bus stop and brought home news – who was on his deathbed, who gasping his last in which malik's house. Then they would wash their lengths of black cloth. Put them on. Knot some churan into their anchals.

Munching on a churan, they'd hurry along to the big house.

Sanichari negotiated with the malik's gomastha. Their negotiation followed a fixed pattern.

'The way we'll weep and wail, huzoor, we'll drown out even the chant of Ram's name! For five rupees and rice. On the day of the kirya ceremony we'll take cloth and food. Nothing more, nothing less. And if you need more rudalis, we'll arrange it.'

The gomastha would agree to everything. What option did he have? Everyone wanted them after seeing their performance at Bhairab Singh's funeral. They were professional. The world belongs to the professional now, not to the amateur. The gomastha himself is professional at manipulating the fieldhands' accounts and increasing the interest owed by peasant debtors. So professional is he, in fact, that on a pittance of a salary, a mere ten rupees a month, he manages to acquire his own fields, cattle and even, if he so desires, several wives. Professional mourning for the unmourned dead is a regular business. In the big cities, prosperous prostitutes competed for such jobs. In this region, it is Sanichari who has taken up this business. After all, this is not the big city. There are no prosperous prostitutes thronging Tohri. So far, he has to agree to Sanichari's demands.

'Just for wailing, one kind of rate.'

'Wailing and rolling on the ground, five rupees, one sikka.'

'Wailing, rolling on the ground and beating one's head, five rupees, two sikkas.'

'Wailing and beating one's breast, accompanying the corpse to the cremation ground, rolling around on the ground there – for that the charge is six rupees.'

'At the kirya ceremony, we want cloth, preferably a length of plain black cloth.'

'This is the rate. Over and above this, you people are like kings, can't you spare some dal, salt and oil with the rice? You've got the goddess Lakshmi captive in your home, you won't miss it! And Sanichari will sing your praises everywhere she goes.'

Business prospered. There was such a demand for the pair who wailed at Bhairab Singh's funeral, that it was almost like a war of prestige. Soon, not just the landlords and moneylenders but lalas and sahus began to ask for Sanichari. In fact, when Gokul lala's father died, he said, 'Come every day till the kirya ceremony, Sanichari.'

Gokul gave them sattu and gur every day, saying, 'We acquire virtue by feeding you.'

He also gave them good quality cloth, unlike the malik-mahajans who palmed off the cheapest cloth. Sanichari and Bikhni sold it in the market.

When he heard about the treatment they received at Gokul's house, Dulan said, 'Good. From now on, you must keep visiting your clients' homes every day right till the kirya ceremony. They're bound to give something to rudalis. At such times no one really keeps a strict eye on expenditure.'

'Yes, they'll surely give something.'

Sanichari exhaled tobacco smoke in sharp contempt. She said, 'These people can't summon up tears even at the death of their own brothers and fathers, won't they count their kirya costs? Do you know that Gangadhar Singh, a rich man like him, was stingy enough to use dalda instead of pure ghee on the funeral pyre of his uncle?'

'If they could cry for their own, where would you be?'

'They could shed a tear, at least.'

'Anyway, let's talk of something useful.'

'Go ahead.'

'Rich people's goings-on. Nathuni Singh's mother is on her deathbed. His house is quite far away. He's said that he wants to hire you.'

'She's dying, not dead yet.'

'Arre, if you hear Nathuni's story you'll realize what sinners these people are. Nathuni Singh's land and wealth are all from his mother. Do you know who she is?'

'No. No one keeps track of everyone's affairs the way you do.'

'She was the only child of Parakram Singh. The kind of oppression that man practised! When I was a child, I remember how he pushed out one of his tenants, Hathiram Mahato. He tied the old man to a horse and set the horse galloping.'

'Yes, I heard about that.'

'Parakram's daughter inherited all his wealth. Nathuni owes everything to her. For some time she's been suffering from wasting fever and coughing up fresh blood. Apparently this disease is highly contagious.'

'No, no. Budhua had the same thing.'

'Budhua was a good man. Nathuni's ma is definitely evil.'

'Whatever. What were you saying?'

'Nathuni is such a worthy son that he's isolated her in a single room at the far end of the compound. Aside from tying a goat to her bed, he hasn't bothered with any treatment. No hakim, no kabiraj, no doctor. No herbal remedies, no medicines, no injections. She's still alive. Meanwhile, he's stocking up on sandalwood and sal wood for a sensational funeral pyre. Bales of cloth are arriving, for distribution at the kirya ceremony. He's preparing to feed Brahmins and purchasing loads of ghee, sugar, dal, flour. He's buying utensils as well, to give the Brahmins.'

'My God! And his mother's not even dead yet!'

'His mother's left to lie in her own excrement all day. Once every evening Moti the dushad woman cleans her up – no one's concerned about loss of caste or defilement any longer, it seems. They've kept a maid to sleep beside her at night. He's not willing to spend a paisa on trying to cure her, but plans to spend thirty thousand on her funeral!'

'You don't say!'

'He's shouting it from the rooftops. That's why I say their whole attitude is topsy-turvy. They don't care about the living, but once they're dead, they hold grand funerals and try to raise their prestige. In this cold weather, he's taken away her warm quilt and given her a thin covering instead. He wants her to die quickly. You must visit their house every day till the kirya ceremony.'

'And what if they don't give us anything?'

'Don't worry, they will. Nathuni won't want to be outdone by Gokul lala. It'll be a loss of face before his community.'

There's a saying that even the tiger shivers in the bitterly cold month of Magh. The cold soon kills off the old lady. Sanichari presents herself every day till the kirya. Nathuni has three wives. The eldest reluctantly doles out atta and gur, grumbling. After all, she died of old age. Why spend so much on her kirya?

Nathuni's middle wife is the daughter of an extremely rich jotedar. Nathuni himself was rich because his father married the only daughter of a rich man – he wanted to do the same. It's bad luck that neither the eldest nor the youngest but only the middle wife is treated as the beloved. She looks down on her marital home as poor compared with her father's and resents her co-wives because they are mothers of sons, whereas her child is a daughter, which lowers her status in the eyes of others. Overhearing, the eldest wife sneers. 'What's thirty thousand rupees for a kirya ceremony? – less than nothing. May my father live long – but when he dies, then I'll show everyone how a kirya should be held!'

The eldest co-wife replies sharply, 'Of course you will! After all, you have to cover up the fact that your father's sister has the blood of a lowly barber in her veins.'

'Don't make me laugh! My aunt and barber's blood! Everyone knows my aunt's husband in Gaya. But what about your widowed sister who lives with her dead husband's brother? How come you don't mention her?'

This causes a major fight. But the middle wife must be truly virtuous. Her words were heard by the gods, and soon after her father was stricken by smallpox. She sent for Sanichari. She said, 'It must be true that those who die on an inauspicious Tuesday tug at the living. Otherwise why would my father get smallpox so soon after my mother-in-law's death? Here, Sanichari, here's a rupee tip.'

'Smallpox?'

'Yes.'

Sanichari puts on an innocent air and asks – 'But I heard that the upper castes never get smallpox? That it is a disease of the poor and lower castes? That's why we take the government vaccination to appease the gods.'

'The government vaccine is like cow's blood.'

Saying this, Nathuni's middle wife changed the topic. She said, 'You were there, weren't you, when the eldest wife and I quarrelled? With my father gone, I have no one. Here I'm surrounded by enemies. The others are given respect because they have sons. I'm the mother of a mere girl.'

'They respect you as well.'

'That respect is not for me, it's for my father Mohar Singh's wealth. My father didn't want to send me far away, that's why he arranged my marriage in a household where there are co-wives. Otherwise, as Chauhan Rajputs, would we ever have married into such a family?'

'It's all a question of fate.'

'That's true. Listen, I'm off to my father's place. You and Bikhni will be required, plus another twenty randis. They'll get one hundred rupees plus rice. You two will get fifty rupees plus rice. You'll stay there till the kirya ceremony, you'll get your meals, and return after you've got the cloth from the kirya ceremony.'

'Huzooran, your father's not dead yet.'

'The rot has set in. He has such a fit physique, fed on milk and ghee, the soul is reluctant to leave his body. When my mother-in-law died, you were given coarse rice and khesari dal.'

'And oil, salt, chillies.'

'Don't I know what they gave you? I know exactly how generous my eldest co-wife is! I'll give you rice, dal, oil, salt, potatoes and gur.'

'Huzooran is a great benefactor of the poor!'

'And listen, you must really do a good job of the wailing.'

'Certainly – and shall we roll on the ground as well?'

'Yes, roll on the ground.'

'We'll roll on the ground, and shall we beat our heads too?'

'Yes, beat your heads.'

'Our foreheads will split.'

'Five rupees each extra for the two of you? Money's no problem, Sanichari. My father's cremation and kirya will be the stuff legends are made of. Everyone will talk about it. I want my husband and co-wives to burn with jealousy. I'm my father's only child. The lavishness should match what my father is bequeathing me. He drank his milk from a silver glass everyday, had whores when he was a young man, kept them till he grew old, wouldn't touch anything but foreign liquor. He refused to remarry in case his second wife didn't treat me well.'

'Please give me some money, I'll have to pay the marketplace randis in advance. They're regular rascals.'

'Here, take.'

The whole situation was quite complex. When someone died in a malik-mahajan household, the amount of money spent on the death ceremonies immediately raised the prestige of the family. The status of the rudalis also rose. The price for this was paid by the dushads, dhobis, ganjus and kols, from the hides of whom the overlords extracted the sums they had overspent. Mohar Singh's lavish death ceremonies became much talked about, with the lion's share of the profits going to the Brahmins. Nathuni's middle wife never returned to her husband, and to prevent him laying his hands on her father's wealth, she began to spend lavishly on preparations for her daughter's wedding – this, however, took place after some years.

Sanichari reported her good fortune to Dulan. He smiled slyly and said, 'The coalminers have a union. Why don't you form a union of rudalis and randis? You can be the pishiden.'

'Hai Ram!'

'Will you look for market-place randis now?'

Bikhni spoke up – 'I'll get them. It's the women who are ruined by the malik-mahajans who turn into whores.'

'Nonsense, they're a separate caste.'

'No, no, you know nothing about it.'

'Hordes of them gather at the Tohri marketplace.'

Suddenly, Dulan asked, 'Arre, Sanichari, remember Nawagarh's Gambhir Singh?'

'Baba! Don't I just! The one who used to roam about the Diwali mela on his elephant. He had a huge nose and a big goitre on his neck.'

'He's done something terrible.'

'What now?'

'Motiya was his kept woman. He maintained her like a wife. As for Motiya's daughter Gulbadan – he dressed her in silver anklets and let her play on his lap. He had vowed to marry her off respectably after Motiya died. Today I saw Gulbadan walking towards Tohri, her eyes red with tears. She was saying, "They know how to produce children but not how to look after their offspring. He's thrown me out." I asked, "Why?" She said, "I merely complained to him that his nephew was pestering me, and he glared at me and said, 'Your mother's been dead three months and you're still hanging around here! Listen to my nephew's offer, or get out. You're the daughter of a whore, after all.'"'

'What a swine he is!'

Dulan cleared his throat. He said, 'I felt terrible. Gulbadan said, "How could he tell his own daughter to sleep with his nephew? And when I have a child by him? One day, they'll kick that child out in the same way. I'll have to work in the marketplace."'

Sanichari heaved a sigh. 'With that face, she'll get snapped up by some rich merchant.'

Bikhni said shrewdly, 'She's learned from her mother's fate, she won't let herself be tied to one man.'

Bikhni went to Tohri and returned, saying, 'My goodness! At the chance of earning money, a whole crowd of women gathered around!'

'Got a good look at them?'

'That I did.'

'What're they like?'

'Cheap whores, selling themselves for a few annas, all old now. It's a hard life. They still have to stand around, eyes lined with kohl and lamps in their hands. They'll come as soon as they get to know that the old man's dead. One good thing!'

'What?'

'I saw your Budhua's wife, your son's wife.'

'In Tohri?'

'Yes. She looks older than you.'

'Don't talk about her.'

'She herself came up to me. She's been there ten years. Asked about her son.'

'What did you say?'

'What should I say? Why should I say anything? I didn't talk to her.'

'Good.'

As she ate her vegetables and rice, Sanichari thought of her daughter-in-law – of her huge appetite. When did she leave? It was the year the elephants overturned that railway engine. The year Budhua died. The mango tree was just a sapling then, now it bears fruit. Ten years at Tohri. Good thing Haroa ran away. At least he didn't find out about his mother.

After eating, the two of them took tobacco. Sanichari said; 'It was her fate. I wouldn't have turned her out after Budhua's death.'

'No, no, of course you wouldn't have.'

'Did she look very poor?'

'Very.'

Sanichari fell silent.

Then Mohar Singh died.

The kirya was held with much pomp and splendour. Afterwards, when the old whores took leave, they addressed Sanichari and Bikhni respectfully: 'Huzoorain, if you need us again, just send word, we'll come.'

Sanichari and Bikhni got a brass bowl and a bamboo umbrella

as well as cloth. Bikhni sold them in the marketplace and with the money bought a sackful of worm-eaten corn. She said, 'We can grind it into wheat or make porridge.'

As time goes by, they settle into a rhythm. When someone dies, they work as rudalis. The rest of the time they survive on half-empty stomachs. And when there's nothing available? No problem. There aren't more than a couple of deaths a year. For the rest, like everyone else, they labour in the fields or work for the malik, clearing land, or gather roots in the forest to feed themselves.

Bikhni surprised everyone. She didn't go to visit her son even once. She grew chillies in Sanichari's courtyard and sold them, then said: 'We should try growing garlic. Garlic sells well.'

Gradually, their reputation grew. Everyone wanted them as rudalis – sure, they weren't cheap, but they really did provide their money's worth, really did weep and wail and hit their heads in the dust. The praises these two sang in honour of the deceased made even their relatives think of them not as the dyed-in-the-wool devil's henchmen they were, but as divine beings born on Earth to beguile them.

Things were going very well. In between two years were bad – Nathuni's eldest wife's brother was on his deathbed, but recovered after a stint in hospital. Lachman Singh's stepmother was virtually declared dead until a dangerous vaid, a natural healer, came along and cured her.

Sanichari heaved a sigh of relief and said, 'Fate.'

The village barber, Parashnath, was unhappy as well. He said, 'All this goes against dharma.'

'Why?'

'Look here, Budhua's ma. Earlier people fell sick, and in the natural course of things, they died. Along with births, there should be deaths as well. Otherwise how will the world carry on? When the old become sick, they should die. All this business of old people being saved by doctors, vaids, hakims – I ask you, is it correct?'

Sanichari sighed. 'Well, you're still better off than me. After all, you're in demand for births and marriages as well as deaths. No sooner is a wedding discussed than you're summoned! What will become of me?'

Bikhni was not despairing. She said, 'Their time had not come, so they didn't die. No one lives beyond their fated time.'

Dulan said, 'There's nothing to worry about. You're eating better than before, so you're worried about things going wrong. Don't you see the malik-mahajan's attitude? Lachman Singh's stepmother would weep at the sight of a good harvest because the money earned this year might not be repeated next year!'

Sanichari said, 'Go on with you! Think you can turn everything into a joke?'

After that, Sanichari's luck improved. Bikhni returned one day, laughing. 'Great news!'

'What?'

'I'll have to sit down comfortably before I can tell you.'

'What's the news?'

'Getting irritated?'

'Get on with the news!'

'Gambhir Singh is dying.'

'Who told you?'

Bikhni told her everything. She'd got the details straight from the barber, a reliable source. Does Sanichari remember that Nathuni's mother had the wasting fever and cough?

'Yes, yes, of course I remember. Go on, Bikhni.'

The way Nathuni treated his mother is now the norm in their community. This disease is considered beyond Shiva's skill. Any treatment or medication is seen as a grave insult to the god. Gambhir Singh has no close kin. His nephew is his heir. The nephew has isolated him in a shack in the yard, left him there with a black goat. At the sight of the goat, Gambhir Singh said, 'This means I'm going to die.' He gave instructions to arrange such a kirya for himself that it would leave everyone stunned. Everyone would realize a great man had died.

'Then? Go on, Bikhni!'

'Gambhir Singh is a really strange man! He's refusing medication, just does pujas and yagnas and havens all day long. His wife insisted on calling a doctor. Even the doctor holds out no hope.'

'He isn't dead yet, is he?'

'He's bound to die! The nephew can't do a thing. The old man summoned his lawyer and ordered that at least a lakh be spent on his kirya.'

'Why?'

'He's saying he's going to use up all his money. His nephew can take the proceeds from the land. He has no children, and he refuses to leave any money for his nephew.'

'So then?'

'Today or tomorrow, he's sure to die.'

'Meanwhile?'

'Meanwhile, I'll make a quick trip.'

'Where do you want to go?'

'Ranchi.'

'Ranchi? Why?'

'I met my nephew-in-law at the marketplace. He asked me to come, his daughter's getting married.'

'Daughter's getting married?'

Bikhni let out a sigh. 'He says that wretch, my son, will probably be there. You're bound to ask why, if I want to see him, I don't just visit him at his in-laws. But that I can't do. However, if I do come across him on a visit to my nephew, no one can say anything. Even he won't realize that it's him I've gone to see.'

Sanichari said, 'Well, since you put it like that, I won't say anything. You say you want to see your son. But will you come back soon? Or will you stay on there?'

'How can I? That day I had walked out of my home and I met you by chance. If you hadn't been there that day, what would I have done?'

'Don't forget about Gambhir Singh.'

'Oh, I'll be back within four days.'

It was a three-mile walk to the bus stop. Sanichari accompanied Bikhni, saw her onto the bus, advised her – 'It's eight rupees for a seat, squat in the aisle, you'll have to pay only two rupees.'

Walking back, she mused on the exciting events taking place – to think of her friend, who knew nothing but footpaths, actually riding in a bus, and going all the way to Ranchi. All that way to attend a relative's wedding! One's relatives live around one – not in far-off big cities like Ranchi!

Sanichari strolled home chatting to people on the way. Everyone said, 'She's led such a hard, sad life. But finding Bikhni has been a blessing. What a hardworking old woman! The whole look of Sanichari's home has changed! This is what they call the game of chance – people who come from far away, strangers, can become as close as one's own kin. Like the bark of one tree grafted onto another.'

At home, Sanichari felt restless. Out of habit she went into the forest to collect firewood, and returned with a bundle of dried twigs. Bikhni would never return empty-handed. She'd bring back something or other – either a couple of withered twigs or a length of rope she found on the path, or a pat of cow dung. Her most recent scheme was to rear a calf. Sanichari can't understand how, even at this age, she's so interested in domestic and household matters.

A few days passed. In this manner, Gambhir Singh's condition worsened as expected. Sanichari went there one day and discussed everything with the gomastha. In the process she learned that although it was being said that he had tuberculosis, actually he was dying of another disease. The excesses he had committed with untold women had given him venereal disease, which was rotting his flesh. That was why he was holding so many pujas and prayers, refusing medicine, courting death.

The accounts-keeper said, 'He's decided to die during the period of the waxing moon.'

Sanichari asked, 'Why?' She thinks, 'Can the all-powerful

malik-mahajans, who can do whatever they want, die when they want as well?'

'Who knows?' replied the accounts-keeper with philosophic detachment. 'If you die during the period of the waxing moon, your soul goes straight to heaven; otherwise, like Yudhistira, you have to visit hell first.'

Sanichari is not too familiar with puranic characters, but has no doubt of their greatness. Through calendar art the images of the epic and divine characters merge with the film actors who play their roles in movies. Trilok Kapoor and Yudhistra, Abhi Bhattacharya and Sri Krishna and so on, and so forth. Astounded, she asks, 'What? Is the malik-mahajan Yudhistira?'

The accountant explains patiently to this illiterate woman: 'Whatever the malik-mahajan says, happens. Right or wrong is a question of one's point of view. Now, wicked people might say that the malik committed dacoity when his father was alive, in the time of the British, that he stole Lachman Singh's father's horse, that he burned down many dushad settlements with his own hands, that he ruined hundreds of young girls, that he's a big sinner. But the malik doesn't see it that way. So he's gathered astrologers and pandits to determine what sin it could be that had caused him to be inflicted with this terrible disease.'

'Have they found out?'

'Found out what?'

'What the sin was.'

'Of course. When he was a boy he hit a pregnant cow with a stick and killed it. This is his only sin.'

Still she asks, 'Will he really die in the period of the waxing moon as he wants to?'

'Most definitely. Haven't you seen, till now, that whatever he wants he gets? And I'll say this, he's done the right thing – if the money gets into his nephew's hands, it won't last.'

'Why?'

'All the malik's women have been Hindu, even the untouchables. But the nephew's randi is a musalmaan.'

'Hai Ram!'

'Be prepared. I've worked here for so long. But after the kirya I won't stick on here. When the kirya is over, I'll leave. Malik has instructed that his kirya should be so grand that everyone forgets about Mohar Singh's funeral. We'll go all out, huzoor.'

Sanichari came away.

She returned home worried. Six days had passed. What's the matter with Bikhni? They live in an isolated village, not much communication with the outside, no one takes the bus anywhere. Who can possibly carry news of Bikhni from Ranchi? She sighed, and put some quilts out to sun. Ground a little corn. Then she went to do her obligatory share of repair work on the panchayat meeting place. If not seen to regularly, these mud huts got eaten away by termites. She returned home carrying a load of twigs on her head, straightened, and saw the stranger.

Unfamiliar man. Shaven head. Bare feet.

'Is Bikhni dead?'

In a trice she understood everything. She asked, 'Are you her nephew-in-law?'

'Yes.'

She felt a landslide within. But many deaths, deceptions, injustices, had hardened her endurance and self-control. She asked the stranger to sit down. She herself sat down, sat quietly for a while, then asked, 'How many days ago?'

'Four days.'

Sanichari counted backwards and said, 'The day I went to Gambhir Singh's. What happened?'

'Asthma, complicated by a chest cold.'

'Something that started here or there?'

'She drank a glass of sherbet on the way.'

'Then?'

She recalled how Bikhni could never resist colourful sherbets, digestive tablets and candied fruit.

'Then the wheezing became worse. My brother-in-law works in a hospital, he called a doctor, we started medicines and injections.'

'I never did that.'

She would catch a few cockroaches, boil them and give Bikhni the water to drink. The wheezing would improve immediately.

'Did she get to meet her son?'

'He didn't come. I'll be going to his place next, to give him the news. Did my aunt leave any belongings here?'

'No, nothing. You call her aunt, and she died in your house but all these days we didn't even know she had family of her own, she was roaming the countryside alone, homeless ...'

'I didn't know or I'd have fetched her before.'

'You'd better be off. You have a bus to catch, it's a long way from here.'

He left. Sanichari sat by herself and tried to comprehend the situation. What did she feel? Grief? No, not grief, fear. Her husband had died, her son had died, her grandson had left, her daughter-in-law had run away – there had always been grief in her life. But she never felt this devouring fear before. Bikhni's death affected her livelihood, her profession, that's why she's experiencing this fear. And why, after all? Because she's old. Amongst them, one works, if one can, till one's last breath. Ageing means growing old. Growing old means not being able to work. And that means death. Sanichari's aunt had lived to such an old age that they carried her in and out of the house like a bundle. In winter, they left her outside while they all went off to work, and came home to find her as stiff as wood, dead.

Sanichari didn't want to die like that. And why should she die? Her husband died, her son died, she didn't die of grief. No one does. After the worst disasters people gradually bathe, eat, chase away the goat nibbling the chillies in the yard. People can do anything – but if they can't eat, they die. If Sanichari has survived so much grief, she'll survive the loss of Bikhni. She's devastated but she won't cry.

Money, rice, new clothes – without getting these in return tears are a useless luxury.

Sanichari went to see Dulan.

He grasped the gravity of the situation at once, said, 'Look, Budhua's ma, it's wrong to give up one's land, and your profession of funeral wailing is like your land, you mustn't give it up. Can't you see how amusing it all is? One by one they're dying, you're going to wail, they're taking the pomp and splendour of the mourning so seriously, making it a matter of honour, they're fighting over it. Take Gambhir Singh, for example, he could easily call in a doctor and get cured, but he's not interested. He's more attracted by all the hoo-haa of a fancy funeral.'

'It's their business, what they fight over, what brings them honour.'

'It's your business too.'

'How will it help me to know all this stuff?'

'When Budhua's father died, didn't you take over his work in the malik's field?'

'Of course I did.'

'In the same way you have to take over from Bikhni.'

'How so?'

'You have to go yourself.' Dulan spoke forcefully, angrily, 'It's a question of survival. You must go yourself.'

'To Tohri?'

'Yes, to Tohri. You'll go there, you'll find the whores, fix them up. Otherwise between Gambhir Singh's nephew and the gomastha, they'll keep all the money.'

'I'll go.'

'You must.'

'But what if ...'

'Your daughter-in-law's there, is that it?'

'You know?'

'Of course. But so what? Isn't she also a ruined whore like the others? Get her as well.'

'Her?'

'Definitely. She needs to eat and earn like everyone else. This business of getting whores to mourn is really amusing. The wealth of these malik-mahajans is unclean money. There's no limit to it. Let a few whores from the bazaar come to their funerals. It's the malik-mahajans who've turned them into whores, ruined them, then kicked them out, isn't that so?'

'Yes.'

She's not too clear about how they've become whores. She recalls how hunger drove her daughter-in-law to leave home, how Gulbadan looked upon her father's nephew as her brother, though both her father and the nephew considered her nothing but a whore. It all seems very confusing to Sanichari, who ponders the matter but can't fix on any direction to her thoughts. What does Dulan have to say?

'Don't weigh right and wrong so much, leave that kind of thing to the rich. They understand it better. We understand hunger.'

'That's true.'

'So then, go on.'

'Won't the village speak ill of me?'

Dulan laughed bitterly. 'What one is forced to do to feed oneself is never considered wrong.'

Sanichari understood what he was trying to say.

Gambhir Singh died on the seventeenth day. When he was breathing his last, the gomastha sent Sanichari a message. She sent word that she was on her way with some more rudalis.

She got into her black clothes and went to Tohri. She felt no embarrassment about asking directions to the red light area. Considerations of the stomach are more important than anything else. She walked in calling, 'Rupa, Budhu, Shomri, Gangu, where are you? Come along, there's rudali work for you.'

The known whores gathered one by one. Soon there was a crowd, from the five-rupee whores to the one sikka ones.

'Huzoorain, you?'

'Bikhni's dead.' Sanichari smiled. Seeing a familiar face in the crowd, she asked, 'Budhua's wife? You come too, bahu. Gulbadan, you come along as well. Gambhir Singh has died; by wailing for him and taking their money you'll be rubbing salt in their wounds. Don't hold back. Take whatever you can. Come, come. Five rupees a head. Everyone will get rice and cloth at the kirya ceremony.'

There was an eager bustle among the whores. The young ones asked, 'And us?'

'All of you come. When you grow old you'll have to do this anyway, so while I'm around let me initiate you.'

Everyone was enjoying themselves hugely. Gangu brought Sanichari a mora to sit on. Rupa brought her a cup of tea, a bidi. There was an air of excitement. Then they all set off for Nawagarh.

Gambhir Singh's nephew, his gomastha, everyone was astonished at the sight. The gomastha hissed – 'Have you brought the entire red light district with you? At least a hundred whores!'

Sanichari said, 'Why not? Malik said make a great noise, a big fuss, something people will talk about. Is that possible with a mere ten whores? Move, move, let us get on with our work. The malik belongs to us now.'

Gambhir's corpse stank of rotting flesh. The randi rudalis surrounded his swollen corpse and started wailing, hitting their heads on the ground. The gomastha began to weep tears of sorrow. Nothing will be left! Cunning Sanichari! Hitting their heads meant they had to be paid double! He and the nephew were reduced to helpless onlookers. While hitting her head on the ground and wailing loudly, Gulbadan turned her dry eyes in the direction of the nephew, cast him a leering wink and grinned. Then, listening to Sanichari's cry, she rejoined the chorus.

Translated from Bengali by Anjum Katyal

A Movement, a Folder, Some Tears

Charu's message came by email.

I haven't yet got rid of my jet-lag. When others are asleep, I'm awake. When they are awake, my eyes feel heavy. Hence this letter, written while the CD plays. The usual song. Tamal's favourite, in Hindi:

Alone
in this city
a man
seeking a living
night and day
seeking a nest ...

You didn't even turn up at the airport. I waited until the last moment. Every time someone passed by with cropped hair, wearing a kurta, my heart leapt, certain it must be you. Sakina and you must have been together that day.

*

True, Sakina didn't say much as they travelled together on the electric train. Dark circles under her eyes. The fan where they stood wasn't working. Sakina's face was covered, all over, with sweat. She could never stand the heat at the best of times. In the swelter of May, she hung on to the chain in the crowded compartment, streaming with sweat. Her neck and shoulders – once burnt by fire, now swollen, twisted, scarred, changed in colour – were wet through. She didn't even notice when her face was gently blotted with her dupatta. Ten years ago, when she came home from the hospital after the event, she had said, 'Look at my neck and shoulders! It's as if some strange creature is lying upon me. You said, didn't you, that a snake tumbled about your Sivan's neck? Now I too have a snake around mine.'

Exactly six months later she broke down.

'They're here. They've come. They are throwing torches dipped in oil into the house,' she began to scream as she ran about.

A whole month passed during which she screamed and wailed and shouted. After that, gradually she quietened down. She wrote about that day for the psyhiatrist, with complete lucidity.

It was a Friday. Only Ammi and I were at home. Although it was December, the afternoon felt really warm. We had left the window open, to let in a little breeze. Ammi was asleep. I was reading a book. In the distance, I heard a cry rising to a crescendo. An outbreak of noises, screaming, roaring, clamouring. Suddenly it became a great deluge. Before I could get up, rolls of cloth smelling of kerosene thudded into the room. Following them came burning torches. I had a nylon dupatta about my neck. I hastened to throw it away, but it had become stuck. I prised it off and flung it. It fell on Ammi, who was hard of hearing, and still sleeping peacefully. Before she could get away, screaming, two more burning torches were on her. I fell down in a faint. When I became conscious, Ammi was beside me, a blackened corpse.

Her voice, recorded onto a tape, spoke in English, without falter.

Doctor: Sakina, do you harbour any anger in your heart?

Sakina: (Laughs) Doctor, when I heard the shouts of those crowds, I was reading Sahir Ludhianvi's poems. The poem that begins, 'That dawn will break some day.' The next instant I was burnt by the fire. Until I broke down, I felt no anger. Only despair. Now, I have a feeling I have saved myself from drowning in my grief. Now, yes, there is anger in my heart, doctor. That is my support. My strength. My anchor. Have you been told to remove the anger from the minds and hearts of those who have been caught in these riots, doctor? Don't do it. I'm going to keep this anger knotted up in my dupatta. I'm not going to scatter it away. I shall go about, hereafter, wrapped in it. Listening to it. Learning from it. I need that anger to help make sure it never happens again.

'Sakina, tabyat thiik nahiin hai, kya? Don't you feel well? Did you take your blood pressure tablets?'

'Mm,' she said.

'Charu must have packed up all her luggage.'

'Mm.'

They didn't say anything more as they got off the train and made their way to Hutatma Chowk where the meeting was to take place. A small pandal had been put up there. There would be songs, speeches and discussions until late evening.

At five o'clock, Sakina touched her shoulder and said, 'I'll just walk up to Nargis Khala's house, and come back. We'll go to the airport together, later.'

But she hadn't come back even when the meeting was over at eight.

Nargis Khala said, when she rang her from a public telephone, 'I've just heard the news about Sakina.'

'What news?'

'Sakina fell down.'

'What? She isn't hurt or anything, is she?'

Khala's voice broke. 'She fell from above.'

'From above? Has she broken any ...?'

Khala wept. 'She fell from the seventeenth floor ... From the terrace of the building where Iqbal Maamu lives.'

She listened to all the details, and then hurried there ...

Sakina's neck was broken. She had fallen onto the grass lawn. No dreadful sight of splattered blood. Her head hung down like a chicken whose neck had been wrung. Her body waited for the routine post-mortem procedure.

When she touched Sakina's arm, it felt cold. She stroked Sakina's neck. Gently she pinched her ear. Kissed her forehead. All the while, tears spurted from her eyes. A pain inside, as if she were being hit by a hammer.

At what moment did you decide to do this, Sakina? When you saw the grass far beneath you, what did you think? What came to your mind? Did you think, wretched girl, that if you fell, the grass would be soft beneath you? Did you place your foot on the hook set into the wall and climb onto the parapet? Did you stand right up there? Did you gaze at the mountainous buildings all around, reaching up to the sky? Did you see the ocean beyond the building, blue and flowing? Did you lift your arms and dive like a swimming champion? Or did you slip and slide as you fell? Did you scream, kannamma? Did your voice dissolve away in the wind, thangam? At what instant did you die? When you touched the ground? On the way there? Or had you died already, even when we travelled together this morning?

She continued to stroke Sakina's head.

What was it that shattered you? What defeated you? What came upon you in that instant's whirlwind and pushed you over? Was it what happened last month? Charu and you went to Ahmedabad to prepare a report. Charu's father's sister has a house there. An aunt who knew you from the moment you became Charu's friend. The same aunt who always looked forward to the vermicelli payasam you brought her at the time of Id. This time she refused to allow Charu and you inside her house. Her daughter and son-in-law stood at the doorway, blocking your entry. When Charu proclaimed loudly that the upstairs room belonged to her father, she was handed the key and told to use the outside stairs to go up. Charu and you stayed there for three days. There isn't a soul who has not read the report you two prepared. When Charu, you and I were together on two different evenings, you spoke about a couple of things that happened.

First. The front door, through which Charu and you had to pass, was sometimes ajar. When you glanced inside, once, the aunt's three-year-old grandson was playing with dolls. A small sword and shield, a few plastic dolls – these were his favourite toys. He sliced off the doll's arms and legs with his sword. He struck a blow even in that shiny place where the doll had no organ.

You called him to the door. 'Kuber!' He turned round and smiled.

'Should you cut up the doll like that? Isn't it like a little baby?'

Tiny sword in hand, he came to the door, with shining eyes.

'It's a Muchlim. I've killed it,' he said, in his childish language.

'Kuber, Sakina Mausi also is a Muslim.'

Still smiling, he stuck his toy-sword into your stomach.

'Jai Cheeram,' he said.

Second. There was a celebration in the temple at the street corner. Singing loudly and shrilly, Charu's aunt leapt up and down, calling on god's name. The devotional bhajans came out like hisses. At one stage, she and her bhajan companions whirled round in what appeared to be a frenzied dance, streaming with sweat, their hair loose, while the floor shook beneath their heavy tread.

When her aunt returned home, Charu called down to her, 'Bua.' Her aunt turned her gaze towards the upstairs room.

Those were not Bua's eyes. In the fading twilight, lit by the street lamp's yellow light, they glinted like a wolf's eyes.

Now, Iqbal Maamu laid his hand on her shoulder. 'Selvi Beti,' he said, patting her, consoling her.

*

The whole family came to the airport. Kalavati Mausi's son sent a car and a driver. You won't believe it. Tamal's parents were there. Tamal's son, Manush, had brought them. Amala, Tamal's wife, too. She said she could understand, at last, my relationship with Tamal for twenty-five years. She wished me success in my journey towards further research. Tamal's father stroked my head and blessed me. He said, 'Who knows whether we will still be here if and when you come back; go safely and return safely.' At that moment I wasn't at the airport. I was on the train to Matunga. In 1993. To us in the women's compartment, the bomb blast sounded only like Diwali celebrations. That instant when the train stopped and I peeped out with the others is still sharply etched in my mind. It goes on extending, extending, extending in my mind, like batter spreading out and out in a pan. Because of the crowds, I had joined the women, while Tamal stayed in the general compartment.

'There's been a bomb blast in one of the general compartments.' When I jumped down, went forward a little and pushed my way through the crowds, Tamal lay on the ground. Both legs reduced to a blood-porridge below the knees. His chest covered in blood.

When I rushed to him, calling out 'Tamal', I realized that for an instant he himself didn't know what had happened.

'What happened?' he asked. As he was carried into the ambulance, he raised himself a little and looked down towards his legs. He looked at me and folded his hands, as if to say, 'Save me from this'. Next to him was an old Muslim man, covered in wounds. The games of history. Historical games. Nobody was with him. Some good people from the train helped me to take him and Tamal to the hospital. Tamal remained conscious until his name was registered.

'Tamal Mukherji,' he said, without faltering. Fifty years of age, he said. His religion was Humanity, he said. There was no one to introduce the old Muslim gentleman.

The police investigation came from a strange and oblique perspective. 'Did these two conspire together to place the bomb, or was it only one of them who did it?'

With the help of many people, I reclaimed Tamal's body and had it cremated in the crematorium attached to the hospital. Even when it was all over, the Muslim gentleman's family was wandering about, waiting for his body. His aged wife, who didn't have the least idea about the severity of the regulations, came to me and began, 'Beti, if an accident happens when you are travelling by train, can you claim compensation? I have two daughters. I must get them married. It was to arrange for some money that he set out this morning.'

I stood there holding her hand. You will remember. We tried to claim compensation for her. We failed. Then we set up a fund and made a collection for her.

All this came to mind, lit up as if by a lightning flash. And once again, as I write this.

*

Sakina put an end to herself. She was a lawyer. She was not unaware of the procedural confusions following such a death. It was not unknown to her that she should have left a letter. Surely her death could not have been predetermined. It must have been the result of an aberration, a sudden whirlwind attack, a wave of vivid emotion that overcame her. Attempting to lean over just a little, she must have tipped over completely. She suffered from high blood pressure. She had received psychiatric treatment in 1992.

After Sakina's death was recorded in the police files, complete with all these explanations, in a language peculiar to government offices, her body was handed over. And buried.

Sakina had gone to collect a folder, which had been left in Iqbal Maamu's flat. That is what she said to him on the telephone. Soon after she arrived, she had a cup of tea, and went to the room where the books were kept.

The file was there, in an almirah. The door on the far side of the room gave onto the terrace. Fifteen minutes later, the caretaker of the building rang the front door bell and kept on ringing until the door was opened.

'A woman has jumped from the terrace of your ...'

'Don't talk nonsense,' said Maamu, 'I'm alone in the flat ...' Before he could finish, he remembered Sakina's presence. He ran to the library. No Sakina. The door to the terrace stood open. The door of the almirah in which the file was kept had been unlocked. The lock and key together had been left on top of the almirah. Far below, Sakina lay, a crooked line. Her black dupatta was caught at the wing-tip of the topiary bird in the garden, and was swinging in the wind.

Running downstairs, laying her in his lap, weeping aloud. The neighbours supporting Maamu ...

Again and again Iqbal Maamu described it all. His beloved niece. He had supported her throughout her legal studies. He had accepted all her decisions. He spoke of them repeatedly.

The almirah was still unlocked. He opened it, took out the folder and gave it to Selvi. The cover bore the name of their organization: Jagruti. Awareness.

*

When it was time for me to go in, a silence fell over all of us. Then the goodbyes. Choking throats. Tears in Ba's eyes. Bapu wiping his eyes with his handkerchief. As I went in, I saw my own reflection in the glass door. I was weeping. I am weeping, I told myself. I have wept before, many times. In the upper berth of a railway compartment. Waiting for a train late one night at a railway station empty of humanity, looking up at the stars. In a bullock cart, staring at the animal's tail. In the bathroom of an airport. Sitting in the corner of the upper deck of a bus. Driving at speed down the middle of a road. So many leave-takings. So many farewells. Another goodbye. Another bout of tears. In the glass door, a fifty-year-old woman holding onto her shoulder bag and setting off for further research. Long hair, uncut. Cheeks streaked with tears. I held on to the rubbish bins for support, and let the tears flow.

'Do you need any help?' A woman, a fellow traveller, had stopped in front of me.

'No, thank you,' I said, and walked on towards the inner door.

Even now as I write this, at this instant when everyone is asleep and I'm awake, the tears flow from my eyes. It's as if a long era of which we were part, as makers of history, has now come to an end.

I can't understand it. I sometimes wonder if it's part of the tiredness that comes with the menopause. But I think I have never felt such weariness before. When did the body control us, ever? When did it dominate us? Were we ever afraid of it? We never even thought of old age. How would it occur to us to be concerned about old age with the example of Nargis Khala in front of us? She has never stopped working for her organization from home, has she, even though she is eighty-seven years old now, and crippled besides? Whenever I think of Nargis Khala, I remember the sound of her typewriter. The sound of her typewriter – placed on the table by the window, so that she can look out – as she taps out a statement on human rights, or writes a letter to a newspaper about freedom of speech. Last month she told me she was considering buying a computer. I said, 'Don't, Khala. I can relate to you only with this typewriter.' She answered, 'Can I keep from changing, just for the sake of your illusions?'

I argued a lot with her that day. I shouted at her. 'Just be quiet, Khala. Why did people like you – people who spent the best part of your lives with Gandhi, who fought for Independence – end up later on in ashrams and small towns? Why did you decide not to enter politics? If you had given your country half the devotion you gave to Gandhi, the politics of this country might have taken a different course. Who asked you for your renunciation? In 1942, you marched through all these streets without fear, like the queens of the locality. How often have we been thrilled by the photographs of your processions, you with your banners held high? Don't provoke me. You, your khaddar and your spinning wheels. You have all become mere symbols. Symbols which we hang on walls or wear as fashionable clothes and caps. Useless, marginal symbols. Cowardly symbols. Frivolous symbols. You left us no other political heritage.'

Perhaps I spoke like that out of the emotional state in which I returned from Ahmedabad. As I spoke, I went up to her wheelchair and shook Khala. Khala didn't stop me. Then I buried my head in her lap. She laid her hands on my head, like a blessing.

*

The folder lay on the table. All the other books and papers from the room were in cardboard boxes. The boxes still gaped open. The schoolboy who lived downstairs and his two friends had offered to tie them all up. The arrangement was that they would be paid enough so that all three could go to a Hrithik Roshan film.

She asked Nandini that morning, 'We have to vacate the room, Nandu. Could you take a day off? I can't, on my own ...'

Nandini answered, 'I have a lot of work at the office. Otherwise I would have helped. I have to go to Pune as well, on Saturday, because of work. Won't it do if you clear it next week?'

'The landlord insists ...'

Nandini was embarrassed. She felt sorry she couldn't help. She knew Charu had gone to the United States, Sakina wasn't there any more, Selvi was on her own. Because of this, she answered without annoyance or irritation, without barking at her mother. Otherwise, she certainly would have retorted, 'Please, Amma. I work in a Private Company. This is not a government post from which I can take time off as I please. Nor is it a women's organization where I'm allowed a day's leave if I have my periods, or my child sneezes, or my husband has a headache, if there is a feast or a fast. If we want equal employment with men, we have to be prepared to work with them on equal terms.'

Sometimes, Selvi wanted to say in return, 'It was we who laid the way so that you could find a job suited to your intelligence, earning an equal wage with men. We weeded the thorns from your path, removed the obstacles, made you aware of your rights.' But such discussions had ceased between them, long ago.

Three years ago, Charu, Sakina and she had finished some work in Dongri and returned home past one o'clock at night. They had all three decided to go straight to Selvi's place, as it would delay them even more if they stopped to eat on the way. They rang the front-door bell until their hands ached, to no effect. No signs of anyone inside. At last they woke up their neighbours, jumped across from their balcony to Selvi's, pushed open the door, which was just closed, and went in. It was a fifth-floor flat. Quite a circus feat, leaping from one balcony to the next at one o'clock at night. They were desperately hungry. Used plates and empty vessels lay strewn all over the kitchen work-surface. In an instant Charu cleaned the worktop. Sakina began to mix the dough for chapatis. Selvi put the potatoes on to boil. When she took out the already-boiled dal from the fridge, Charu seasoned it with chopped onions, tomatoes, ginger, garlic and green chillies. A piping hot meal of chapatis, dal and potato-sabzi at two o'clock in the night.

Ramu was alive then. When she asked him angrily, the next morning, why he had not opened the door in the night, he snapped back, 'If you come home at twelve and one, I can't be expected to keep awake and open the door.'

'Why, haven't I opened the door for you when you came back at three, after a night out with your friends? Haven't I fed you?'

'I was tired. I fell asleep. So must you make such a song and a dance about it?'

'We had to jump across the balcony to get in. Sakina suffers from high blood pressure. You know that, don't you?'

Charu and Sakina intervened, preventing the argument from growing worse.

Later, while they were having tea, Nandini turned up and Selvi asked her, 'How could you have been so fast asleep? Didn't you hear us ringing the front-door bell?'

Nandini said, 'Amma, I could hear quite clearly the way you were fighting early this morning. That is what is known as oppression. Go on. Go and write another book.' Then turning to Sakina and Charu, she added in English, 'Isn't that right?' When Selvi explained to her friends what Nandini had said, their faces tightened.

Even though Ramu died in an accident, the relatives spoke as if it was all owing to her lack of care. 'A good man. Half the time he made his own coffee, and drank it all alone ... And for all that, it was his own choice to marry her ...'

Yes. That happened twenty-five years ago. It still remained their complaint.

Nandini too had said, 'You should have looked after Appa better, Amma. You were always running off to some procession protesting against dowry or rape or whatever. People who think like that should never get married.'

At that time she had not had the strength to explain to her daughter that in their youth Ramu and she had belonged to the same group of friends, and that he had married her precisely because he admired her activism.

The landlord came and looked in.

'Udya kali karnarna nakki? You'll definitely vacate the room tomorrow, won't you?'

It was an old-fashioned tiled house. As you climbed up the wooden stairs, there was a small room to the right. Their office for the past twenty years.

'Yes,' she assured him, and turned away. The sharks of the building trade had their eyes on this house. It was in an area that had become popular among actors and the newly rich. The landlord had been muttering for the past two years about so many women coming here. When Muslim women came, he said, the house stank. As if the winds emanating from him with the speed of jet were perfumed! Perhaps our own farts smell sweet to us. He said they stank because they ate beef. Having endured the many odours he expelled, lifting his thigh and contorting his body, they had no wish to explain to him about Vedic times.

He was concerned that they might ask for some compensation because they had rented the room for so many years. Sakina had said that before they looked for another place, they should really hold out for the money.

When she took up the folder and placed it on her lap, it was as if Sakina was beside her. Snake-neck woman. She who knotted up her anger in her dupatta. The folder had a purple cover.

*

You were angry when I began to apply for research grants. You shouted at me. You charged me with being a coward. You said I was running away to hide. I accept all your accusations. But my dear friend, I am also the woman who saw her lover's legs reduced to a mess of blood. I didn't give way then. I didn't run away. I stood. I opposed. I fought. These past ten years, I gave all my breath and being to the work of Jagruti. I immersed myself in music. How many Kabir dohas I sang, in how many places! Do you remember the devotional song, 'Aaj sajan moré' which begins,

> Embrace me today, my love,
> let this life reach fruition.
> Heart's pain,
> love's fire,
> let all be cool ...

Rising higher and higher, the song would go,

> Quench my thirst, Giridhara,
> enchanter of my heart –
> I thirst from the very depths of my being,
> I have thirsted for many generations.

When I sang the words 'I thirst – I have thirsted', repeating them over and over again, didn't all three of us – you, me, Sakina – weep?

It wasn't just a thirst for human love. It was that unquenched thirst within us. We are people who continue to wander about with that thirst. Even now, when I say, 'from the very depth of my being', an ache like a cold wind enters my whole self. You must believe this. If I decided, in spite of that, that I had to come away, should you not understand that I had a strong enough reason?

Selvi, Kumudben Bua is not just my aunt. She became a widow at an early age, and came to live at our house with her young son. She gave me her entire support in all my decisions. She accepted Tamal. Just because Tamal loved fish, she allowed it to be cooked in her house. She called our house-dog 'Arjun Beta' without any hesitation, and fed it the offering from her daily puja. After Arjun died, she gave the offering every day to a street dog, in Arjun's name. She was never held back by the requirements of ritual. She never allowed anyone to be held back in that way. It was she who taught me about humanity.

The first shock came when she refused to allow me inside the house in Ahmedabad. The look she gave Sakina was the second blow. The third whiplash was the change in her eyes that evening. There was a further blow, which felt as if it ripped my flesh away. I never told you both this. Bua used to go out with other women, from time to time. Always when she returned, there would be a kind of energy in the way she walked. Once, on her return, I came face to face with her. She lifted her hand to stop me from touching her. Selvi, the stench of kerosene came from her hand. My whole body began to shudder. We left that very day.

I didn't say anything to anyone. That evening, when I was at home, Bapu said at the dining table, 'The Muslims have learnt a good lesson.' Ba added, 'Let them all go to Pakistan.' These people are all of my blood. The food stuck in my throat. How did this lake of poison come about? How could I have been so blind? Why did we never see the growth of this horror, which was capable of dividing parents and daughter, brother and sister; which could come between all relationships?

Several little incidents appeared in a new light, suddenly. No one asking after Sakina for many days. Ba's simple puja of lighting her lamp becoming more and more complex over the last two years. A sticker on Bapu's car mirror, saying, 'Say with pride, I am a Hindu.' My sticker on top of that one, 'Say with pride, we are human beings.' Ba's comment when I bought a green sari, 'Why did you go for this Muslim-green?' Buying bread no longer from Mohamed Kaka's shop as we have done for years. Various conversations in relatives' houses. Tiny incidents, whose violence was striking, when added together. Each and every one had been a drop of poison. It felt as if the kerosene I smelt on Kumudben Bua's hand had pervaded our house.

A fear that this storm of madness might never cease caught in my mind, like a hook. It's a good thing Tamal died. He could never have borne this.

There's a little story in a Paulo Coelho novel. In a distant land there lived a wizard. He poured a drug that induced madness, into the town well. The people drank it and began to go about as they pleased, in a totally crazy way. When the king tried to bring about laws to control them, they told him to leave the throne. So the king decided to abdicate. The queen, though, counselled otherwise. 'Oh, King, don't give up your throne. Come, let us also drink from the same well.' And as soon as they drank, they became like everyone else. The problem was over.

I was afraid there was no well left that the wizard had not touched, Selvi. It was then that I decided to leave the country. I did not have the strength to live with this day after day.

Today I write this to you alone. It will take me days to write to Sakina.

*

In the folder, there were notes for the Jagruti newsletters, descriptions of some of their events, details of women who had come to them for legal advice, summaries of discussions, details of arguments. Records that Sakina had collected and kept with care.

There was even a note on the occasion, in 1980, when they had cut their hair. She wrote, 'On the dais, there was a debate going on about physical beauty. A professor-poet began by saying that the beauty of an Indian woman is signalled by long hair, big breasts, tiny waist and sword-like eyes, and went on to sing a purana to long hair. Selvi and I exchanged glances. Since Nandu was born, Selvi scarcely has time to comb her hair. As for me, travelling about constantly, long hair is a real burden. What's more, as the professor went on and on, gushing and melting about long hair, the trail of peacock's feathers, the spread of dark clouds, etc., everyone's eyes were on us. We went straight off and had our hair cut. We felt light-headed; headstrong no longer!'

Selvi remembered it well. Those were times when they faced everything with an energy that said, 'You can't define us. We will break your definitions, your commentaries, your grammars, your rules.' They felt an urgency to defy everything. She and Sakina had gone to a Chinese beauty parlour and had their hair cropped close to their heads. When she went home, Ramu only asked, making no fuss, 'Well, Selvi, was it a pilgrimage to Palani or to Tirupati?'

'Neither; it was to China,' she told him. Lively times, those were.

There was a little notebook containing the songs they sang in the eighties, during their marches:

Don't surrender,
don't submit,
don't drown,
don't die.
We are the Revolution
to all injustice
We are the reply.

Charu always led the singing. All the rest joined in the chorus.

There was a copy, in the folder, of the sticker printed with the Mandir-Masjid song, which they had pasted on all the railway compartments after the Babri Masjid was demolished.

Temples, mosques and gurudwaras
 they divided from each other.
They divided the land,
 they divided the sea.
Don't divide human beings
Don't divide human beings.

Charu had written a note on the occasion when Sakina was to give a speech at a meeting in a women's college near Churchgate, at the time of the Shah Bano case. The question of maintenance was being re-examined.

They had announced that the meeting would be at six in the evening. When Sakina and I went there, there were many burkha-clad women outside the college, carrying placards which said things like, 'Shariat alone protects women', and 'We will only listen to Shariat.' I looked at Sakina. 'There are two sides to everything, aren't there?' she remarked. There was a huge crowd in the hall. Sakina's lawyer friend, Shahid, sat down beside me. When Sakina began to speak, the burkha-clad women rose up in a wave. They moved in on Sakina, shouting, 'You are not a true Muslim. You don't know the Koran. You don't say your prayers. You are an enemy of Muslim women.' When they insisted again and again, 'Tell us, are you a Muslim or not?', Sakina became distressed, unable to move any further back. Her voice broke as she said, 'I really am a Muslim. I have read the *Koran*. I know my prayers. Let me speak ...' Shahid tried to restrain the man next to him who was jumping up and down, and said, 'Why don't we listen to her at least?' The man yelled back, 'Shut up, you are not a Muslim.' Shahid replied, 'I am, actually.' The crowds became uncontrollable, and the police arrived.

Shahid and I brought Sakina away through the back door. She was shattered. 'This is going to be a huge battle, Charu,' she said. 'It begins with someone else giving me an identity.'

Like a sequel to this, there was an incident in the house of Charu's relatives two years later. Selvi remembered it, as soon as she read Charu's report.

The discussion had begun in an apparently light-hearted manner. 'Every Muslim has four wives.' Charu and she had interrupted to say that it wasn't true, and that in any case, many Hindus of their acquaintance had more than one wife. At this, Charu's uncle's son remarked, 'Of course, Charu, you have to say that. It concerns you, after all. You are Tamal's rakel, his mistress, aren't you?'

'Very well, let me be a rakel, Sudhir. But how many wives did your grandfather have? And do you know the story of your great-grandfather? He scattered his seed all over Gujarat very generously. Watch out, there are several of his great-grandsons walking all over Gujarat, with the same features as you.'

'All that is irrelevant. Selvi, have you read Tulsiramayan?'

'Why would I read Tulsiramayan? I've read Kambaramayanam, certainly. As Tamil literature.'

'Isn't Sri Ram your god, then?

'Life is my god.'

'If I ask you whether you are a Hindu, can you answer yes or no?'

'I can only say I was born into a Hindu family.'

'Yes or no? Tell me that.'

'Yes. No.'

They didn't hit out. They didn't kick. But that was all. They roared. They thundered. They ridiculed. They spoke with contempt. When she refused to eat, they said, 'Che, this is only a friendly discussion.'

The interview with Nargis Khala was on green paper. An interview, which all three of them had held with her. She had talked of her days during the Independence struggle, and had ended by saying, 'You might ask me, what I achieved in my life. I'll tell you a story in reply to that. A Zen master went away to live in a cave in a remote mountainside. On his return, the king summoned him to the court and asked him to give an account of the wisdom he had attained. The master was silent for a while, and then he took out the reed-flute that was tucked in at his waist, and played a cadence on it, very softly and sweetly; then walked away. Some things can't be said. They can't be wrapped up in words. If you ask me about my achievements, I will touch you with these hands. Hoping that through my fingers, the warmth of my experience will reach you. I will touch your heads with my hands. What else can I do? What do I know except that?'

How often had Nargis Khala touched her? Stroked her cheek? When Sakina and Charu returned from Ahmedabad, and poured out their distress, she put her arms around both of them, embracing them. She looked like Jatayu at that moment.

'Broad views about life have shrunk into religions, and we have been turned into their symbols. They regard us as empty symbols. Symbols of a religion, a nation. We mustn't be trapped by that. In this war, let that be the ground of your contest. A ground that cannot be reduced to definition and detail.'

'But what are our weapons, Khala? What, if anything, can be our weapons?'

'Only this,' she said, laying the palms of her hands, wrinkled like withered leaves, against their cheeks. She smiled.

*

'Aunty, may we come in?' The two young boys were strikingly tall. A girl of the same age was with them. All three worked fast. When they stopped for a rest, halfway through, they danced to 'Bole chudia' and 'Shaba shaba'. Then they returned to their work. All for the sake of Hrithik Roshan.

One of the boys said, 'Our Baba told us Amir Khan is Muslim. We mustn't go to Amir Khan films. And we mustn't drink Coca-Cola.'

'Really? Hrithik Roshan's wife is Muslim. Amir Khan's wife is Hindu. Don't drink either Coca-Cola or Pepsi. Your teeth will rot. Tell your Baba.'

'I'll tell him,' he said, hesitantly. He was afraid the money might not come into his hands.

As soon as they were paid, they fled, shouting, 'Thanda matlab Coca-Cola.'

*

It's night-time here. I'm sitting in a cyber centre, writing this. I'll tell you later why I'm here.

First there is some important news. Sakina is dead. She fell from the terrace of Iqbal Maamu's seventeenth-storey flat and died. Her neck was broken. How much violence there has been in our lives. Tamal's death in the bomb blast. Ramu's death in the car accident. Now Sakina's ill-fated death. These are violent times. We cannot redeem our lives until we have passed through them.

Sakina's death stabs at my heart even now. She was with me that day until early evening. She seemed a little weary. I was distraught because I could not understand why she told me she would go to Nargis Khala's house, but changed her mind and went to Iqbal Maamu instead. She was my friend from our school days. I agonized over why she committed suicide when there should have been so many more years of friendship ahead of us. I couldn't accept that it was suicide. Before she went she had said, 'Let us go and say goodbye to Charu at the airport.' I thought and thought about what could have happened between five o'clock and the moment of her fall; I retraced her steps again and again. Some things became clear to me.

The night before, she returned from her second visit to Ahmedabad. When she called by telephone, her voice didn't sound right to me. I insisted, 'Come round to my flat at once. You don't sound good at all. I'm sure you haven't eaten at all, properly.' She came. I made her favourite soft rotis, and a potato and bell-pepper sabzi. She ate. Later, as we lay down and talked, she told me about an incident that happened the previous evening. It was rather late when she reached the refugee camp. A young Muslim woman was walking in front of her, she said, one child on her hip, and another clutching her hand. She walked along, supporting both children, and managing at the same time to carry a bag in one hand. The tricolour flag was stuck between her fingers and she was walking along, extending it in front of her. Like a protecting shield. As if she were proclaiming, I too am a citizen of this country.

'I wept and wept, Selvi, when I saw this. Why has it become so necessary for just a few of us to have to do this? My Khala was a freedom fighter. My Maamu heads many charitable institutions in this city. My Ammi retired from an administrative post in a school. She died, a blackened corpse. My father was a high-ranking official. Here am I, walking about with a snake neck. That girl might have come from a similar family. Or she might have been one of India's many, many poor women. I couldn't bear to see her stumbling along with her children, her bag and her tricolour flag.' She wept for a long time. She repeated again and again, overwhelmed by the thought, 'The time has come when I have to establish that my Khala was this, my Ammi was that, and so on and on ...'

She was devastated by the thought that the actions of her family – performed naturally and as a matter of course – had to be presented now, as her credentials. She said, 'Selvi, do you remember what Charu used to say? That when certain birds decide to die, they swallow many pebbles; then when they try to fly, they cannot because of the weight inside them. So they crash down and die. My heart feels as heavy as if I've swallowed many stones.'

'You go to sleep now,' I said, patting her. She dropped off like a child.

But there was no cheerfulness in her expression the next day. Later we stood together in the heat in Hutatma Chowk. She was participating in the hunger strike, besides. At first, she really must have set out for Nargis Khala's flat. Then, remembering we had to vacate the Jagruti office in the next few days, it could have struck her that she might as well collect the folder from Iqbal Maamu's flat, since she was in that part of town. I conjecture all this from Iqbal Maamu's memory of his conversation with Sakina, over tea, that last day.

It seems that while she was waiting for a taxi to take her to Iqbal Maamu's house, she met Nandini. She asked Nandini where she was off to. Nandini said to her, 'Sakina Mausi, I have to tell you something. Keep away from Amma and me for a while. I hold a responsible position. I don't wish to be caught up in any kind of trouble ...' This from the girl whom you and Sakina brought up. When she was a child, she thought of Sakina's Ammi and Khala as her grandmothers.

Already Sakina was a bird that had swallowed many pebbles. Nandini made her swallow a block of granite. It seemed Sakina just patted her on her back. Soon after she got to Iqbal Maamu's flat, she went and opened the book-almirah. I went to Maamu's flat myself, and made myself go through all her actions. The instant she opened the almirah, she would have seen the photograph of Ammi, holding Nandini in her arms. Sakina must have been deeply moved. I think she didn't take her blood-pressure tablets that day. She must have felt dizzy. She must have opened the terrace door, gone outside and taken a few deep breaths. She might have remembered the topiary bird. She might have held onto the parapet wall, raised herself a little and peered down. Empty stomach. Seventeenth floor. Suddenly her foot might have slipped. I believe that's what happened. She fell against the topiary bird, and then crashed to the ground. And that is how our Sakina met her end.

Now please read the attachment I have sent with this message.

Finish the letter later. When the girl who worked in Sakina's house had her baby, it was the fiftieth anniversary of Independence. Sakina wrote this then. I found it in the folder. I think she must have written it for us, all that while ago.

*

Attachment: For Roshni, a morning song.
A few weeks ago your mother invited me to your home to give you a name; to whisper it in your ear. In that tiny hut, where there was scarcely enough room to sit down, your mother had hung a cradle which she had bought for a hundred rupees. She had strung flowers around the room. She had bought a new frock for you. A couple of months ago I had seen you in the hospital within three hours of your birth. You looked like a peeled fruit, then! Now your face and your features were bright, radiant. When I whispered in your ear, like a secret, 'You are Roshni, you are Light,' you swivelled your eyes round and gazed at me.

Every night, your grandmother, who gave up her share of a small piece of agricultural land and left her village to come and work in the big city and bring up four daughters in this slum colony by the seaside, will sing you to sleep with lullabies. As you grow up, she will tell you stories to the sound of the waves, until you fall asleep. Stories of kings and queens, stories about the devil, about valorous mothers and noble wives. At dawn, the calling of the azaan from the mosque will wake everyone, summoning them to prayers. I have heard that in the temples too, they sing the tirupalli ezhuchi to wake up the gods. Roshni, this is my azaan for you, my dawn song. To wake you up and keep you awake. This is the song of my generation. The generation that has lived through these past fifty years. A generation that wants to tell many stories, in many voices, in many forms. You will hear many tunes here. And there will be some discordant notes, too. Because it spans many years. It touches many lives. Lives that are similar, and very different. But do listen to it.

During these years, it wasn't easy to grow up, to live, to make the right choices in life, in education and work. Several of us, even now, keep changing those choices. We had to oppose the mainstream and swim against it, taking care not to be caught in the whirlpools. They told us many stories too. They told us that for women, marriage was the most important thing in life. But we had also heard of the Sufi saint Rubaiya, and of Meera. We knew about bhakti. All the same, several among us were atheists, didn't believe in rituals, or didn't accept that one religion alone was true. Even now, that is so.

From our childhood, the Independence movement and its ideals had merged into our lives. The men and women who had been part of it were our role models. Many of them lived among us. They came and spoke to us in our schools. You could say there wasn't a home without a picture of Gandhi, smiling. From our schooldays we learnt the song about Gandhi's life, which began, 'Suno, suno e duniyavalo Bapuji ki amar kahaani.' When we were still in school, we saw the film, *Jagruti*. In that film, a teacher takes his pupils all over India, and sings to them, 'Take this earth, and wear it on your forehead as an auspicious sign. This is the land of our sacrifices.' For our generation, it became almost a national song. We were stirred by other Hindi songs, such as the one that went, 'We have saved the boat from the storm and brought it safely ashore. Children, safeguard this land.' We wept. There were some among us who had grown up learning the poems of the poet Bharati. Iqbal's lyric, 'Sare jehan se accha' rang out in every school. We learnt to sing Tagore's songs, 'Ekla chalo' and 'Amar janmabhumi', making no discrimination against any language. In another picture, *Kabuliwallah*, the hero, from Kabul, sings a song, remembering his country. 'My beloved land, I dedicate my heart to you. You are my desire. You are my honour. I greet the winds that come from your direction with a salaam. Your dawns are most beautiful; your evenings most splendidly coloured.' We used to apply these words to our own country, and weep. Of course there were other labels amongst us – as Marathi, Kannadiga, Tamil, Telugu, Punjabi, Assamese and so on. But for us who grew up in the years following Independence, the country as a whole was the important thing.

But these were not the only songs we heard. There were other sounds and voices. Proverbs, discussions, the voices of everyday life. Listen to some of them: rubbish and daughters grow quickly. Women and cows will go where you drag them. Women and earth become fertile with beating. A woman learns by giving birth; a man learns through trade. A daughter is like a basket of snakes on the head. A leaking roof and a nagging wife are best abandoned. A woman's virtue is like a glass vessel. If a husband batters or the rain lashes, to whom can you complain? You may sit on any ground, you may sleep with any woman.

Sometimes the older women in our homes, or travellers we met on journeys, sang yet other songs. Work songs, dirges, lullabies. Women spoke of their tribulations in such songs. Such sounds brought us down to earth from the idealistic heights where we were floating. I found some of those songs in books, too. One remains in my memory: it's a song by a widow who says she might have served society better had she bloomed as a flower on a tree and not been born a woman. The metaphor in the song refuses to leave me.

There was also something called national culture. Motherhood was at its core. A woman like Jija Mata. A woman who suckled her child with the milk of valour. Before our time, women had already left their homes to work for the country. They had accomplished extraordinary things. But we who came after them had to safeguard our homes. We were instructed that our duty was to reap the benefits of the previous generation, to listen without opening our mouths, never to raise any questions. Our responsibility was to create a home, set up a good family, learn what was useful to society. The advice to us was clear: sit still. Otherwise you will rock the boat.

Our bodies grew heavy. We carried a heavy burden of stones that we did not choose to carry. I say all this, Roshni, with the clarity of hindsight. But at that time we were clear and confused, both. We were not silent, though. Do you know, there is a Bengali proverb that says, no one can control a woman's tongue? So we never stopped talking. We spoke up through poems, stories, political essays, music, drama, painting; in many different ways. Many of us aimed for higher education. If you look at many family photograph albums, there will be one photograph of a young woman in a graduation gown, clutching a rolled-up degree in her hand. Wearing an expression of fulfilment. Head held high. A keenness in the eyes. I too have such a photograph. But it was also customary, as soon as this photograph was taken, to remove the graduation gown and take another one, which would be sent to prospective bridegrooms. I told you, didn't I, there were all kinds of pressures on our lives? It wasn't easy to deal with them. A woman called Subhadra Khatre has said, 'It would be good to deposit one's femininity in a safe-deposit vault and move around freely in the outside world.' She was an engineer of that time. She writes, 'Had I been a typist, I would have picked up a job easily. As an engineer, they looked at me as if I were trying to usurp a man's place.'

Until the end of the '60s we fought only within our own homes, and our narrow surroundings. It was a battle to stop others from directing our lives. In 1961 the law against dowry came into force. We debated it in schools and colleges. There were some women in politics even at that time. But it was in the '70s that a serious networking among women with varying views began through conferences, workshops, protest marches and dialogues. We wrote many songs for our movement. We sang them. We raised our voices against price rises, against dowry, against rape, against domestic violence, against liquor and against the exploitation of the environment. We worked together and independently. We gained victory. We saw defeat. Sometimes we were divided as activists and academics. But one thing we understood clearly. Just because we had similar bodies we did not need to have similar thoughts. The political atmosphere made some of us disillusioned with the movement. Some of us opted out. Others became isolated. They retreated into their shell, refusing to communicate. We became aware of one thing. We needed to learn humility. However much we celebrated sisterhood and love, there were still many demons within us such as jealousy, competitiveness, arrogance, insolence, hatred. Some of us emerged with renewed strength. Like so many Sitas who couldn't be banished to any forest. Like so many Rubaiyas who walked their own path, singing the stories of their own lives.

Roshni, Light, I have strung together for you fifty years of doubts, rebellions, battles, struggles. This is only a song. When I write an epic for you – and I will write it one day – I will speak of all this in detail. But don't think the song is complete. It is true communal violence, caste-wars and human degradation have all dispirited us greatly. But our battle continues. We still raise our voices to safeguard rivers, trees and animals. To safeguard human beings, above all. You will hear in this song, resonances of our joy, despair, disappointments and exhilaration.

Sleep well, Roshni. And when you wake up, let it be to the sound of our song. You and I and many others must complete it.

For we believe that a song, once begun, ought to be completed.

*

Now read on.

As soon as I realized how Sakina's death had come about, I left for home. I waited for Nandini. When she returned, the questions I put to her confirmed for me, what she said to Sakina that day. At once I telephoned Susie, who manages a working women's hostel, and booked a guest room there, until further notice. I told Nandini to pack whatever clothes she might need into a single case. I told her I would send on the rest of her belongings, later. Then I asked her to leave my house. She was shocked. She had assumed it was I who was leaving, and I think she was preparing herself for a histrionic farewell. She became furious. 'Don't I have any rights in my father's house?' she demanded.

'The house is in my name. Your rights to it will come after me.'

As she was about to leave she said, 'Don't expect me to come to your aid when you fall ill, and take to your bed.'

I said, 'I know how to live alone. And I know how to die alone. You can go.'

'How can people like you call yourselves mothers?'

'I count myself a real mother. Those others live with the illusion of motherhood,' I said, closing the door.

I sent on all her belongings, including the computer. That's why I write to you from this place.

I have put all the things from the Jagruti office in the warehouse of a factory belonging to one of Iqbal Maamu's friends. A go-down without any windows. A go-down which never sees any sunlight. Someone belonging to another generation, perhaps one of the little girls we educated, like Roshni, might one day open the warehouse and let the sunlight stream inside. We'll wait. Until such a time, we'll take up other kinds of work; little drops falling into the great ocean.

Sing a song for me, during a quiet moment there. 'From the very depths of my being, I thirst.' I shall hear those words. I send you, with this, some tears. Take them. Let me know when they reach you. Selvi.

*

She clicked on 'Send', and as soon as she got the message 'Sent', she disconnected. She rose to her feet, and paid her fee to the manager of the cyber centre. Outside the glass door, a fine rain was descending.

'The first rains of June, madam,' said the cyber centre fellow.

'Yes,' she said.

She came outside, lifted up her face to the sky and received the cool raindrops. In that instant, time stood still.

Translated from Tamil by Lakshmi Holmstrom

Numoli's Story

What is Freedom
For him or her, for you or me?
What does it mean
To each one of us?

Freedom means to love and to share,
To help and to care,
To be unafraid
And to love everyone.

Safdar Hashmi

Numoli began working at the loom before the pale light of dawn touched the sky. Now, her finger joints had begun to ache. She put aside the shuttle and the half-finished pattern, and cracked her knuckles. For a while she looked, absorbed, at the slowly emerging motif, in red, of a xarai that she was weaving into the white gamosa. This time her brothers would be really impressed. They always teased her, calling her a simpleton and an idiot, but this time they would realize her true worth. This was no common pattern she had found and copied from somewhere. She had taken the motif from a book of patterns brought by Makon's city-bred sister-in-law. Working very fast, she finished the pattern and thought of wrapping the woven cloth around the beam, but she stopped and ran her fingers lovingly over it once again. How lovely the xarais in red looked with their tips complete against the heron-white background. Resting her hurting fingers on the reed, she called out to her mother excitedly, 'Bouti, O, Bouti, I've finished another one.'

A little sparrow fluttered down and parked itself on one of the poles of the loom. Then, suddenly, it flew off, frightened by the sound of the treadle. Numoli laughed, and looking at the little sparrow now perched on a branch of the mango tree, said, 'You're scared now, aren't you? But I know you're the one who sat on the flower on my second brother's gamosa yesterday and tangled the yarn, I know now.' A little cuckoo started to sing from somewhere on the just-fruiting mango tree on which the sparrow sat. Numoli stared at the mango tree and noticed a beautiful orchid blossom in the fork of its trunk. It seemed as if suddenly that row of red xarais in the gamosa, within the heron-white background, had spread out over the mango tree, the song of the cuckoo, the petals of the orchid and the whole sky. Touching the red xarais yet again, she called out once more to her mother, 'Bouti, O, Bouti, please come, I need your help to wrap the cloth around the beam.'

Numoli's mother was getting lunch for her sons. The eldest would go to work at his job in a school, the second to work in his office and the youngest to college. She was cleaning fish. Hearing her daughter call out, she walked up to the loom from the kitchen without washing her hands. Her eldest daughter-in-law was pregnant and had gone to stay with her mother. So Numoli's mother was having to manage everything by herself. At such times she wished her second son too would get married. But he had been saying that he would not bring a wife home before he had built a decent house. The youngest had already taken out his bicycle to go to college. The fish was still in the bamboo sieve. 'Why are you bringing down the skies with your screams?' she rebuked her daughter. She wanted to say something more but stopped, and looked at her daughter's innocent face fondly. How quickly she had grown! She was now a young woman. Soon it would be time to get her married. Just last week there had been a proposal from her best friend, Sakhi's son. She really liked that healthy, hard-working lad who had crossed the river, tilled the land and set up his own fields on the side of the river. But the brothers did not want to give their only sister away to an uneducated farmer. They kept scolding her, 'You haven't even finished your matriculation! Who will wed you now but a village bumpkin!' As a mother, she was saddened when she heard them taunting the girl in this way. How did it matter if she could not finish her schooling and go to college? Not many girls in this area could work such intricate patterns on the loom as deftly as she could. You felt soothed and calmed when you saw her working, humming a bihugeet or a biyanaam to herself.

The bell-metal plates she cleaned gleamed like gold, the fish tenga she cooked was like nectar, the coconut laroos she prepared were as white as tagar blossoms, the pithas she made were absolutely special. Her brothers felt they lost face just because she could not be a fashionable college girl. She had blushed pink seeing the silk churidar-kameez that her youngest brother had bought for her from the city last pooja. 'O, Bouti, look what Xaruda has brought for me. Where and when will I wear such fancy stuff?' And sure enough, that pretty dress, mauve like ejar flowers, was left unworn in her suitcase. She wore cotton mekhela-sadors that she wove herself. The way she had cried when they had bought her a silk mekhela-sador set for a thousand rupees from a Sualkuchi trader! 'After Pitai died, my two brothers have had to work so hard to keep our house going. And now you go and waste their hard-earned money to buy silk clothes for me! That old man counted and took not one, not two, but as many as ten hundred rupee notes in front of our very eyes! We could have bought a cow with that money or a bundle of tin-sheets for our roof.' That girl cared for nothing other than the house. She did not go out anywhere, nor did she spend a penny on herself. It was hard to find a young girl who was as domesticated as she was. Numoli's mother could not help sighing.

Numoli was weeping, holding the batten of the loom. Big teardrops fell from her doe-like eyes. Nearby, her youngest brother, getting ready for college, was wrapping a book in newspaper and shouting at her, 'Why do you bother about these newspapers? Do you ever read a word of what's in them? Is there anything in your head that you will be able to read? Whenever somebody takes an old newspaper to wrap something, you come swooping down on them. What do you do with those old papers?' Numoli sobbed even more. Her mother couldn't restrain herself. She ran her fingers through her daughter's hair and looked sternly at her son and said, 'With the money she gets from selling old newspapers in Ramu's shop, she buys things for the three of you. She has bought these soap dishes and shaving bowls for you from that trader who sells things at three rupees apiece!'

When he heard his mother's stern voice and the sound of Numoli's weeping, the second son, who was polishing his shoes before heading out to work, said, 'If she did not waste her time on all these useless things and concentrated on her studies instead, she could have been in a college by now.' The mother took her daughter's hand and led her to the kitchen. 'Come with me, Maajoni, and help me clean the fish, my dear.' Wiping her tears with her asal, Numoli followed her mother into the kitchen and started working on the fish. The eldest son came into the kitchen to check if his food was ready and the mother's grief overflowed. 'What's the point of scolding and taunting her? God did not give her the brains to go to college. A goddess for a god, a mare for a horse. Like everyone else, she too must have someone destined for her.'

The son sat down on a low wooden pira and answered, 'Bouti, you're the one who pampers her so much and spoils her.'

The spoilt daughter of the overindulgent mother was at that

moment completely lost in staring at a bheseli fish. She had left half-done the fish she was cleaning and, putting this tiny fish in a bowl of water, was kneeling and watching it. 'Bouti, look, look, she's still alive. She looks so pretty when she swims.' The mother came and took some of the fish that Numoli had finished cleaning. After washing the fish, she placed them in the kerahi of hot oil over the fire to fry, and scolded Numoli. 'Your brothers don't scold you for nothing! All you need is a little fish or a bird to forget everything! You're old enough now to look after a household but you don't seem to have lost your childishness!'

'Whose childishness, Khurideo?' Everyone turned around at the sound of a deep voice and the clack-clack of boots. Prasanta. Even on this warm April afternoon, he had a jacket on. As he pulled a mura to sit down, there was a sound from inside his jacket. He pulled down the zip. Numoli could clearly see three revolvers inside. Prasanta was her cousin, her Borpita's son. 'Oh my God,' she wanted to scream, but stopped, biting her lips. Once before, when she'd seen a revolver in his jacket she'd asked, 'Kokaideo, why do you carry them around?' and had been roundly scolded by her mother and three brothers.

Prasanta had changed completely in the last few years. He had been missing from home for about two years. Then, he began to come home every now and again. Today, they were seeing him after nearly six months. Whenever Prasanta came, there was silence. Her eldest brother was already locking the main door of their house.

'Xarubapu,' Prasanta was telling her youngest brother about some meeting, 'Tomorrow we have a meeting of the Xangathan, it will be in our house.' Having said this, he left, as abruptly as he had entered. The whole kitchen reeked of the sour odour of stale sweat, which even wiped out the strong smell of fried fish.

'Xarubapu, what did he ask you to do?' The eldest brother's face showed clear signs of worry.

'I have to keep my eyes and ears open. The whole village is swarming with the military. It's only because of Prasanta that they are after all of us. Prasanta killed two of their men in our village, didn't he?'

'Who knows what will happen next?' the mother cradled her head in her hands and sat down near the hearth.

Numoli did not like all this moaning and sighing. Moments like these when one could not laugh, or say anything, weighed on her like a curse. How could people live like this? She felt like teasing that little cuckoo singing away on the mango tree. She felt like sucking one of the pieces of seasoned, garnished and pounded ou-tenga drying in the sun. But how could she do that when all around her the others were so grave? They were all sitting motionless like numbed doves. Let Prasanta do what he wanted to, what difference did it make to them? Xarudada had given up Prasanta's company after Bordada had scolded him for it. And the military presence everywhere! After two of them had been killed in the fields, the army had swooped down on the village, descending in truckloads and surrounding it completely. Before she could even take in the situation, her eldest brother had taken her and his wife and had left them at his in-laws' place. But where was the military now? Everyone seemed rooted to their seats. She had finished cleaning the fish ages ago. The little bheseli fish was still swimming in the half-pail of water – like a little red and silver flower-petal. She would have to keep it alive in a bottle. She wanted to get up to look for a bottle, but couldn't. How could she do anything when everyone remained like this?

'Bouti! Are there any military here these days?' she asked, unable to tolerate the silence.

All of them turned to look at Numoli. Her doe-like eyes gave her face the innocence of a little baby girl.

'Maajoni! These things are beyond you. Go and wash the fish. You have been working on the loom since the crack of dawn. It is almost ten o'clock now. Go get yourself something to eat.'

She picked up the fish with her hands and glanced at her mother's face. Mother's eyes were brimming with tears. Numoli could not bear to look and her own eyes welled up. Her mother was telling her sons something, her face pale with fear. 'I heard in the naamghar that day that the military do not come openly these days as they used to do earlier. It seems ten military men roamed around in Bongaon for a long time disguised as fishermen before they were discovered.'

'These are bad times.' Her eldest brother poured water over his half-eaten meal and got up. Even her youngest brother, who was always on the lookout for something to eat, left home without eating. The food served to her middle brother remained on the plate – untouched. Numoli began to feel sick with anxiety – her three brothers would remain hungry all day. She sat on the doorstep of the kitchen and dug her head between her knees – large teardrops wet her mekhela at the knee. Her youngest brother removed the bamboo pole at the entrance to the compound and came in. He leaned his bicycle against the wall but stopped when he noticed Numoli crying at the doorstep. Subconsciously, all three brothers loved the sound of Numoli's sweet voice calling out to their mother announcing their arrival the moment they touched the wicket gate. The first thing they did when they came home was to look at Numoli's innocent face, to say something to her and only then get on with other things. It seemed to them that something was really amiss if she did not go about her work humming a cheerful tune. Last night six of Prasanta's accomplices had entered the village. Of course no military or policemen had been spotted yet. Still, Xarubapu thought of what Mother had heard in the naamghar and he shuddered involuntarily. His chest seemed like a dry field of hay, which could catch fire with the smallest spark and get destroyed immediately. He'd got his things together to go to college but had not gone. His elder brothers were not home. If something happened, what would his mother and sister do? He could not get rid of a feeling of disquiet. And when he saw his little sister sob her heart out, his mind filled with sorrow. He walked slowly up to her, 'Numoli, what is the matter?' Hearing him call her by name, she looked up at her brother, a little surprised

– he usually found other names to tease her. 'Dada, didn't you go to college?'

'No, don't know what might happen ...' he wanted to say, but he stopped short. He didn't want to frighten her unnecessarily.

'You did well. What would you have learnt cycling ten miles to college on an empty stomach?'

'Have you eaten something yourself? Bouti was saying that you have been at the loom all morning and have not eaten.' He placed his hand gently on her back.

Smiling at the affectionate little pat from her brother, Numoli wiped away her tears and said happily, 'Let's go and eat. The food must be cold by now. Just wait a minute, I'll go and pick some mint leaves. They will taste wonderful ground with a little tamarind.'

She knelt near the mint-patch in the garden – thin blades of sorrel were pushing their way up between the lush mint. She plucked a couple of stems – with little violet flowers. They wilted instantly, the flowers drooping in her hands. How easily these tiny plants wilt! She thought of removing all the sorrel stems to clean out the patch but didn't. Let them be. They were not doing the mint any harm. Then spotting some tiny yellow flowers growing in the grass near the mint, she stopped again while plucking the mint. How lovely they looked! Like gold! If only I could wear one as an earring! She plucked two tiny flowers and placed them on her palm. They began to wilt almost immediately. Makon's sister-in-law wore a pair of earrings that looked like these flowers, only slightly bigger. As it is she is a very pretty city lady. On top of that, her lovely woven clothes and sparkling earrings really set her beauty off. When she becomes a bride, will she too ... Her mother's friend, her Xokhi, had taken the size of her bangles when she had come the last time. Would she really become her daughter-in-law? Her mother had told her about her Xokhi's home – she had fish swimming in her pond, there wasn't a tree that couldn't be found in her back garden. They said also that the boy was very hard-working. Tall, medium-complexioned and handsome, he had come visiting one day and had brought three kinds of bananas for them from his kitchen garden – Malbhog, Jahaji and Senisampa bananas. What ripe and firm bananas! Her brothers had teased her while eating those bananas. 'Did the ploughman bring these for our little bengi?' He tilled his own land, how could he be called only a ploughman? If everyone went to work in offices and schools, who would work the land? She would also go to the fields to sow and reap. Not once did she get to go to the fields, even to take food for her brothers. They wouldn't allow it. She opened her palm. Although wilted, the two little flowers were not completely crushed. In front of her floated the spectacle of the tall sunburnt son, her mother's Xokhi standing beside a bride, dressed in a beautiful handwoven set of clothes, wearing those golden earrings like the two little flowers on her palm. No, how silly! They would look like ivory and ebony. The sharp-tongued women who sang wedding songs might even start singing.

> Oh, my little heart
> How pretty is the bride
> But the groom?
> Oh my little heart.

She really started singing the refrain of the wedding song aloud, 'Oh, my little heart ...'

'Come on, bengi! You came here to pick some mint leaves and now you're sitting here singing wedding songs! Let's go.' Numoli covered her flushed face with both hands. As if her brother had caught her in the arms of a tall, sunburnt, well-built lad in the middle of a golden mustard field. Three cuckoos started singing from three directions all at once, as if to tease her. Her innocent, childlike face reddened even more.

'My stomach is growling. Half the day is already gone waiting for your mint chutney!' said her brother. The youth in the mustard field vanished forthwith. Numoli hastily picked up the mint leaves and ran to the kitchen. 'Bouti, O, Bouti, where have you kept the tamarind?'

She had found everything a little strange this morning. Her youngest brother normally worked through the night and got up late. But today he woke up just a little after her. Usually, as soon as he awoke, he would begin to shout for his tea and would not get out of bed before she had served him a cup. But this morning he, who relished his tea so much, had left it untouched despite the milk and sugar she had lovingly put into it for him. And then he'd headed out towards the village crossroads, without even washing his face. And once back, he'd declared, 'Nobody should go near Borpitai's house today.' Every day, she and her mother went to her Borpitai's house many times. This house was just beyond the mound. What was special about today? Was it because Prasanta was there? What had he done that people lost their voices the moment he arrived? How would the police or the military know that he had come? Why was her youngest brother so upset today? Numoli sat at the loom, holding the spindle in her hands. There come Ratul and Prabin, her youngest brother's friends. Normally they would sit in the soraghar or the bat soro-ghar, but today they walked straight into the backyard. She got up from the loom and was walking to the kitchen to make some tea for them when she overheard them talking about various people being put up at various places. No, they left without waiting for tea.

Baroda, her eldest brother, was not at home. Although he did not speak much, Numoli was very happy when she saw her grave and dignified brother sitting on the veranda. She glanced at the chair on which he normally sat in the mornings. If only he were home, she would not feel so uneasy. The time for her sister-in-law's confinement was drawing near, and he had gone to see her at her parents' home. He had gone there directly after school yesterday and would come home only after school today. Her other two brothers were sitting with their mother in the kitchen. Again that uncomfortable, frightening, frozen period. She was a little scared to sit alone at the loom. God knows what was going on. She was scared even in her own house. Everything was just the same – the mango tree that was drooping under the weight of its blossoms, the lau that was creeping over the kitchen roof, the rows of areca-nut trees with betel leaves growing on them lining the path, the long back garden, the pebbled road in front of their house and the people going back and forth, the lemon trees growing on the little mound near their Borpitai's house, nothing had changed. Sitting a little apart from the others, she took out some flattened rice in a sieve and started cleaning it for her brothers' snack later on.

Her ever-smiling, cheerful youngest brother, Xaruda, seemed so different today – it was as if he was frightened about something.

'Majuda,' he asked the middle brother, 'can you not stay at home today? What if something happens?'

'How long will they be here?'

'Yesterday Prasanta said they'd disperse tonight immediately after the meeting.'

'Has he kept anything in our house?'

'He wanted to, but I didn't allow him.' Numoli heard her mother's voice and wanted to ask her what it was that they had wanted to keep in the house but were not allowed to. Even her mother was sitting there so sullenly. She would get irritated if she asked her anything. After soaking the flattened rice in water in a big bowl, she went to get four bowls to serve it in, but, on second thought, left one behind. She did not feel like eating. With what would she serve the rice? She had not milked the cow yet. What was wrong with her today? On other days, she would have milked the cow, cleaned the courtyard and also worked on her loom for a while by this time. With the bowls in front of her, she waited for some time and then said, softly, to her mother, 'Bouti, I'm going to milk the cow ... breakfast ...'

Her youngest brother interrupted. 'No! You mustn't go to the cowshed. The room next to the front room of Borpitai's house is right next to the cowshed ...' he gulped and did not continue.

'I'll go instead. You don't have to,' her middle brother said, getting up and starting to walk towards the cowshed.

Their back garden was short but wide. It extended a long way along the road, but their house was right next to their Borpitai's. Their father had built this house so close to his brother's that they could call out and hear each other in case of an emergency. The cowshed was also there. Every now and then, cows were stolen, so their father had built the cowshed right next to the house. Of course they did not have a shed full of cows now, as there had been in her father's time. Her eldest brother had sold the cows. All three men went out early in the morning. How could the two women manage so many cows? Now there was only a year-old calf and its mother. The cowshed was very close to the front room of Borpitai's house. Numoli had often asked her brothers to move the cowshed to the back. If they had a flower garden there instead, then that new soraghar of her Borpitai's house, with its full brick walls, built at the time of her cousin's wedding, would look so much nicer. Although they kept promising to move the cowshed, nobody had actually taken it seriously. Just there, Xaruda had planted a little sapling he had bought in the city. She could never remember the name of the plant. That little plant, growing in that fertile spot near the cowshed, grew tall and luxuriant in no time. Last year, it was so laden with orange blossoms that passersby stopped in their tracks to look. The soil around there was very fertile – the betel-leaves that grew on the areca-nut plant had a very special taste, and each paan leaf was as soft as the tender leaf of a segun tree.

She felt a little sorry to see her middle brother going to the cow shed with the dung pail. She did not like the idea of her neatly-dressed and spotlessly clean brother handling dung. She ran and snatched the pail from him. 'Majuda, you don't have to throw the cow dung. I'll do that. You go and get the cow instead. I need to milk her, the calf is crying for milk.'

'You don't need to throw the dung today. Just milk the cow,' said her white pyjama-kurta-clad brother, putting the dung pail down.

Prabin and Ratul came in. Her mother gave them two cane muras to sit on in the courtyard. The very fair Ratul was flushed and agitated about something. There were beads of perspiration on his forehead. 'We'll tell Prasanta this time. He can do whatever he wants outside this village. We cannot tolerate this any more. Last time they killed two military men and vanished, and we had to pay the price for that,' Ratul said, enunciating each word carefully, as if he was frightened of something. 'How many days has it been since we've started sleeping in our houses again? We've had to hide in jungles and forests.'

Numoli heard Ratul's words. Her hands, which were milking the cow, began to tremble. The cow got annoyed and lifted one of her hind legs. What was Ratul saying? Would it all happen again? After staying in her sister-in-law's house for a fortnight last time, she had come home to find everything in a mess. The ripe and heavy paddy grain lay trampled flat in the mud. The young women would go to the 'reserve' every night. Truckloads of military men were everywhere. For days on end nobody in the village could rest even for a moment. Those days again! She could not milk the cow today with her trembling hands. She managed to get barely half a bucketful and then tied the cow to her haystack and came back.

Her middle brother went in ahead of her and said to their mother, 'It doesn't look as if anything untoward will happen. Let me go to work. I'll work half a day and come back early. Xarubapu is here.'

'Xaruda, are you going fishing?'

'Yes.'

'Can I come too? I don't need your worms, I'll make do with ata instead.'

She wanted to run to the kitchen to fetch some ata, but stopped when she heard her brother's harsh voice. 'There's no need for you to come with me. I'm not going to fish hoping to catch fish. I just want to keep an eye on the road.'

It was possible to sit on the bridge over the pond and keep an eye on the main road. But who was her brother going to keep an eye on?

'Xaruda, who are you going to watch?' she could not stop herself from asking.

'Why do you need to know all that? Go and do your work. And listen, if anyone asks you anything about Prasanta, say you don't know. And if you see the police or the military, tell me, but don't come out yourself.'

She wanted to squat near her brother and ask him what Prasanta and his friends had done to be hounded by the police and the military in that way. Where do the military and the police come from? What meeting were Prasanta and his group having today? Why did her brother have to use fishing as an excuse to keep an eye on the road? Who was coming? Their village was a full ten miles away from the town, and her Borpitai's home was even further, deep inside the village. How would anyone get wind of when and with whom Prasanta was having a meeting there?

Her mind was in a flutter. The consequence of working on the loom with a mind so restless reflected clearly in the xarai pattern she was weaving – the red xarai appearing in two disjointed bits, separated by a white line, as if someone had driven a sharp knife through it, slicing it into two. The two bits lay scattered on either side. It was as if someone had run a knife through her mind too, and left one half with her muddled confused thoughts, while the other remained, on the gamosa pattern. She sat staring at the two bits of the xarai, holding her face in her hands. Even this dull afternoon held something frightening. On other days her mother would join her after finishing her work in the kitchen, and help her fill a shuttle or untangle the yarn. Today her mother was still groping around in the kitchen. She had not even finished cooking yet. First she had burnt the vegetables, then she had spilt some water, and then the milk boiled over even while she was watching. Should she go and help her mother? She decided she should, but kept sitting. She didn't feel like going into the kitchen. Suddenly the godhuligopal tree near the fence came to life. She stood up and looked at it. Had the cat got in, chasing the mouse? When she clapped her hands, saying, 'Shoo ...', a big fat snake came out and disappeared. That snake did the rounds of the backyards in their neighbourhood. She had seen it many times, it was at least four or five yards long, pitch black, and invariably vanished when it sensed humans were around. It kept away from people. Only today had it come as close as the threshold. It had probably come out to catch some frogs thinking nobody was around. There were many frogs under the godhuligopal tree. She would have to tell her brothers to get that place cleaned – who knew, there could be many more snakes lying in wait under the tree.

Her youngest brother emptied the fish he had caught from the casket onto the sieve – all sorts of fish, quite a few of each kind – garai, magur, rou and puthi. Watching the fish jumping about in the sieve, Numoli began jumping too. 'Dada, that's a lot of fish you caught today.' She touched the fish, turned them over and then cried out again with childish pleasure, 'Xaruda, look at these two tiny golden-red xenduri-puthi.'

Scraping the husky covering from a large ripe areca-nut with a sharp kaari, her brother answered, 'Fry those two for me today.'

'No'; she sounded so sad and upset that her brother stopped scraping the nut. He looked at her and said, 'Okay, you eat them.'

'How can anyone eat such lovely fish? They're still alive, I'll keep them.'

'Fish caught with a bait don't survive too long.'

'They'll stay, I'll take care of them. They're not dead yet.'

'The areca-nut tree near the pond has given very good fruit this year,' he said, splitting the nut into two, revealing the thick coconut white inside.

She did not hear anything. In a trice, the two tiny fish, jumping around like two streaks of vermilion, occupied her mind completely. Those unnecessary worries, the xarai that lay split into two on her loom, the big fat snake under the godhuligopal tree, all these thoughts got left behind, like the outer covering of the areca-nut that had just been pared. The red vermilion spot on the white fish was so pretty. Her long braid got dirty in the dust as she sat on her haunches to look at the fish. But she noticed nothing.

'Oi, Bengi, go and get me a paan please. Don't forget to put some suun on it!' said her brother, lifting her braid gently from the ground.

Everyone in the house called her names and asked her to run small errands. Numoli, do this. You fool, bring that. You little idiot, get that, etcetera, etcetera. And her overabundant love for her three brothers would find expression and fulfilment in these little chores she did – in getting them the paan, or the stool or the newspaper, or the shoe-brush, a shirt or a glass of water. Since morning that day, nobody had asked her to do anything. So when she was asked to fetch paan for her brother, her suspended breath seemed to somehow flow again.

'Wait, Xaruda, it'll take me only a moment,' she ran to the kitchen with her braid swaying from side to side. Not a single paan leaf was left in the broken-handled bowl where they were usually kept. All it held was a black rotting remnant.

She ran towards the cowshed to get a fresh leaf for her brother. Everyone liked the paan from one particular betel-leaf creeper. The leaves from the others were either sold or given away to neighbours on festive occasions. The long-handled hook used to pick the leaves was standing against the fence bordering the road. While getting the hook she looked at the lovely flowering tree her brother had brought from the city. There was not a single leaf on it. What a strange plant it was. New leaves were sprouting on all the other trees nearby, but not on this one. Was it dying? She scratched the stem to see: inside it was still juicy and soft green like young leaves.

While she was stooping to check on the exotic plant, a man spotted her and came up to her. Tall, stiff, dark, strange – she could not remember having seen him before. He was wearing a dhuti and punjabi, on his shoulder was a gamosa with a large flowery pattern, his hair was closely cropped, and he sported a big, impressive moustache. Who was this man? He was not from this village. Who was he looking for? Was he a relation of Makon's sister-in-law? He also had a golden-coloured seleng-sador with a jari border over his body. The man came very close to the fence.

'Which is Prasanta Hazarika's house?' His voice was as rough as he was stiff. The tone was somewhat unpleasant. Why did he want to know Borpitai's house? There was a marriage proposal for Lata from some family in the city. She had finished her graduation and was studying for her Master's in the city. This man looked like someone from that family. One did not dress up so much unless one was visiting for a special auspicious occasion. She hesitated a moment before pointing out the house to him. If somehow this man went back to the city without finding her Borpitai's house, everyone would blame her. They would accuse her of sending him away out of jealousy, for not having made it to college herself.

In her mind's eye, she could see the picture of her city-bred cousin with her cropped hair and red lipstick, wearing a bright, colourful sari with large flowers on it. How distasteful that sight was! But why should she be jealous? She was happy if everyone was happy. She pointed out her uncle's house to the man.

'That one there.'

Instantly the man stood up, erect. The whole area suddenly reverberated with the sound of bullets and filled with the smell of explosives; the shots seemed to be coming from the direction of her uncle's house. Before she knew what was happening, the man with the sador caught hold of her. With the pressure of a strong hand holding her, Numoli was pressed against his chest, her face towards Borpitai's house. The man was aiming his revolver at her uncle's house. In reply to every shot he fired, bullets rained down on them from all sides. The man kept jumping up and down like a cat. He went forward once, then back, and he held her like a shield to his chest. Suddenly something pierced her bosom. She wanted to cry out, 'O, Bouti!' but could not roll her tongue. She heard her mother's voice once. 'What has happened to my darling Maajoni?' After that a deafening sound behind the cowshed. And with that sound, her little world of red-dotted fish, the singing of cuckoos, the blossoming of mango flowers, her mother's love, her brothers' affection and the red patterns on the gamosa that sparkled on her loom, all fell silent. Her head wilted and drooped like the little blades of sorrel after being plucked, on her white mekhela-sador appeared the red colour of blood, the stains rough and ugly. As if some careless unskilled weaver had tried to weave a confused red border on sparkling white cotton. The man lowered her body to the ground. It writhed and shook, a bit like the two red-dotted fish that tried to move on the sieve before dying. The man knelt near the body and fired a round of bullets in the air. After that he took out a walkie-talkie from his pocket.

The spring wind seemed to carry the smell of the blood flowing from her bosom through the entire village. Like her limp and drooping head, the whole village seemed to wither away at the smell of bullets, the sound of firing, and the deafening impact of grenades. The notes coming from pipes and horns here and there, fell silent in mid-afternoon. The people on the streets and in the fields all went into their houses. Everything wore a deserted look. People locked themselves indoors. The strangely dressed military man who had come to get news about Prasanta kept guard over Numoli's body. The news spread from house to house in no time. Those who heard it could not restrain their tears. How could that innocent girl who never went out of the house without her mother die such an unnatural death? In everyone's pots, food remained uneaten that day. If someone had served himself, he fed it to the cats and dogs. The terror-stricken people who had locked themselves inside their houses got to hear another piece of news – Prasanta and his gang had fled by the side of the naamghar through the fields. And in their mind's eyes floated the spectacle of the paddy fields laid waste last year, full paddy sheaves trampled flat by the boots of the military ... Those wounds had not healed yet, and now once again ...

When she heard the first round of firing, Numoli's mother was in the kitchen draining rice. She had called out to her youngest son, 'Xarubapu, what sound is that?' And when she heard round after round of the same sound, she stiffened, the steaming pot of rice still in her hands. Then she put it down and had only just begun looking for her daughter when she heard her son's anguished voice from another room, 'Bouti, we're finished, our fates are sealed.' She rushed to the room and found him sitting and weeping. Out the window she saw a big, rough man firing his gun, holding her daughter to his chest. He was trying to shield himself from the bullets coming from Prasanta's house using Numoli's body. The mother could not see her daughter very clearly, she was partly hidden by the man. She could not hear Numoli's voice either. In the midst of the smell of bullets and smoke, her daughter's thick, serpent-like braid would suddenly swing in the air, then vanish from sight again.

As his mother tried to open the front door to go out, Xarubapu went and locked it. 'Bouti, Pitai is already gone and now if you too ...' Just then the bloody red flowers blossomed on Numoli's white dress. Thereafter, a frightening earth-shattering roar. This time, Xarubapu, red with fury, tried to open the door to go to Numoli's side. But his mother held him back saying, 'I've already lost one child, how can I bear the loss of two ...'; her voice died out. She often had dizzy spells. Now she lost consciousness. The son laid her on the floor, brought some water from the kitchen and sprinkled it on her. She woke up and started muttering. 'My dear sweet Maajoni ...' It was getting quiet in the direction of Prasanta's house. When he saw the injured man firing in the air and trying to contact his associates Xarubapu wanted to go out again but he held back. As if an injured tiger was guarding his prey. If he went and something happened to him, what would happen to his mother? In his mother's distraught mind, hovering between consciousness and unconsciousness, floated the picture of her sweet innocent daughter, walking back from the pond, crying, in great pain. Once, during their holidays, all the three brothers had drained the pond. Numoli was hovering around her brothers like a little girl, running small errands for them, helping them, when a tiny sting-fish pierced her finger. She had run crying to her mother, 'O, Bouti!' She had cried so much on being pricked by a little fish. On that same girl's bosom today ... Her mother tried to get up again and open the door to go out – Numoli was lying face down on the stones on the road, around her a pool of red blood. Sitting beside her was the big rough man with a revolver in his hand. He also had bloodstains on him. Every now and again he let out a roar in Hindi like an injured tiger – 'Keep away!' The line between consciousness and unconsciousness once again became very hazy in the mother's mind.

Not too long into the afternoon, four truckloads of military men descended on the village. They surrounded it completely, no one could go in or out. People returning home from work, students returning from school or college, small traders returning home with empty baskets after selling their wares in the city, all were stopped on the road to the village and asked to turn back.

Raghu had managed to get a good price for the ahu-jika from his garden. He had bought half a kilo of fish on the way and was imagining how tasty the fish would be when cooked with fresh gourd, when he was stopped on the road by the military. He was terrified at seeing their guns. Girls returning from college had to seek shelter in the hospital for the night. Most of the men decided to see the night out in Ramu's little tea-shop at the end of the road. They sat up the whole night.

Numoli's eldest brother was returning home from school after spending the previous night at his in-laws'. The bag on his bicycle was bursting with things his wife had sent for Numoli – some bamboo-shoot pickle, some kharoli, some patterns for the loom ... He spent the night at Ramu's shop along with the others. All night long he kept hearing about the girl or bride killed in the firing. Unable to sleep, he worried constantly about his mother and little sister, his heart beating uncomfortably.

Numoli's second brother had returned home early as promised.

On the way he heard about a girl who had been killed in the firing. His heart missed a beat – people were assembling near his house and there weren't any girls in Borpitai's house. For a while he was overwhelmed. God knew what had happened. Cycling furiously, he had tried to enter the village when that flock of military men obstructed his way. There were orders from above, nobody was allowed to enter the village or to leave it. He almost forced them to let him in. In broken Assamese and Hindi he tried to tell them that his mother and sister were alone at home and that he had to go home to them. But they did not relent. There was the whole village inside. Why was he so worried? How could he tell them what was going on in the house next to theirs? Seeing him standing on the road with his bicycle, one of them just pushed him aside. With a heavy heart, he proceeded to the home of a friend who worked in the hospital and spent the night there. Throughout the night, he kept hearing about the girl lying on the road. And with every mention, a shiver of dread and fear ran down his spine. His friend had often invited him to spend the night at his home, and today he even put together a nice dinner for him. But he wasn't able to eat even a morsel.

They loaded Numoli's body onto a truck when it was time for the sun to set. At that time, Xarubapu was fanning his near-unconscious mother. Looking for just a moment at his sister's body, lying amidst upright guns and khaki uniforms, he could not contain himself. He went to the edge of the pond and started howling. He bit his lips hard to stop himself from crying – he did not want his mother to hear him – so hard that blood started dripping from them.

Nothing stirred anywhere ... his almost unconscious mother, his sister's lifeless body that they had carried away in the truck ... in his life of one score years he had never encountered a crisis like this. His father had died in that very house two years ago because of hypertension. The whole village had come and seen them through that crisis. Some took charge of their distraught mother, others showered all of them with affection and understanding, yet others cooked and made sure they got their meals at the right time. During their sorrow, the whole village had surrounded them, protecting them like a big bird sitting on her eggs. In the warmth of their affection the wounds had healed quickly. Remembering the hustle and bustle of people going in and out of their house, bringing them food and provisions, fruit and vegetables, he suddenly felt very lonely. He was not a city lad. No, he had grown up being nurtured on the affection of the entire village. He succumbed to the terror of the present situation and his stifled sobs rolled down the banks of the pond.

By then, the sun had set into the reserved forests and darkness enveloped the still benumbed village. In the gradually increasing darkness, the military went from house to house. They collected all the men from these houses in the big yard in front of the naamghar. They gave Rajat Barua, who had come to the village from the city for a couple of days to meet his sick mother, an extra kick or two when they came to know he taught in a college – this for being an educated man yet allowing terrorists to enter the village. For that same crime, they also kicked around the old arthritic village headman. Old and sick, young and immature, all sat quietly in the naamghar courtyard, shivering. In the houses where there were no men, they left a trail of devastation behind, trying to find the birds that had flown in the pots of rice and the jars of salt.

When Xarubapu reached the naamghar from the edge of the pond they all looked at him. The dried coagulated blood on his lips and his bloodshot eyes swollen with incessant crying were similar in colour. Seeing all those familiar people, he started weeping again, tucking his head between his knees.

The jawans who went into Xarubapu's house looking for terrorists knew only one thing – the gang of terrorists had fled from somewhere very close by. They entered Xarubapu's house in the middle of the night. The doors of the house were still open. After searching the whole house, when they reached the front room, Xarupapu's mother was still lying there, unconscious. 'Dead or alive?' they asked in Hindi and left, after prodding her from side to side with the muzzle of their guns. The flash of guns, the sound of boots and the unfamiliar smell brought back Xarubapu's mother to consciousness. She sat up on the bed with a start. And her mind saw again and again the image of a long braid like a big fat snake, swinging in the wind. She wanted to get up and scream, 'Oh my dear Maajoni!' but stopped herself when she saw the armed men swarming about in her courtyard. She wanted to call out to Xarubapu but her voice seemed to have got stuck in her throat. She sat down on the floor, dumbstruck with fear. When she thought that one or two of them were approaching her, when she heard the heavy tread of their boots, she crawled under the bed like an animal. A sharp sliver of light licked the house. The woman tried to shrink further into herself. After that the sound of boots died down. The middle-aged woman shivered and sobbed silently with a terror she had never before experienced in her entire life. Alongside her, the mellow spring night in the village too wept.

Just before dawn, Numoli returned to the village. Her virgin body had been cut open by a doctor's scalpel and sewn together again. After Numoli entered the village, the blocked road was opened again. When they set foot on the road, all the frightened people, returning home after spending the night wherever they could, saw the body of the much-loved sweet girl that they all knew, lying on a little wheeled carriage, that looked like a cow-cart, attached to the jeep. Her body jumped with the jeep as it drove over the bumpy pot-holed road. It seemed as if she would sit up that moment, flash a smile and say, 'Raghukai, have you come back from the market?' Raghu would put his yoke down and stop for a moment. And from the basket he would take out a paper packet and show it to Numoli. 'I've bought a sador for your Mami. It cost me full score and five rupees.' She would inspect it closely. 'It's quite nice. The woven ones are much better, this is flimsy.' Raghu would let out a sigh. 'What can one do? The lady who used to weave for everyone in the house is now crippled with pain.' Once, during that Bihu, Raghu's sick wife had cried inconsolably after putting on a green-bordered white sador that Numoli had woven for her. The same Numoli is reduced to this today. Raghu put his yoke down on the roadside and began howling loudly. Seeing Raghu crying like that a military man standing nearby started hurling abuse at him. 'Your own boys have become terrorists, you hide them in your houses, then they kill your own people and now you come and cry ...' All this was spoken in Hindi, of which Raghu did not understand a word. In his chest was a heart full of love on a white sador with a green border. He could not stop crying. The jeep carrying Numoli began to circle the village. Someone from the jeep kept saying something at regular intervals, the gist of which was: 'Your own people are being killed by terrorists, this is what will happen if you shelter terrorists, the people should cooperate with the police and the military in catching them, otherwise such incidents will keep happening.' A few villagers understood a word or two, most of them not a word at all. No one was allowed to come close to Numoli. When the jeep passed by Makon's house, the mad-with-grief Makon tried to touch Numoli but she bit her tongue and stopped in her tracks at being told off for wanting to do so.

The people who had spent the night in the main courtyard of the naamghar had also been allowed to go home. Almost all of those who had spent the night waiting outside the village had also returned home by then. But nobody had entered their homes. The wicket gate of Numoli's house was wide open. The people kept entering the courtyard, one by one, silently. The womenfolk of the village also came and filled the house. The cows and calves were still tied in the sheds, nobody swept their courtyards that morning, all the people who had eaten nothing since the previous day had still not thought about lighting the kitchen fire. The housewives had fed the very young and the old and infirm with whatever was available and had rushed to be beside Numoli's mother. No one was bothering about others' cows ruining their gardens, no one had checked whether the ducks and hens had all returned to their coops or had been devoured by cats and jackals. In the minds of all was an overpowering, overwhelming fear, an all-consuming terror.

Meanwhile, Numoli's two brothers had returned home. They came in to find their mother lying almost unconscious. And Xarubapu? Four or five men together could not hold him down. He was screaming, 'What did she understand of terrorists, of the army? Why was she killed?' He was beating his head on the floor. Four or five men tried to restrain him, and he almost toppled over. When he saw his two brothers, he started rolling on the floor, like an old tree that had just been axed, 'I couldn't save her, in front of my eyes they ...'

Just at that moment, the jeep stopped in front of Numoli's house, after doing several rounds of the village. Numoli came home, borne by two jawans, and was laid down in the courtyard. Over her body cut apart and sewn together, covered by her blood-stained clothes, a military officer had laid a garland or roses, and he took off his hat as a sign of respect. The other jawans, who were creating a lot of noise with their boots and guns, followed suit. The handsome and polite officer stood for a while, head bowed. With him stood the other jawans as well. The truckload of jawans who had accompanied Numoli's jeep entered and filled her house and compound. The waiting villagefolk understood they were looking once more for Prasanta and his gang. One of them even yanked at Xarubapu, who was crying with his face tucked between his knees, and stared into his face. After about five minutes they all trooped out with heavy footsteps and climbed into the truck. The officer saluted Numoli's body one more time and got ready to leave. Before he got into the jeep he said in English, 'If you shelter terrorists, things like this will happen.' Xarubapu shouted back, 'Everyone tries to victimize the innocent. I'll have my revenge on all of you, just wait ...' This time, Xarupabu's brothers held onto his arms. His old Borpita, Prasanta's father, approached him slowly. 'My son, don't try to stir up a hornet's nest.' He kept hearing again and again, all through last night, that the bullet-riddled body of his six-foot-tall, well-built son, who had been away from home these last two years, was lying in the reserved forest, or in some field, or on the river bank. The old man put his entire weight on his walking stick and started weeping uncontrollably.

Numoli was lying asleep in the courtyard with the garland of roses on her chest. Her long, thick plait lay on the grass. She was encircled by a ring of dumb people whose stomachs ached from hunger, and whose eyes burnt from lack of sleep. No elder was reminding anyone about the rules and rituals of performing the last rites. Nobody was trying to organize the wood for the pyre. No one had even thought of taking the body to the tulasi plant, no lamp had been lit ... All the frightened people just stood around her like deer hunted by a tiger. The only sound was that of stifled sobs, and Xarubapu's screams, 'I'll teach them a lesson, I'll spare no one ...'

Who would put Numoli's body on a bamboo bier and take her to the riverside cremation ground? How would they do that? Numoli seemed to spread over the entire village. There sat Numoli on the tree of large and oval limes in Raghu's garden and would burst into song if anyone came near,

> O, cowherd of the village
> My dear friend and my brother
> O, listen to my plea
> Pluck not this lime nor another.

Numoli became a gourd creeper and spread all over the mounds of the village. She would break into song if anyone came near,

> Stretch not your hand
> Nor pluck this gourd
> O, old lady
> Whoever you are from wherever.

Numoli began to bloom and sway as lotuses in the pond do, and would cry out if anyone tried to pluck her,

Stretch not your hand
Nor pluck this flower
O, dear boatman!
Whoever you are from wherever.

She will weep and wait in the village as the limes, as the gourd, as the lotus. One day, someone will come to her and say, 'If you're the little Numoli, then eat this little bit of chewed betel-nut.' She will eat that and turn into a little sparrow. Then he will say again, 'If you're the little Numoli, if you have love in your heart, then wear this gamosa and you will become a human again.' Numoli will come back to life again. Her heart is full of love. She will wait until she can come back to life again.

Translated from Assamese by Meenaxi Barkotoki

The Story of a Poem

Sushama is writing a poem. The first two lines form themselves very easily on a sheet of paper.

> A teardrop sways my lashes
> as I think of you – even now.

These are very ordinary lines. Any romantic or postmodern poet can write them. If they deserve special attention at all, it is because they are written by a woman. You know, in our society – which incidentally includes Sushama's husband Reghuraman too – people always go out of the way to unearth autobiographical elements that are believed to underlie women's writings. If Reghuraman reads these lines though, he's likely to look at Sushama with suspicion. He is very particular that his wife, like Caesar's, should be above suspicion.

Sushama's poems thus take birth in a hostile and suspicious world. Look at her, writing the poem at the kitchen table on which lie scattered some sheets of paper, a broken pencil, a knife, diced vegetables and a few plates. The chopped-up circles of ladies fingers can be used for frying or for making a kichdi. The unripe bananas, drumsticks and tomatoes speak of the possibility of an aviyal. Sushama: just watch her. She leaves the half-sliced vegetables on the table to write the first two lines of the poem, then leaves the poem and comes back to the vegetables. Now she has sliced a whole lot of ladies' fingers into beautiful rings. Her lips are moving, she mumbles something that's barely audible as she puts the vegetables away and turns to the unripe bananas. Look how easily she peels them, with the tip of her knife. Suddenly, she stops, and picks up the pencil and we see four lines of the poem being born effortlessly:

I remember –
how we walked huddled under an umbrella,
how the torrential downpour drenched the lonely street,
how you put your hand on my left shoulder,
how my whole body shivered at your touch.

A slow brightness lights up Sushama's eyes. The movement of her hands slows down as if she is falling asleep. She is going off – into another world that has rain, the rhythm of rain and electrical fingertips. Let us leave her there and go to meet Reghuraman.

*

Reghuraman is standing at the bus stop near the children's school for a bus to take him to the office. Usually he goes on his bike, but today the bike refused to move. So he dropped the children at school in an autorickshaw and is now waiting at the bus stop. The bus must come soon, for Reghuraman has to reach his office before a red question-mark appears against his name in the attendance register.

Reghuraman's table in the office is near Shriranjini's. Reghuraman likes Shriranjini. He has fantasised about several parts of her body as if they belonged to Sushama; but, strangely, he has never wished to have Shriranjini as his wife. As a wife he prefers only women like

Sushama – who is quiet, does not talk much, does all the chores without ever complaining and who is excellent in culinary arts. Shriranjini is good – but only as a friend. A good friend to talk to when your mind feels dry. Someone good enough to be taken to the Indian Coffee House and got into an argument with – about Borges or Aravindan or Deconstruction – over a cup of tea and masala-dosa. If she objects not, he is willing to go a bit further – but only to a point from where he can turn and walk back. No, he would never wish to have Shriranjini as his wife; let feminists be the wives of other men.

As Reghuraman thus reflects on Shriranjini a bus pulls up in front of him. Children in school uniform clamber down and the bus is almost emptied out. Reghuraman sits comfortably near a window and continues to think about Shriranjini. Now he hopes that she will come to the office today clad in red silk. As he entertains these simple thoughts the conversation of two self-styled critics seated behind him falls upon his ears.

A: Did you read E's latest story?

B: Yes, I did. I think the dissatisfied wife in the story is the author herself.

A: I thought so too. But how can you be certain?

B: You see, a colleague of mine lives near her house. He told me that ... er ... there are some problems in her marriage. Haven't you noticed – all her heroines go in for extramarital affairs. They hate marriage.

A: You're absolutely right. So the affair of the girl in the story ...

B : ... is, of course, the author's.

Reghuraman, who knows E, the author, and is familiar with her happily married life, listens with curiosity to the stories about her. He feels relieved that Sushama is not a writer. Else such curiosity would have found its way into his bedroom as well. Instead, people only say of him that he is a happily married man. He thanks his stars for saving him from being the husband of a writer.

Shriranjini writes poems in English and people do talk about her too. Why should all these women have the urge to write? He has read Shriranjini's poem, the one that won a prize from the British Council. It begins:

> Strip me and see the real me with naked vision
> And be frightened, shocked, morally decayed.

Who else but Shriranjini can write such beautiful lines? Strip me ... what an interesting deconstruction it could lead to! Reghuraman's tongue passes over his lips.

*

Now there are three more lines in Sushama's poem. They are:

> how each raindrop blossomed into a flower,
> how fire burned in each of its petals,
> how the redness and warmth spread through the body.

The incomplete poem rests on the dining table. Sushama, all her chores done, is bathing. As the water flows down her body we can see that her mind is still in a daze with the half-born poem. The afternoon sun blazes hot around the house. Unable to bear the heat, the plants droop, their heads bent low. But where Sushama is, it rains. It rains in Sushama's mind. And suddenly one more line is born in her:

> how your eyes were hidden by my scattered tresses.

And we see Sushama, naked, dripping, running to the dining table to add that line to the poem – hurrying to catch it before it vanishes. She scribbles it down without even bothering to check if the curtains are drawn or if the idle neighbour's vulture-like eyes are seeking their prey. As she writes, a little puddle of water forms around her feet; she runs back to the shower shaking her dripping hair. As she does so, she catches a glimpse of herself in the bedroom mirror.

Once again she stands under the shower, now remembering Reghuraman's flippant remarks about her body. He'd said to some of his colleagues who had come home for tea – 'You see, there is only one difference between my wife and Miss Universe. The curves are in the right places on Miss Universe and in the wrong places on my wife.' He laughed, enjoying his own joke, while his colleagues, evidently uncomfortable, made a pretence of smiling. Only one lady – a Ranjini or so – expressed her dislike at what he'd said. She came to the kitchen later and tried to comfort Sushama – 'Take it easy, Sushama. Reghuraman is really proud of you. He talks about you in the office at least a hundred times a day.'

Sushama, knowing full well that if he talked about her at all, it would only be to negatively compare her with other women, did not ask for details. In fact she did not like the memory of that afternoon to intrude into her poetry-dazed mind. Go away, she told that memory. Don't stand in the way of my poem. Get lost!

*

Reghuraman comes back from the canteen, his hands and breath smelling of roast chicken, and asks Shriranjini – 'Aren't you eating? Are you fasting today as well?'

'Yes,' she tells him. 'Today's Thursday, the day on which I observe the Santana Gopala Vrata for the benefit of my children.'

'What a combination of contradictions you are,' remarks Reghuraman. 'You hold such free and fearless opinions, and then you sometimes behave so conventionally.'

When Shriranjini refuses to respond, he adds: 'But I must tell you that your contradictory nature adds to your charm.'

To steer him away from the subject Shriranjini asks, 'Why can't you bring lunch from home? Sushama would prepare it happily for you.'

'I don't like cold food,' he says. 'I enjoy only hot or warm food. That is why I was particular about marrying an unemployed, unambitious girl. You know there is no refrigerator in my house. Sushama tried her best to make me buy one, but I was firm. Now do you understand, Shriranjini, the secret of my healthy body?'

Shriranjini's eyes steal over his firm hands and broad chest.

She withdraws her eyes guiltily, gets up and moves away, mumbling some excuse.

*

The poem now rests on Sushama's lap. She has added a few more lines to it.

how our paths forked in two different ways,
how our memories were blotted out by hands unseen,
I remember all these forever and ever.

Sushama reads the poem again and again and makes some changes. Outside the house, the sun has started to lose its heat. Sushama is happy now. There is no trace of any fatigue though she has risen with the sun and moved with the sun. There is a celestial rapture on her face as if she is an apsara who has come to the green woods to give birth to a baby in secret. Her eyes rise from the poem and wander round the room, not really seeing the snacks and the tea kept on the table or even the time on the clock.

*

'I'm leaving early,' says Reghuraman to Shriranjini. 'I'll not come back as usual after dropping the children at home. I've got to go to the workshop to see how my bike is.'

Shriranjini looks up from a file and gives him a smile.

'See you tomorrow.' He pauses at her table to whisper in a low tone, 'Will you wear the red sari tomorrow? Please – it's a request.'

He walks away quickly without waiting for a reply. Shriranjini looks after him with confusion in her eyes and mind. His firm footsteps seem to tread on her heart.

*

Sushama's trembling hands are now dialling a telephone number. She cradles the poem in her lap like a baby. She hasn't added any more lines to it; so we can safely conclude that it is complete. After dialling the number Sushama sits back restlessly.

We can hear the faint ringing of a telephone somewhere far away. It stops. Someone picks up the receiver. We can hear a masculine voice saying, 'Hello?' Sushama's face tightens like a heart that is about to break. After a slight pause the voice asks again, 'Hello? Please say who you are. How can I know unless you tell me?'

Sushama suddenly replaces the receiver. Her pulse-rate slowly comes down to normal and her face relaxes. She is now adding a few more lines to the poem.

Though you no longer hold me in your mindscape
You are still the teardrop on my lashes.
As each raindrop falls from the sky
You fill my thoughts like the waves of the sea.

*

Reghuraman and the children have arrived in an autorickshaw. Sushama hears the sound, jumps up and tears the poem into small pieces. She throws the scraps out the window and rushes to open the door before the doorbell rings, for she is the ideal wife and the ideal mother!

Since Sushama has destroyed the poem, reader, if you want to read it in full, you can pick up the verses scattered in this story, put them together and read them.

Translated from Malayalam by the author

WAJIDA TABASSUM

Cast-offs

'No, Allah! I feel very shy.'

'What's there to feel shy about? Haven't I taken off my clothes too?'

'No-oo!' Chamki was embarrassed.

'Take them off now! Shall I tell Anna Bi?' Shahzadi Pasha, who knew nothing beyond giving orders, threatened. Scared and bashful, Chamki, with her small hands, first removed her kurta then her pyjama. On Shahzadi Pasha's command she then jumped into the soapy tub with her.

After they had finished, Shahzadi Pasha smiled indulgently and, with the arrogance of a mistress towards a servant, said, 'Now, tell me, what are you going to wear?'

'This, my blue kurta-pyjama,' Chamki said seriously. Shahzadi turned up her nose in amazement. 'These ... these dirty, smelly clothes? Then what's the use of bathing?' Instead of answering, Chamki popped a question in reply. 'Pasha, what are you wearing?'

'Me?' Shahzadi spoke with easy pride. 'That glittering Bismillah outfit which my Daadi Amma made. Why do you ask?'

Chamki became thoughtful. 'I was thinking ...'

'What?' Shahzadi Pasha asked, bristling with curiosity.

Suddenly Anna Bi roared, 'Pasha, did you banish me from the hammam to be alone with this miserable little wretch? Get out at once or else I will go to Bi Pasha right now!'

Chamki quickly blurted out what she had been thinking.

'Pasha, I thought ... if you and I exchanged dupattas and became sisters then I too could wear your clothes.'

'My clothes? You mean all those clothes lying in my trunks?'

Chamki nodded hesitantly, feeling apprehensive. Shahzadi Pasha doubled up with laughter. 'Oh, no! What a silly girl! You are a servant. You people only wear my cast-offs. All your life you will wear nothing but that.'

Then, with great care, born more out of pride than kindness, Shahzadi picked up the clothes she had taken off before her bath and tossed them at Chamki. 'Here! Wear these. I have many others.'

Chamki flared up. 'Why should I? Why don't you wear my clothes?' She pointed at the filthy pile lying in a heap.

Shahzadi hissed with anger. 'Anna Bi ... Anna Bi ...!' Anna Bi banged at the door. Since it was not bolted it flew open at once. 'So, you two are still naked?' Anna Bi placed a finger on her nose and spoke in mock anger.

Shahzadi pulled a soft pink towel from the stand and wrapped herself in it. Chamki stood as she was. Anna Bi glared at her daughter and said, 'And you! How dare you enter the hammam of Pashas?'

'Shahzadi Pasha said ... you also bathe ... with me.'

Anna Bi looked around, terrified that someone may have overheard. Then pulling her out of the hammam she spoke roughly, 'Now go to the servants' quarters, quick! Or you might catch a chill.'

'But my clothes?' said Chamki, cringing with shyness.

'Don't wear these dirty clothes now. In the red trunk there is a kurta-pyjama that Shahzadi Pasha gave the other day. Wear that.'

As she stood there, naked, the little seven-year-old spoke

haltingly. 'Ammini, if I am the same age as Shahzadi Pasha, why can't she wear my cast-offs?'

'Wait! Wait until I tell Mamma that Chamki said this to me!'

Anna Bi, scared, picked Shahzadi up in her arms. 'Pasha, she is mad, the whore! Why tell your Mamma of her ranting and raving? Don't play with her ever again! Just throw your shoe at her and forget her.'

Then she dressed Shahzadi, combed her hair, got her ready and served her a steaming plate of food. After finishing her work, when she reached home she found Chamki standing there, stark naked. Looking neither right nor left, she immediately started walloping her daughter.

'Picking fights with those who feed you! Whore! ... If Barre Sarkar throws us out where will we go? Such airs!'

In Anna Bi's reckoning, it was her great good fortune that she had been hired as a wet-nurse to Shahzadi Pasha. Her diet was the same as that of any Begum's because, after all, she nursed the only child of the Nawab Sahib. There was no dearth of clothes because it was essential for a wet-nurse to remain clean and tidy. And the best part was that her child got all Shahzadi Pasha's innumerable cast-offs. Handing down clothes was an established custom. It surely surpassed the limits of generosity that even silver toys and ornaments were given away as cast-offs! And this scoundrel ... as she grew older she protested only about one thing: 'Why should I wear Bi Pasha's cast-offs?' Sometimes she stood before the mirror and said with great wisdom, 'Ammini! I am prettier than Bi Pasha. Then why doesn't she wear my cast-offs?'

Anna Bi worried about this. These were big people. If anyone ever got the slightest inkling that Anna's daughter had spoken such words, her nose and hair would be chopped off and she would be thrown out on the streets. In any case, the wet-nursing was long over. But it was a tradition of the house that annas only left when their bier left the house. That was why she was still here. Even so, pardon could only be granted if an error was worthy of being pardoned. She said, twisting Chamki's ear, 'If you say anything ever again ... Just remember, all your life you will have to wear Bi Pasha's cast-offs. Do you understand, you donkey?'

The donkey sealed her lips but the lava kept heating up in her mind.

When she turned thirteen, for the first time Shahzadi Pasha could not say her prayers. On the eighth day when rosewater was sprinkled to mark the occasion, her mother had such a shimmering outfit stitched for her that her eyes were dazzled by its glitter. The costume was sequinned with little pairs of gold ghungroos. When Shahzadi walked the bells tinkled musically. In keeping with the traditions of the household even that ... that invaluable costume was given away as a cast-off. Anna Bi was thrilled. She brought the clothes to Chamki who by now had grown wiser than her years. 'Ammini, accepting these cast-offs as a matter of compulsion is different. But don't look so pleased at receiving such gifts.'

'Oh, beta,' she said, softly, 'even if we were to sell these clothes, we would get at least two hundred rupees, solid cash. We are indeed lucky to be living in this household.'

'Ammini, how I wish ...' Chamki said with great wistfulness, 'that I too could have given some cast-offs to Bi Pasha!'

Anna Bi struck her head with her open palm. 'Allah! You are no longer a child. For God's sake come to your senses. If anyone hears this nonsense, what will I do? Have some pity for this white-haired old woman.'

Chamki fell silent.

Maulvi Sahib had started them off together on reading the Koranand, the Urdu primer. Chamki was quicker than Bi Pasha. When they completed the first reading of the Quran, Barri Pasha, out of the goodness of her heart, had a new set of clothes stitched, in slightly cheaper material, for Chamki. Although she ultimately also got Bi Pasha's heavy set of clothes as cast-offs, Chamki loved hers better than her own life. There was no insult associated with it. That saffron-coloured outfit was better than any of Bi Pasha's glittering clothes.

Now that Shahzadi Pasha had attained puberty and had studied as much as she needed to, the question of her marriage arose. The household started being frequented by goldsmiths, tailors and traders. Chamki decided that on the wedding day she would wear the very same saffron outfit, which was no one's cast-off.

Barri Pasha, who was a kind-hearted woman, always treated her servants like her own children. That was why she worried equally about Chamki's wedding. At last she was able to prevail upon her husband and find a suitable boy for Chamki. She thought that in all the bustle and preparation of Shahazadi's marriage, Chamki's nikah could also be managed.

When there was only one day left before the wedding, the haveli was overflowing with visitors, and the young girl had taken over from the elders. Shahzadi was sitting among her friends getting her feet hennaed. Suddenly she said to Chamki, 'When you go to your in-laws, I will put henna on your feet.'

'God forbid!' Anna Bi said with affection, 'may you never touch her feet. It is enough that you have said these kind words. But just pray that her groom too turns out to be as kind as yours.'

'But when is she getting married?' a pert little girl asked.

Shahzadi Pasha laughed an arrogant laugh. 'When all my cast-offs are discarded and with her, then consider her dowry ready!'

Cast-off, cast-off, cast-off. A thousand needles pierced her heart. Chamki brushed aside her tears and flung herself on her bed. As evening fell, the girls started their dholak. All the lewd marriage songs were sung in girlish voices. The previous night there had been a ratjaga, and tonight again there would be one. At the back of the courtyard the cooks had lit their fires and were preparing the most delectable dishes. The brightly lit night already carried the illusion of the wedding day.

Chamki's tearfulness enhanced her natural beauty. Her saffron-coloured clothes elevated her to the heavens from the depths of her inferior status. They were no one's cast-offs. Made of new material, this outfit was unique! All her life she had worn Bi Pasha's hand-me-downs. And now her dowry would also consist of Bi Pasha's clothes, she was destined to wear her cast-offs for the rest of her life. 'But Bi Pasha, you mark my words, a daughter of Syeds can only be pushed thus far, no further. Just wait and see. You gave me things to use, didn't you? Now wait ...'

*

Carrying a tray of maleeda Chamki reached the chambers of the groom's party. The place was brightly lit ... the nikah was the next day. No one took any notice of her in this confusion. Making gentle enquiries Chamki reached the bridegroom's room. Tired from the rituals of haldi and mehndi, the groom was reclining on his masehri. When the curtain moved he turned around, and was transfixed by what he saw!

Her saffron kurta coming down to her knees, tight pyjamas stretched on her rounded calves, saffron dupatta sprinkled with light kaamdaani, tearful eyes, curved arms peeping out of the short sleeves, strings of jasmine entwined in her hair and on her lips a daring smile. There was nothing unusual about this. But for a young man who had spent several nights fantasizing about a woman ...! No matter how restrained, he becomes almost uncontrollable the night before his wedding.

Night, which lures the flesh. Solitude, which spurs temptation.

The way Chamki looked at him, he succumbed immediately. She deliberately turned her face away. Agonized, he climbed off the bed and stood in front of her. Chamki's glance from the corner of her eyes reduced him to a pulp.

'Your name?' he managed to say, swallowing.

'Chamki!' A glittering laugh transformed her face to moonlight.

'It's true! Whatever it is that's shining inside you, it is only right that your name should be Chamki!'

Trembling, he put a hand on her shoulder. He spoke in a voice which was not the voice men use to seduce a girl, but softly, lifting his hand from her shoulder and holding her hand in his own he asked, 'What is in this tray?'

'I have brought maleeda for you. Last night was ratjaga.' Chamki encouraged him. He was wounded, without a weapon. 'I have brought it to sweeten your mouth,' she smiled.

'I don't believe in sweetening my mouth with maleeda.' He bent down to sweeten his lips with hers. Chamki fell into his arms. To rob him of his purity, to lose her own.

On the second day after the bride's departure when, according to the tradition of the household, Bi Pasha returned home to give her wedding night clothes to the daughter of her wet-nurse, Chamki smiled.

'Pasha, all my life I took your cast-offs. But today, you too ...' she started laughing wildly. 'All your life ... you will use mine ...!' She could not control her laughter.

Everyone gathered there realized that it was the thought of separation from a childhood friend that had temporarily unhinged Chamki.

Teaser

Rakesh leapt onto the bus, feeling like a red, hot chilli. The bus was a tongue in the mouth of the world and by placing his foot upon it, he scorched it with his power.

His power resided in the fork of his pants. Most of the time it slept. But when it was awake, such as when he boarded the bus he took to college, it was vibrant, it was radiant. It generated heat, light and truth.

Some mornings, he would surface from sleep to find that the power had arisen before and was gazing at the dawn world with its single blind-slit eye. He would feel abashed then, that he had been asleep and unaware of its presence. And relieved that he had a space to himself, a portion of the dining room, which had been walled off just for him to sleep in. He would have hated someone else to witness his miracle.

Today had been one such morning.

He believed the power to be a manifestation of the divine, made flesh upon his body. A baton pressed into his keeping for a brief but sacred period. It was not given to Rakesh to understand whence the baton was passed to him, by what mechanism it lodged in that mystic, hair-bound space at the junction of his legs nor why it twanged and hummed with a life of its own. Out of the void it appeared and trembled, fluoresced and passed onward to the void again.

He asked no questions. The priest of a one-person religion, he performed his devotions dutifully. And felt cleansed, uplifted, serene.

Thus, on this morning, as on previous mornings, his first conscious moment was that of being enveloped in a fine mist of sweat and cosmic light. He washed, dressed and ate his morning meal in an electric daze. His mother nagged at him for dawdling, his father called him a lazy good-for-nothing, his elder brother teased him about some trivial thing. And all the while, he felt safe across his lower belly, the sign of higher approval. The sign that he was blessed in ways that these minor mortals could never share.

He went downstairs, down three flights of stairs and outside to the nearest bus stop, all in the same sparkling state. As if his feet didn't quite reach the ground. Each hair on his scalp was distinct. He could feel air moving between the strands, his nerves were bright and polished, like the ends of shiny new pins. From the place covered by the zip of his jeans beamed a powerful invisible light, triple-Xrays, laced with dark stars, sprinkled with electrons.

Within minutes, the bus had materialized, summoned to the stop by the sheer force of his will. He entered it and immediately his potential of light and heat spread its tendrils out, not only across the entire lower deck but the upper deck as well.

He barely bothered to check with his eyes what his highly attuned senses had already revealed to him: there were several targets present on the bus.

This was not always the case. Sometimes there were none suitable to his purpose. Sometimes they sat in inaccessible places. Sometimes there was such a surfeit of choice that he was slow to select the one most ideal from among those available. There were even occasions when targets appeared in such profusion that he felt intimidated by the strength of their numbers and held himself in painful check.

But today, he knew, was going to be special. Hopping up from the boarding area to the raised floor of the lower deck, his left hand met the waiting strap as if it flew there of its own volition. The interior of the bus was still relatively uncrowded. Right away, he saw three targets.

One of them was the tender, chubby type, with long plaits and an expression of sweet and perfect stupidity. A target who did not yet know what it was. This type would take a long time to merely register his presence, leave alone notice his flashing beam of light. Sometimes, such a target would remain innocent and unaware of him for the entire duration of their relationship. He would pity it then. Such extreme ignorance was distressing.

Of this species, even those that did become aware of him never progressed far. At most, as he pressed his attentions, they would squirm and wriggle and move themselves ineffectually about. But they remained unconscious of the source of their difficulty. They acted from instinct rather than knowledge. While Rakesh enjoyed being an agent of their education, their lack of depth afforded only a fleeting challenge.

He knew that the most he could inspire in such a target was fear. But it was a dim fear, a ten-watt fear. A fear such as one might expect to find in the mind of an animal or some other such low-born entity. And in any case, it was not fear that he sought to inspire but a submissive reverence.

Thus it was easy, today, to turn his attention to the other two targets. At first glance, they both seemed more to Rakesh's taste.

In his experience, the ideal was between the ages of sixteen and twenty-three. It would be well dressed and smart, but not too smart. Overconfident targets tended to respond in silly ways. Sometimes even causing a commotion to break out in the bus. Rakesh had developed the ability to identify and avoid such targets. He had no interest in confrontations.

His preference in clothes varied from day to day. For instance, he could never decide whether he liked short skirts or not. They were enticing, but then again, so obvious. They fairly screamed for attentions of his kind. And he didn't like to feel that he was being manipulated. Yet the sheer sight of that bare skin, those exposed lower limbs ... well. There was something to that. Something undeniable.

But in general he preferred tight clothes. A target with seams bursting from under the arms, yet clad from head to foot, suggested the perfect mix of modesty and turgidity. Ripeness awaiting puncture, like cloth balloons. But kurtas only. Sari-clad targets were, as a rule, to be avoided. He didn't think it out clearly, but if he had, he would have readily admitted that they reminded him of his mother.

The positioning of the target was another important factor in determining his choice. There were three kinds of seats in the bus. The majority accommodated two passengers and faced towards the front. In some buses, the last row of seats was one long bench, which could support six passengers. In other models, especially double-deckers, the boarding area was in the rear. In these, the passengers entered the lower deck by passing between a pair of seats placed across the aisle from one another. Each seat could accommodate three passengers.

The young chubby target was sitting on one of these three-seaters and the other two were further in, one by itself at a window seat and the other, sharing the seat with someone else, sat primly, with its lower limbs stuck into the aisle at an awkward angle.

The window-seat target wore a kurta and had longish hair blowing loose and open in the breeze. The hair was being held down with one slim hand. Rakesh could see a portion of the neck. He had an impression of someone gentle and refined. Such a target would tense up the moment he sat down near it, like a hi-fidelity receiver, registering his broadcast at the first tentative announcement. But it would nonetheless endure the whole journey squashed into the side of the bus rather than push at him or create a fuss of any kind.

Such targets could turn out to be angels, goddesses. That modesty, that delicacy which abhorred the slightest aggressive gesture – ah! Depending on what it was wearing, he might even get a chance to touch bare skin, with his forearm or his elbow.

Then again, the aisle-seat target seemed the most challenging of the group. The awkward pose in which it sat would provide Rakesh with the ideal opportunity to make his initial contact. To begin with, he could pretend to lean against the backrest of its seat. If he timed himself just right, this could happen as the bus began to fill up. Then, unless it reached its stop, the target would effectively be pinned there while he bumped the whole side of his body against it with the motion of the bus.

Today's aisle-seat was wearing a short-sleeved blouse and jeans. Even from where he stood, Rakesh could see that it looked plump and ripe. He was on the point of moving towards it when suddenly it turned and he caught a glimpse of its face. Glasses! How he detested them. Not merely because they were disfiguring, but because they very often appeared in combination with a dangerous, pugnacious expression.

Such targets, it seemed to him, should be whipped, stripped bare and paraded in public places to teach them the error of their ways. To teach them that their true nature was to present themselves as attractively and appeasingly as possible. So that devotees of higher purpose, such as himself, could fulfil their ritual obligations.

This was his ardent quest, his daily mission. To pursue his private religion. To worship at his secret altar. He needed targets to complete his rites, in the same way that a flame needs a wick. He expected no more than submissive acceptance. It was so little to ask. Just to sit there, just to permit him to build his heat on their fuel. It always amazed and saddened him that there were those who resisted. Those who were incensed.

He stopped in his tracks, needing to make a lightning decision.

The bus was moving and the other passengers who had boarded from the same stop as he were pushing him onwards. As he turned, to buy time, the realization struck him that this was no ordinary morning. There was a wider than usual range of attractions.

The tendrils of intuition which sprang to his command whenever the power was awake in his jeans wandered ahead of him and scoured the upper deck. Now they brought to him an intimation of something still to be discovered in that area above his head, but further forward. The impression he received was so sharp and strong that he looked up reflexively. A fantasy occurred to him: of the floor of the upper deck made of clear glass, the seats padded with transparent foam, and every passenger a target! What a wonder *that* would be! The pressure beneath his belt purred aloud, just to conceive of such a sight. It was appropriate, then, to go to the upper deck.

Rakesh had to struggle through the passengers in the boarding area to reach the diminutive spiral staircase tucked into the rear corner of the bus. Grabbing the slick steel handrail he advanced a couple of feet, feeling as he did so the entire helical strand of shallow metal steps writhing sinuously with the headlong motion of the bus, which had, by this time, picked up momentum.

He found himself immobilized behind the rump of a large old woman who was struggling to propel herself upwards. He fancied, as he stood there, that he could smell her rancid and hanging flesh. When the bus shuddered abruptly to a standstill at a traffic light, he was pitched forward, so that his nose came within nanometers of disappearing into the unseemly depths of that ancient crevasse.

But even as his mind recoiled and the beam of solid light inside his pants wavered dangerously, the bus shuddered, groaned, hissed and in its pre-acceleration convulsion, gave the antique leviathan in front of Rakesh the necessary impetus to hurtle up the last few steps to the top deck. Relieved to be spared the ghastly prospect which had briefly presented itself to him, Rakesh clung to the curving rail of the stairwell till the passengers immediately below him gave him an impatient nudge.

An open stretch of road lay supine before the bus. The vehicle charged towards its next stop at full throttle, roaring, bouncing, swinging and lolloping along so that the human flies trapped within it experienced brief spells of zero gravity. Rakesh found that he could climb effortlessly by floating between bumps, with only his hold on the handrail keeping him from being launched into orbit.

He surfaced like a diver inside an air-lit space of a receiving hatch. It was bright upstairs. The ceiling was low, heightening the effect of a cramped, submersible vessel. Rakesh stopped slightly at the top step, to avoid bumping his head. Then he stumbled and almost fell as the bus, sighting its next stop, homed in on it, eager to devour its bait of waiting passengers.

It was at this moment, withstanding the tumultuous forces of public transport that he saw It.

Sitting at the very frontmost seat. With the window open. Its hair streaming back in the wind. A target.

But *what* a target!

Not only was there an empty seat beside it, but its shoulders were bare! Even from the back of the bus, Rakesh could see that it was wearing something utterly minimal. A confection made of thin straps and bright clingy material. In Rakesh's experience such clothing was only ever one layer deep. There would be no underclothes beneath. Such clothing revealed more than it concealed. He had seen countless examples worn by models and the type of ethereal targets who floated beyond his reach in private transports. But on a bus their presence was so rare as to be all but extinct.

He had of course seen pictures of targets wearing nothing at all. But he had found them deeply disturbing. Their wanton pinkness. The predatory expressions. The incomprehensible willingness of creatures who posed in magazines conspired to make him wonder whether they were, after all, figments of some artist's fevered imagination. An artist who viewed the body as a gross physical entity, a collection of soft, moist organs. Exuding, excreting, inhaling, ingesting. A fantasist who had never actually encountered real targets in real life on real buses. Targets with their steely nubs thrusting and straining against the confines of clothing. Targets resisting, with sweet despair, the potent attentions of their natural foe and patron – these were more enticing by far than the barren, lifeless pictures.

He moved slowly towards the front of the deck, deliberately delaying the moment of truth. There was an absolute clarity, an absolute certainty of purpose, as he propelled himself forward, hanging onto the overhead rails. No one could challenge his claim on that empty space glinting beside the target. It was his and his alone to claim. He was a bird, his arms were wings and he glid with the tilting motion of the bus as it sped down the endless ribbon of the road.

The stiff, unbending material of his jeans relayed the movement of his legs to the wild creature, which sat coiled and thudding within its den, causing it to breathe out a vertical halo of light. His whole mind became like a vast glowing bowl, his scattered thoughts scrabbling feebly at the rim. He caught himself wondering whether his light had become actually visible. Whether it was his imagination that fellow passengers seated on either side of the aisle were actually flinching as he passed. Perhaps covering their eyes, lest they be blinded.

Finally he was there. At the front seat. He had expected to savour the moment, hovering just above and beside the target, before sitting down. But the bus chose just then to come to a halt with an ungainly bump. It was almost a disaster. He was knocked forward and off balance, then tossed back again, so that he fell into the seat like a rag doll. He winced as the hard seam of his jeans tore at him. But he clenched his teeth and set his mind tight.

The moment passed away without incident.

He breathed out. Opened his eyes. He was sweating and his

nostrils were wide. The bus started up. Air moved in through the windows. He was in control again. And astounded.

In the sudden crisis which had almost overtaken him, he had not only sat down but had instinctively splayed his knees wide. In so doing, his right thigh had been flung against the left lower limb of the target. Practically plastered down the full length of that miraculous appendage which, to crown everything, was bare from the ankle to just a few inches short of the hip.

And there had been no reaction!

Rakesh was dumbfounded.

In all of his expeience, all targets, even the most non-sentient ones, showed some response to that first touch. It might only be a vague uneasy shifting or an unconscious recoil or a sudden flying up of the fore-limbs to bunch and constrict the top segment of the body.

The first response was one that Rakesh particularly savoured because right until that initial fluttering, wondering move had been made, there was no saying how the encounter would turn out. It was only after the first touch that he could foretell whether the experience ahead was going to be memorable or just mildly amusing or, as in some cases, a no-show. The difference between transcendence and failure, between brilliant, thrilling delight and mysterious, unknowable cancellation.

For there had been times aplenty when, try as he might to prevent it, the mysterious private carnival would dismantle itself and vanish into its night, leaving no trace aside from a small area of scented dampness.

But this, today, was utterly unknown and unfamiliar. The glow that had suffused Rakesh as he approached the seat wavered once more.

Was it possible that this situation was too freakish, after all? Too alien and bizarre? He did not permit his thigh to budge in any direction except for what could not be avoided on account of the motion of the bus. He was not ready to go any farther than he had already managed with the assistance of pure fate, but he wasn't ready to withdraw. His sense, all his senses, were peeled fine, like cloves of garlic. The next few moments would be of the utmost consequence. Surrpetitiously looking to his right, he took stock.

From the corner of his eye, he confirmed his first impressions. There was a lush bloom colouring the skin, which was pale and supple. So the target was youthful. It had made no effort to flinch away from him, which suggested that it was passive. There was something mysterious in such an extreme non-reaction, but he let himself relax. He had encountered any number of targets who took their time to respond. None of them had ever looked like this one. But he did not question the infinite variety of fate. It might be all right, after all.

The incandescence crept back into its saddle. His furtive gaze licked hungrily, slipping quickly down from the face to the chin, the neck and thence to those regions below the neck.

He wanted to groan with ecstasy. He couldn't remember ever having seen a pair of tremblies quite like the two beside him. He knew they had some other mundane name but he disdained words which would link targets to their day-to-day manifestations as women, sisters, daughters, wives. He had created his own lexicon which would neve be loosed upon the air. Words which existed only to describe the relics at the shrine of his own senses.

So tremblies they were. Quivering and jittering, while their owner sat with her arms loose. The gale from the open window had reduced the cloth of her blouse to a thin, seductive film of pale blue beneath which twin lighthouses beamed from their promontories of spongy rock.

As Rakesh watched, barely breathing, he fancied that he could see a resonance. The light that streamed out from his jeans was echoing from her promontories. He was hallucinating, he was levitating. The pulsing within mirrored by the pulsing without. He would have to move soon.

The bus juddered to another halt. It had reached the peak of its route and was starting now to disgorge its contents. The passengers in the seats directly around Rakesh and the target began to vacate their positions. Within minutes, Rakesh was practically alone on the top deck with his inscrutable companion.

How was it possible that she had not noticed him yet?

She had not so much as twitched. Voluntarily, that is. The bus coughed to life once more and Rakesh saw, through a screen of sparks, the promontories jump in unison. They wobbled wildly out of sync as the labouring vehicle heaved itself back onto its course. Was she blind or deaf? Had she slipped into a seated coma? Yet her body was alive and vivid with motion.

Watching her, Rakesh was barely able to contain himself. He clenched his teeth and tilted his head back, hardly daring to breathe. He spread his arms, so that the left arm spanned the aisle. The right one lay across the top edge of the seat he shared with the target. In doing this, he discovered that his right arm had inadvertently trapped some strands of the target's hair. Dimly, without seeing her, he felt her move at last. First, she drew her hair out of the way. Then, beside him, along the length of his leg, he felt her shift. He shut his eyes. It was the beginning, He must prepare his moves.

The classic manoeuvre required the bus to be careening along at high speed, so that he could use its motion to lean with ever increasing insistence upon the target. It must be neither all at once nor too discreet. The quarry must not remain uncertain of his intentions for too long. Today, having started out with such an outstanding surplus, he wondered if he couldn't go much further than he normally dared. Use his hands for instance. Touch her shoulder. Her hair. Or even turn and breathe directly on her. Anything seemed possible.

He had barely finished enumerating the possibilities when he had the strangest impression that he was being looked at. He couldn't say precisely what gave him that idea, but it had to do with the movement she had made, so her knee seemed to be digging into his leg. He was confused. He didn't dare open his eyes now. Given the position of her knee, she must have turned full-face towards him. It was a situation so unprecedented that he was paralysed. He could do nothing at all.

Now he felt her breath. Near his ear. She was saying something, but his mind refused to translate those sounds into words. Through the shut lids of his eyes he could see her.

The woman's face was harshly coloured, like a film poster or a dream. Red mouth, pink cheeks, eyes fringed thick with tar. She was not so young after all. She seemed to be smiling. But strangely. He would have liked to flinch away from her expression, but couldn't move. His skin had shrunk, pulled tight by a knot centred at the tip of his private torch. A tight knot, a bursting knot.

The bus was hurtling towards its final destination. The woman reached with her hand and touched him. Touched the curving ridge of the zip of his jeans. With the hard red talon at the end of her forefinger. Tracing the double track of stitches, up, up, towards his belt buckle.

A hoarse grunt escaped him.

And he emptied out. Heart. Brain. Kidneys, all. Liquefied and discharged through his geyser in the mantle of his body. One harsh pulse. No light.

He opened his eyes.

The woman was looking at him. Her mouth was twisted. She was laughing silently. He could hear the sound in his mind, over the thunder in his ears. She was looking at the damp patch that had appeared under the waist-band of his jeans, on his shirt. 'Silly!' she was saying, 'Silly little boy has wet his pants!'

She stood up then, stepped over his feet, and was gone.

The bus roared as it sighted the terminal stop, gathered itself to make the jump to light-speed, landed at its berth with a shriek of brakes and a violent spasm. Then died. Its metal skin ticked and sighed as it gave up heat and stress.

The voices of disembarking passengers and the clangour of their feet faded as the last of them got down. The conductor, far away, at the head of the stairs, agitated the clapper of his bell. Don't make me come and get you, said the conductor, clanging the clapper's strident tongue, just come on now, let's go, without a struggle.

But Rakesh remained where he was, breathing slowly. He was staring straight out at the blank sky, blinding blue and bright. Just behind his eyes, a feeling like grey rain.

Mayadevi's London Yatra

The day Mayadevi turned sixty-eight, seventy or seventy-five years old (her date of birth was an ever-changing event linked to her moods), she decided to go to London. Everyone in the family was stunned when she announced this, but no one dared to speak out because the old lady ruled over the entire three-storied house with a quiet reign of terror. Whenever she decided to do something, her three sons and their wives quickly agreed, since they had learnt, slowly and bitterly, over the years, that no one questioned the old lady's whims. Though there was no need for Mayadevi to give an explanation to her submissive and docile family, she still called her sons and gave her reasons for undertaking such an unusual journey at her age.

'I want to see Amit before I die.'

This eldest son of hers had gone to England to study when he was eighteen years old and had not returned to India since then. He wrote to his mother on the fifteenth of every month and sent her money regularly along with many expensive but useless presents, but did not come home to see her because he had an acute phobia of flying. He had travelled to England by ship in 1948 and once he had landed there after a traumatic and unpleasant journey, he never stepped out of the safety of the island. There had been a few short, tension-filled trips to France and Italy, but these were either by train or by boat. Around every October as the Puja season approached, he promised his mother that, this year, he would take the plunge and get into an aircraft and come to Calcutta, but his nerve failed him with reassuring regularity each time.

'The wretched boy was always a sissy. He never could cross the road if a cow was standing in the middle. Lizards frightened him and rats made him scream from the time when he was fifteen. I will shame him by going to London – to his very doorstep, even if I have to bathe in the Ganga a hundred times after I return,' the old lady declared and the sons, who thought it a very foolish idea, nodded their agreement as they had done all their lives.

Once the momentous decision had been taken, Mayadevi began planning for her journey on a warlike footing. She first applied for a passport and visa, but filled the forms with a lot of arguments and protests because she did not like the impertinent questions the government dared to ask her. Once that was over, she bought a big register and wrote down her plan of action step by step.

Now she decided to tackle the English language. Though Mayadevi had never been to school, she could read and write Bengali fluently and was far better-read than her graduate accountant sons. She could understand simple sentences in English but had never spoken the language to anyone in her entire life, since the occasion had never arisen. Now she hunted out a tattered old English primer that belonged to one of her grandchildren and every morning after she had finished her puja, folded her Gita away safely and distributed the sanctified sweets, she sat down to study this jam-stained old book. The household, usually peaceful and quiet in the mornings, was now filled with Mayadevi's strange rendering of the English primer. Sitting cross-legged on the floor and rocking herself backwards and forwards, she read each line over and over again in a musical singsong as if she were chanting a sacred verse. Then she would suddenly stop and ask herself questions. 'Did Jack fetch the bucket?' she would ask in an accusing tone, and then reply, 'No, Jane fetched the bucket.' She would get up once in a while, adjust her spectacles and take a short walk around the room, holding the closed book near her chest as she had seen her grandson do when he was memorizing a text. The servants did not dare come near the study area but watched her nervously from the kitchen doorway. They were sure she was learning English only to terrorize them more effectively.

'At her age she should be only reading the Gita, not reciting jack-jack-jack like a parrot,' they said, but only within the safety of their quarters.

The lessons unnerved the cook so much that he stopped fiddling with the marketing accounts and turned honest, in case the old lady, armed with the English language, caught him out. The daughters-in-law too found the lessons very odd and giggled quietly in their bedrooms but they were careful to put on a serious face when they found themselves in the vicinity of the English lessons. The sons also kept their distance from their mother after their eager efforts to help her with her English pronunciation had met with a cold rebuff.

'For sixty years I have managed this house and my life without any help from you or your late father. I do not have any wish to start now,' she said, dismissing them with a regal wave of the tattered book.

So she carried on learning the primer and the household not only got used to the strange sounds, but caught the infectious tone too and the servants began humming 'Jack and Jill' as they went about their chores. Within a few weeks Mayadevi had finished the primer and graduated to more difficult books. She now carried on long conversations with herself to air her newly-acquired knowledge of English and as the days went by the characters from the primer, the *Teach Yourself English in 21 Days* and other books got mixed up with each other in the most unfortunate, tangled relationships.

'Did Jane go to the grocer's shop alone? No. Mr Smith went too.

Mrs Smith is sitting on the bench in the garden with Jack. She is smoking a pipe. How are you, Jack? Quite well, thank you. Where is the tramway?' her voice would drone endlessly till she had learnt all the words in each and every book by heart and so had the rest of the household.

Now there were only three months left before the date of departure, and Mayadevi went into the next stage of her travel preparations for the great journey which had been named London Yatra by her family, though, of course, behind her back.

'Now I am going to wear shoes,' she announced and ordered one of her sons to get her a pair of black canvas shoes and six pairs of white cotton socks.

Mayadevi had always walked barefoot in the house and worn slippers on the rare occasions she went out to visit. The No.3 blue rubber slippers lasted her five years at least and though they hardly ever stepped on the road, they were washed every day with soap. But in England these faithful slippers would not do, and so Mayadevi reluctantly and with a martyred air forced her thin, arthritic feet into her first pair of shoes. For one hour in the morning after the English lessons, and then another hour after her evening tea, the old lady practised walking in her new shoes. Like an egret stepping out on clumsy, mud-covered feet, the white-clad figure paced up and down the house accompanied by a rhythmic squeaking of rubber. Soon, there were large blisters on her feet, but Mayadevi carried on the struggle like a seasoned warrior and no one heard her expel a single sigh, ever. Her sons admired her from a distance, but did not dare to praise her, since they knew she distrusted flattery of any kind and always said, 'Say what you want from me and leave out the butter.' So no one ever praised her, and came straight to the point when asking for favours.

When there was only one month left before the departure, Mayadevi wrote to her son in England and informed him of her plans. He instantly went into a severe panic and telephoned her, which he had never done in the last thirty years.

'Ma. Please do not undertake such a dangerous journey. Planes are crashing all the time. You can be hijacked to Libya. Air travel is really unsafe now. You wait, I will definitely come home by ship next Puja,' he screamed hysterically over the bad line.

Mayadevi listened to him patiently and then replied, 'I may be dead by next Puja. My ticket has been bought. You will come and greet me at the airport and make sure you come alone and not with that giant wife of yours,' she said, and put the phone down firmly though she could hear her son's voice still crackling on the line.

From then on there was total silence from across the ocean, but that did not bother the old lady and she now moved into the final preparations for the London Yatra. She started visiting her relatives one by one and each one was informed of the travel plans personally by her, just as if she were following the norm for issuing wedding invitations. She did not sit for long in any house but simply gave a brief outline of why she was going to England and then left without accepting any tea or even a glass of water. The relatives were surprised not only by this flying visit like royalty, but also by the fact that she chose to tell them why she was going.

'The old battle-axe is losing her strength, getting soft in the head now,' they said, but were secretly pleased that she had condescended to visit them.

After this came the most important stage, and one morning the old lady called her sons and the family priest for a meeting. The daughters-in-law and the servants, not invited, took turns to listen at the door.

'In case I die in that land, though God will never do such a thing to me, bring my body back immediately before they contaminate it. Then see that all the rituals of purification are done properly,' she said, fixing the priest with such an unblinking, cold look that he began to tremble with fear and could not help thinking that the old lady had died already and was watching him from heaven.

Once the plans of how to deal with her dead person had been discussed to her satisfaction, Mayadevi gave them detailed instructions for the purification rites she, if returned alive, would go through on the very day she came back.

'There is a week-long penance to be done, Brahmins are to be fed and the entire house is to be washed with water from the Ganga. So see that you take leave from the office, all of you,' she said to the sons, who understood the importance of the occasion and readily nodded their heads, hoping the meeting had finally ended.

Now only one week was left before the date of departure. A large, battered suitcase, which had been a part of Mayadevi's impressive dowry when she came to this house as a fifteen-year-old bride, was brought out from the dark corner of the store-room and Mayadevi began packing. Six white cotton saris, six petticoats and an equal number of blouses, one white sweater and a grey shawl, along with a small red cloth bag for her Gita and her prayer beads, and a plastic box for her false teeth were the only items she packed.

'Everything except the Gita and my teeth shall be thrown away when I return, so why waste money?' she said.

The suitcase was packed and ready five days in advance and left on top of the stairs like a coveted trophy. Everyone who came or left the house would trip over it, but not a murmur of protest was heard. In fact, the servant proudly dusted it every day and the children approached it with awe.

Then, finally, the day of departure arrived. Mayadevi got up before dawn, bathed and went into her prayer room. She knelt before the gods and whispered, 'Give me strength to endure this ordeal and let me not die in that land. I promise to make you new ornaments of gold when I return. Please bring me back safely to you.'

She sat for a long time in that small, incense-filled room and only when the light began to stream in through the windows did she get up and go out to wake up her sons. Soon the entire household was rushing around, though there was nothing very much to do. The suitcase was dusted a few times and the children made to touch their grandmother's feet every time they passed her way. The sons kept clearing their throats and looking at their watches.

'Has she got everything?' they muttered, but not too loudly since none of them wanted to go and check.

Mayadevi packed five large packets of puffed rice in a cloth bundle and filled up her grandson's plastic water bottle. This was all that Mayadevi was going to eat for the next twelve hours, because she was not going to touch any food 'that God knows who has touched'.

The day passed quickly as visitors came to say goodbye. Each one admired the suitcase and, after bumping into it, remarked how light it was. The plane left at twelve o'clock at night, but Mayadevi and her sons were already at the airport four hours before that. They sat solemnly in a row and watched the clock now, instead of their wristwatches. They had never before spent such a concentrated and confined time with their mother and were finding it very difficult to sit so close to her on the plastic chairs. They took care to change places so that no one had to sit for too long near her and each brother could get some respite. Once in a while Mayadevi spoke to give some last-minute instructions. Her sons only nodded and cleared their throats once again.

At last the flight was announced. The old lady lifted her head and listened carefully. Suddenly one of her sons got carried away by emotion and tried to give his mother a few travel tips, but she got up quietly and joined the long queue of passengers weaving their way to check in. One by one the sons, bending with difficulty under their middle-aged spreads, touched their mother's feet. She blessed them with a rarely-seen gentle smile and as they stood like orphans, she sailed out of their vision and into the gaping door of the security area. The sons were not worried about their aged mother. They only wondered how England would cope.

*

It was raining when the plane landed in London. A flicker of worry crossed Mayadevi's mind as she wondered whether, with her still uncertain shoe-walking ability, she would be able to manage the wet ground. It will have to be done, she said to herself, looking down sternly at the shiny black shoes as if ordering them to obey her. She adjusted her sari, still crisp and starched after twelve hours, and got ready to leave the plane.

Throughout the flight she had sat ramrod-straight and when the air hostess had offered to adjust her seat to a more comfortable, reclining position, she had said, 'Why I sit like that? I am not sick,' in a sharp voice, freezing the pretty young hostess's smile before it could even begin to form.

The hostess ignored the old lady after that, but could not help glancing at the odd white-covered head each time she passed her seat. Mayadevi's neighbour too had stopped talking to her before they had even crossed the Hindukush mountains and now pointedly looked the other way. She had tried to be friendly and helpful and had showed the old lady how to fasten her seat belt. Mayadevi at first did not say a word and the younger girl thought she was just shy about not being able to speak English and became more friendly.

'Everyone was so kind to me in India. Even though the people are so poor, they have such large hearts,' she said, warming to the subject, happily rehearsing what she was going to say many times over when she reached home, when suddenly Mayadevi opened her mouth for the first time and said, 'Why they not be kind? They lick white people's shoes 200 years and now it becomes bad habit like drinking and smoking.'

The girl was shocked. Never in her six-month stay in India – during which she had travelled the length and breadth of the country, staying only with families since one could get to know the 'real India' that way, and also hotels were so expensive – had she ever met with such rudeness. She was gathering her wits to say something sharp in reply when Mayadevi shook her head firmly and also crossed her hands over her lap in the traditional manner of refusing food at Bengali feasts, to doubly confirm her refusal. She then watched the poor girl eat her meal and stared at her with an expression of such distaste that the poor girl left her food half-eaten, though she was enjoying the European meal, even a plastic-covered one, after six months of endless dal and chapatis.

Once in a while, Mayadevi would eat a handful of puffed rice and take a few sips of water from her plastic bottle. The bundle containing the rice and the water bottle had been carried close to her body throughout the journey and when the security men at the airport had asked her to send it through the X-ray machine, she had clung to the bundle like a lioness to her cubs and said,

'Touch it and I shall throw it in your face. I will starve for the next twelve hours and if I die, you and your next fourteen generations will have the sin of an old woman's death on your heads.'

The security men, trained to deal with terrorism, did not know how to handle this and allowed the old lady and her clumsy bundle to pass without any checking. Actually Mayadevi did not really need the rice and could easily have stayed without food for many hours at a stretch, since she had been fasting for some auspicious day or the other from the time she was a young girl and her stomach was quite used to stern starvation regimes. But now that the plane was about to land, it suddenly gave a loud rumble of protest, startling Mayadevi by this uncharacteristic rebellion. The young girl heard the grumblings too and allowed herself a small mean smile. Old cow, hope she has a bad time here, she thought, but then immediately felt guilty and filled in Mayadevi's landing form for her. Mayadevi never said 'thank you' and as soon as the plane came to a halt she shot up from her seat. She marched down the aisle clutching her food bundle close to her body so that no one could contaminate it by touching it and was the first passenger to get out of the aircraft. She then slowed down and attached herself to a group of Indian passengers who had also just come off the plane. She followed them closely, but when they reached the immigration area and began queuing up, she walked past them and planted herself firmly at the head of the line. No one could ask an old lady to move back and, even if someone had, Mayadevi had her steely look ready. The young blond man at the immigration counter smiled at her kindly, even though it was against his principles to smile at immigrants or visitors of any hue. In return for the rare grin he received the famous dead fish stare, under which innumerable men and women of Calcutta, young and old, had quelled. The young official felt sheepish for no reason at all and quickly called for an interpreter, an almost SOS urgency creeping into his voice.

'I speak English. You speak English with me,' Mayadevi said clearly.

The immigration official cleared his throat and said, 'How long do you plan to stay in the UK?' and when Mayadevi said nothing, he repeated the question, adding a 'Madam' this time.

'No need to say again, again. I answer you. I stay in this land one week only. Not a day longer, you can tell your Queen Victoria,' said Mayadevi.

The stunned official stamped her passport with a resounding thump and waved her on as fast as he could.

'This is one old bird who is not lying to me. Won't ever catch her working at Selfridges, for sure,' he said, and laughed nervously as if some ordeal had passed.

Mayadevi again followed the passengers she had marked out, and made sure they collected her suitcase and carried it for her in their trolley. Her son was waiting for her outside when she finally emerged, but even though she saw him at once she gave no sign that she recognized him. The fifty-year-old extremely successful dentist, member of the Royal College of Dentists and a very old London club, did not dare raise his arm and wave to his mother. She walked towards him slowly and, after she reached him, stood staring at him as if he were a total stranger. The son lurched forward and made an awkward, half-bending movement to touch his mother's feet but at the same time surreptitiously tried to look as if he was tying his shoelaces. Mayadevi, who was on full alert, her eyes carefully scrutinizing her son for faults, pounced like an eagle on the first wrong move.

'Ashamed to touch your mother's feet now, are you? A mother who has not long to live but even then has travelled such a great distance, fasting for twelve hours, sitting with all kinds of half-castes so that she can see her son,' she hissed.

Amit, who was wellknown in dentists' circles for his dry, sharp wit, was about to defend himself with a few crisp, well-chosen words, but before he could speak, something clicked inside him. As he looked into that old, lined face, an irrational fear jolted his memory and he said in a whining, childish voice, 'No, Ma ... I ... so many people here,' stammering helplessly.

Now that she had established the old family, Mayadevi told her son to pick up her suitcase and take her to his home. Though the mother and son had not seen each other for more than thirty years, they drove to the semi-detached house in the beautiful, green, tree-lined suburbs in unbroken, stony silence. The mother asked no questions and the son offered no explanations, because he somehow felt that she knew everything about him already, and disapproved strongly. When they reached home, Mayadevi got out of the car in a suspicious, stealthy manner as if she was expecting hidden traps in the neatly laid out garden. Mother and son entered the house like two mourners, and when his wife came out of the kitchen to greet them Amit almost burst into tears with relief.

'Welcome to England, Mrs Banerjee. Hope you had a nice flight,' Martha, Amit's wife, said cheerfully.

Mayadevi looked up at her tall, large-boned daughter-in-law through the top of her spectacles for a few long, uncomfortable seconds and then said, 'I wish to wash hands. Everything so dirty.'

Martha's plain, good-natured face showed a brief flicker of surprise, but she beamed at her mother-in-law and said, 'Come and see your room and then we will have a nice cup of tea. Hope you like the new curtains we put up for you, Amit did not know what your favourite colour was, so I chose blue.'

She prattled on, her voice full of genuine affection for the old lady she had never met before. Amit crept up to shelter behind his wife's ample frame, as his mother examined the room, and cringed each time Martha came too close to her. He knew what would happen if Martha touched her by mistake.

'Are you feeling cold? Should we turn up the central heating?' asked Martha, suddenly feeling cold herself.

Though Mayadevi was shivering in her cotton sari, she said, 'Not cold, only wash hands, so much dirty.'

Martha quickly led her to the bathroom, gaily decorated with trailing plants and fluffy rugs. Mayadevi slammed the door shut on Martha's smiling face and began to wash her hands. First she washed the taps thoroughly, and then she began rinsing the soap, though it was a brand new one. Then she finally washed her hands meticulously four times in a row. When she had finished, she turned the tap off with her elbow, so as not to touch the tap again. She dried her hands by shaking them about in the air, looking scornfully as she did so at the pretty, flowered hand towels Martha had put out for her. Then she went out to search for her son.

'How will I bathe in that jungle you call bathroom? Why has she put carpets in the bathroom? To hide the dirty floor?' she charged full force, happy to have found something to complain about so quickly.

'Ma, she can hear you,' said Amit, glancing nervously at the kitchen door, even though they were speaking in Bengali. 'You must be tired, why don't you eat the rice I have made for you and go to sleep now,' he suggested, desperately hoping she would agree.

Surprisingly, she did.

'If you are telling the truth that she did not make it,' was the only half-hearted resistance she put up and followed him to the kitchen.

'I cooked it, Ma, she did not even touch it. I am not lying to you,' he said, and flushed when he saw Martha watching him even though he knew she could not understand what he had said.

But Mayadevi made sure that the message had got through by giving her a triumphant look. She took out her false teeth with a sharp, satisfied click and sat down to eat. The meal, a bowl of overcooked rice and a muddy brown dal, was consumed quickly and noisily as Mayadevi chewed with her gums and when she had finished, she took her plate to the sink and washed it carefully twice. She shook it dry by waving it in the air and then kept it as far away as possible from the other plates and dishes. Martha's friendly smile had by now faded to a bewildered, confused look and she stood silently, watching the water from the plate drip all over her hospital-like, sparkling clean kitchen floor. She did not know what to do or say. Amit stood next to her, wearing the expression of a sad, unhappy man, expecting worse times ahead.

Mayadevi, quite content now with the way things had gone so far, left them both and went to her room. She dragged the bedcover off the bed, spread it on the floor and then, after saying her prayers, fell asleep at once. She woke up in the middle of the night and sat bolt upright. The greyish-yellow streetlight streamed in through the window and the sky outside was a lighter shade than she had ever seen. Calcutta seemed very far away. 'God forgive me, I will return soon,' said Mayadevi, feeling lonely for the first time in her long, solitary life.

The next day passed very much like the first, only Mayadevi cooked the food for herself and Amit. He felt guilty about not eating with Martha, but his mother's contemptuous 'Ha! A slave to his wife!' plus the delicious fragrance of long-forgotten, favourite dishes compelled him to sit down and eat with his mother every evening, as he came back from work. Martha never complained and he did not dare to ask her what they both did during the day, but he got the answer anyway, judging by the new, unhappy lines on his wife's forever-cheerful face. Like two boxing champions trapped in a ring, Martha and Mayadevi circled around the house, avoiding each other but at the same time keeping a wary eye on what the other person was doing. The old lady would listen as her daughter-in-law went about doing her housework and then she would tiptoe out, her eyes gleaming like a fault-finding laser beam, to check out her work. She opened drawers, peered under the beds and ran her fingers over the windowpanes. But she could not find any dust or cobwebs as she did on her weekly checking rounds in her house in Calcutta. Angry and bored, Mayadevi took to sitting in her bedroom in sullen silence for the entire day. Martha did try from time to time to make friendly overtures but each time she met a solid wall of silent rebuff. Mayadevi would shut her eyes tightly and pretend to chant her prayers every time her daughter-in-law looked into her room. She never wanted to go out to look at the shops, watch television or drink tea, and Martha could not think of anything else to cajole the old lady out of the room. Slowly, the six days of unspoken tension passed, and Mayadevi happily began packing her bag once more.

'Thank God it's over, the wretched trip,' she muttered.

The last day of the visit was a Saturday and Amit had taken the day off from his clinic. He had been hoping that some emergency would crop up and he would have to rush to the clinic, but he knew very well that it was a foolish thought and a dentist had no crisis of broken molars or sudden cavities in his career. He decided bravely to face the situation and take his mother out shopping. Martha, her good-natured spirit still alive, offered to come along too but Amit said in a courageous voice, 'No, you rest, dear, I'll take her alone,' as if he was going off to slay some dreaded dragon. But Martha insisted on coming along to give him unspoken support. They drove to the large shopping centre nearby, Mayadevi sitting in the back, spurning all friendly remarks and efforts at showing her the sights of London. When they reached the huge, glittering building, there was an embarrassing tussle in the car park; Mayadevi did not want to get out of the car.

'Why should I go into this big shop? What do I want to buy from here?' she asked her son, facing him squarely.

Amit stared helplessly at the giant shopping complex with ten floors of the world's best merchandise, but he could not think of a single thing his mother could buy there.

'Well, now that we are here, let's go in. You can tell everyone at home what you saw, can't you?' he said with a wide, foolish grin, as if he was talking to a child.

Mayadevi's sari got stuck in the gap between the steps and she, thinking Amit had stepped on it, kept scolding loudly. They disentangled her and then walked straight into the fairyland of lights, cosmetics, perfume and lingerie. Mayadevi suddenly stood still. She felt as if she had been struck by lightning. In her entire seventy-five-odd years, she had never seen a world like this. Hundreds of bright lights gleamed everywhere she looked. Dazzling blinding mirrors as tall as trees, and walls that had solid gold lamps on them. There were countless, mysterious, colourful objects she could not recognize on every glossy surface. Silken bits of lace were draped all over glass shelves and, though they had an odd shape like two cups, Mayadevi, who had never worn any undergarment, like most women her age, thought they were the most beautiful lace decorations. She could smell the fragrance drifting up from the glittering glass bottles filled with magical potions. It was the most powerful and sweet incense she had ever smelt. There were jewels as big as eggs in boxes that shone with silver and gold threads. Mayadevi felt that she had died and gone to heaven, only the people were wrong.

'There should have been our gods and goddesses in this paradise, not these pale humans,' she said softly to herself, not moving in case it was a dream.

Her daughter-in-law suddenly understood what had happened to the old lady. She took her arm and gently guided her through the mazelike, narrow lanes of the department store, overflowing with gleaming merchandise. For once Mayadevi did not flinch at her touch and followed Martha meekly as if she were a celestial maiden guiding her in paradise.

'I think we should get her a nice warm jumper, Amit,' Martha said to her husband, who had not yet noticed the sudden change in his mother.

They went to the women's department and Martha picked up a pale blue cardigan.

'No, no, only white,' whispered Mayadevi, still in a trance.

Martha found a fluffy white one quickly, and also a lacy white shawl to go with it. She presented them both to the old lady with a friendly smile. But this gift was a greater shock to Mayadevi than seeing the big department store, in all its glory, for the first time. Her late husband, her many children, and countless relatives had always given her what she had asked for, but no one had ever given her a present. Her steely eyes, unused to crying, became almost blind with tears, and through the blur she took Martha's hand and shook it as she had seen people in her phrasebook do.

'Good girl, very well, thank you,' she said to her daughter-in-law, showering her with all the polite words she knew in English.

By the time they reached home, Mayadevi's brief moment of weakness had passed and her vision had cleared. She was her old iron self again. But there was a certain change in her demeanour. She did not actually smile but her eyes had lost that old freezing glare and she called Martha by her name.

The next day, before she left for the airport, she let Martha make her tea and, though she did not thank her when she placed the cup in front of her, Martha little knew how much sacrifice and giving it meant for the old lady. The journey to the airport was silent this time too, but not an unhappy, uncomfortable one. When the time came for Mayadevi to leave, she patted Martha's hand and said, 'When I die, you come to Calcutta for funeral. Let my fool of a son be. You come.'

Then, after making sure that her son had touched her feet properly, she walked into the 'passengers only area'. She did not turn around to wave at them, though she knew she would probably never see her son again. She was content that she had done her duty and now she looked forward to the year-long penance, purification and sacrificial rituals she would have to do to wash away the sins of the London Yatra.

Meenal Dave

Nightmare

Her fingers fly over the computer keys but her eyes search the clock. It's not going to be possible to catch the first MEMU today. Mrs Rao is really the limit! She has to think up this assignment at the very last minute, just when it's time to leave! Sure, she has a point when she says the office has reopened after some ten or twelve days. But, my dear woman, you merely have to ride pillion on your husband's motorbike and you're home for a hot meal of idlis and sambhar. And I? If I miss that train, I have to wait at the station for a good hour, and then ride in the train for another two, fearful and trembling, and what's more, probably in an empty compartment! But how can I expect you to understand that? There! Thank God it's over ... ah! There's already an auto here. Good.

Arre, brother, hurry up please. The curfew's been lifted after so many days, no wonder people are rushing out of their homes as if they have been uncaged. Mindless lot, they're taking off in their cars and two-wheelers now, but one tiny burst of a firecracker and they'll be rushing to lock themselves up again. Good God, did this light have to turn red now? But, as they say, akarmi no padiyo kaano. I've got exactly seven rupees with me, so I won't waste time hunting for change. All these people coming out of the station, but, please, would you make way for those who have trains to catch? And then, these railway people, they're just too much. Trust them to put the staircase right at the end of this long platform, and my train is from Platform 4 and about to leave. Let me run ... just the last two steps and ... there! Damn. Missed it. Have fun!

'Ben,' the chaiwalla says, 'now you'll have to wait for an hour.' Why's he looking at me like that? And now there's not a single passenger on the platform. Just two minutes back it was swarming with people. And now? Taking off like a flock of birds when someone hurls a stone.

Perhaps I should go to Smita's. I'm not likely to have company on the train, even if I spend that whole hour here. The smell of fear still hangs in the air. Even when the chaiwalla looks at me, I'm afraid, who knows, he might throw his tea things at me. Who knows which caste he belongs to. People like us don't believe in caste, creed or community, but he can't know that, can he? He's looking at my chandlo, my mangalsutra. No, no ... everybody's not like that. I'm thirsty. Where's that bottle of water – I think I put it in my bag ... oh, there it is, but it's empty!

Maybe I should call home from this phone booth and also pick up some water. And a magazine. Vikram answers the phone. He's upset that I haven't made the first train. But I hang up on him, I don't allow his annoyance, swinging on the phone, to even reach me. The telephone booth man dispenses advice: 'Ben, don't go home so late by train. Things were different earlier, but now you can't take any risks.' So what has changed in these last ten days, I ask myself. Do people not shed tears anymore? Or don't they love? Aren't babies born anymore? Have flowers begun to wilt before they blossom? Nothing's really changed. But then why this fear, this suspicion everywhere?

Let me do some browsing at the bookstall. Same thing. The newspapers are full of the game of numbers, the dance of death, the game of fire, the fury of bullets ... I pick up two magazines and settle down on a bench.

The platform is deserted. Cooking fires are being put out at tea stalls and the oil used for frying savoury things has gone cold. Boys working at the stalls are half asleep. Bottles of aerated drinks have been returned to their crates. The lame boy who polishes shoes is peacefully asleep, his head resting on his shoe-stand 'pillow'. But the dog near my bench is restless. He roots around, then stands, looks around, cranes his neck, pricks up his ears and seems to be listening. And then curls up again. And up again. There are two dogs fighting on the platform across. Is he frightened of them?

I notice that there is a woman sitting next to me now. She wears a thick black burkha, only her hands are visible. And she carries a large cloth bag. The face-net of the burkha even hides her eyes, but I can feel her gaze upon me.

So many benches free on the platform, why did she have to come and sit next to me? What does she have in mind? Is she carrying a bomb in that bag of hers? What if she leaves the bag here and walks away and the bomb goes off, what will happen to me? That would be the end of my poor husband and children. No, but let me not think that will happen. Poor thing, she's just sitting quietly there. But does that mean she's harmless? Should I move away? Go elsewhere? My tongue is stuck to my palate, it refuses to move. My fingers are clutching my handbag. Despite the cold evening, a drop of sweat falls from my forehead onto my hand.

'Kem Ben? Where are you off to?' Chiman, the daalwada-seller, descends like a saviour. I feel blood surging through my veins again. As if the curfew has been lifted. 'You're late, Ben, the first train has left.' Smilingly, I nod, afraid to open my mouth. What if the words slur?

'Why are you sitting here?' He signals me to get up. 'At such times you shouldn't be sitting here.' But my feet will not move. Chiman smirks at my foolishness and walks away. He's right. I should get up from here. You never know what she might do, this woman. She could pull a knife out of that bag and stab me and no one would know anything. Arre, she only has to kick me and I will collapse. Look at her hands, how big and masculine they are. Is there a hardened criminal hiding behind that burkha? How do I get up? Why did I have to decide to travel at this time? He Ram, please let me get home safely. Should she try anything, I will tell her, listen woman, take what you want but don't kill me. My parched throat hurts, my hands are frozen. The moment I see someone coming, I'll get up. I search around the platform covertly, moving my eyes this way and that. Not a soul now. Where have all the people gone?

It seems like it was only yesterday that this platform buzzed with life – trains coming and going all the time, people rushing from here to there, difficult to find a spot to stand. And the ladies' compartment in which I travel every day – at every station women pour into it like grain being emptied out, and some get off. Then, once they settle in and have found somewhere to sit, handbags and baskets are opened and out come beans, peas, garlic, and they begin to peel, sort, sometimes chop. At times, balls of colourful thread emerge and turn into flowers and petals on saris and kurtas. Somehow, designs make their way onto woollen jumpers. Papads, pickles, packets of chutney and masala are bought and sold. The tears of women tortured by husbands and mothers-in-law are wiped, bittersweet office gossip is exchanged, sweets are distributed to celebrate engagements and weddings, occasionally even blows and curses are traded, ramrakshakavach and gayatri mantras are chanted, or room is made for the namaaz to be read. As more stations arrive, the seating gaps fill up … But where are all these faces today? Where are the bags of peas-beans-garlic-papad-masala? Their place seems to have been taken by terror-filled faces and bags full of suspicion. How can I get away from here?

Arre, the train's here. I didn't even notice its arrival. Okay, now straight into the ladies' compartment. Oh dear, the burkha-clad woman is climbing in after me. Why doesn't she leave me alone? The compartment's virtually empty – barely two or three women.

A fisherwoman fast asleep with her empty basket lying next to her. It's stinking, but never mind, at least there's another human being in here. And that other woman is sitting facing me.

It is dark and black outside just like the burkha she's wearing. Not a sliver of light for me to hold onto and sail through this dark ocean of the night. What shall I do? I shut my eyes, hoping the darkness will go away, hoping to escape those constantly-fixed-upon-me eyes. What must she be doing now? People say that you can't trust them. You never know when they might draw a knife and butcher you. I remember a classmate called Hasina from college. Her brother stabbed his wife. I couldn't help wondering if this woman might also do that.

Oh God, someone's shaking me. I open my eyes – it's the woman in the burkha! Oh no, what will she do to me? Should I shout for help? The fisherwoman is fast asleep. So she won't know if I get killed. Should I jump off the moving train? Oh God, please, please come to my rescue! I promise never to get onto this train again. I'll even give up my job and to hell with commuting up and down. Better to starve than suffer this nightmare!

'Bahanji, sister,' the burkha woman is calling me, 'I'm getting off here. I'm so grateful that you were around, imagine travelling alone at such a time. I was so scared ... you know ... so difficult ...' I can't believe it! She's frightened like me! I burst out laughing.

'What's there to be scared of sister, I do the "up-down" every day.' My voice suddenly acquires more force than the train's whistle.

She places her hand on mine and says khuda hafiz, may God be with you. It's moist and sweaty and as she touches me, my sweat merges with hers. The train stops. I help her with her bag, which suddenly seems light and harmless. She melts away in the faint light of the station. The fisherwoman yawns. She stretches her limbs and takes a bag out of her basket. A beany greenness spills out and pervades everything. The stars begin to shine in the dark and show me the way home.

Translated from Gujarati by Rita Kothari

March, Ma and Sakura

My mother came to Japan and sakura burst into bloom. Somehow I knew how things would be the day I went to the airport to fetch her. I stood in the arrival lounge and, contrary to custom, the Air India plane was on time. The passengers came tumbling out. Very anxious, I peered into each face, looking for her. If she wandered off, she'd just be standing, lost and scared in some corner of this enormous place. People moved along, pulling unwieldy baggage. In Delhi the family must have put her on the plane, had her bags checked in; now she'd have to lift her suitcase off the conveyor belt herself. Would she even be able to spot her suitcase, pick it out in a place where there were only suitcases? It wasn't as if she'd suddenly begin to see these things, especially now that she was old! After all, she didn't even remember the colour and number of our car, the car that Pitaji or Bhai Sahab drove, while she sat in the back.

These thoughts were making their way through my mind when I noticed my mother walking into the lounge with a young boy. The boy was pushing a trolley loaded with his and Ma's suitcases, while Ma came along, a small bag slung on her shoulder. I leapt forward and stood right in front of her so that there'd be no chance of her missing me.

She saw me and came towards me with a shy smile that turned into a shy chuckle as I approached. I bent down and touched her feet and she said, pointing to the young man, 'He's also come to Japan for the first time, he's so nervous. I told him my son will come to the airport, he lives here; you can ask him about everything.'

It was then that I think I had an inkling how things would turn out, though that is what I say today, with hindsight. However, I should have known even then that Ma had come and sakura would bloom this year. Ma drove me frantic by the time March came, but March came only later.

In the first few months I'd call her from work several times in the day – 'Ma, what are you doing?' And she had the same few responses to my questions: 'Son, I've stitched a button on your kurta, now I'm going to bathe,' or 'Son, I've made some carrot halwa for you, I'll run the washing machine now.' Many were the times I told her, 'Ma, it's such a lovely day, why don't you go out? If you don't want to go far, just stroll outside, around the house.' But each time she'd say, and from her voice I could tell that her lips were pursed in a pout, rather like a little girl's, 'No, I'll get lost.'

'Oh, come on Ma!' But my reprimands were lost on her.

'Who's asking you to go far?' I'd say, 'After all, that's the road you walk on every evening with me.'

'Unh, hunh,' she'd say, sounding grumpy and reluctant.

I'd scold her even more, 'The least you could do is to go up to the supermarket and get some milk, yogurt, juice.'

'But I won't even be able to ask anyone the way back home.'

'You just have to come back the way you went, foolish Ma, and if you're such a coward, you can keep my card with my address on it. Anyone will tell you the way ... not just tell you, hold you by the hand and bring you right up to the door!'

'Now look what you're saying! Will I walk holding someone's hand? And what if I can't open the lock, you know what the locks here are like, turn to the right and then to the left ... no, definitely not!'

'Ma, go out!' I'd rebuke her.

'No, dear,' she'd say, her mind made up. 'I'm alright at home. I'll go out when you come home.'

Of an evening I'd try blackmail; 'See, I have to come running back home from the office, can't go anywhere else, all because you've been lying about the house all day, haven't been out at all ... really, you must start going out by yourself, even if it's only to places close by ...' She'd glare at me, shaking an admonishing finger; 'Look son, don't tell me all this now, don't forget how old I am!' And the safety-pin caught on her bangle would begin to shake in agitation.

However, February drew to a close and new shoots began to appear on all the branches. Ma began to talk to the boy at the fishmonger's in faltering English. The Japanese boy would ask Ma in broken English how she would cook the fish and Indian Ma would reply in broken English that she'd make fish pickle; she'd send him a jar too. Their use of English would have made an Englishman see red and turn to pickle!

And then, maybe not more than once, but certainly on one occasion, I saw the boy from the fishmonger's carrying Ma's shopping home for her while Ma tripped along in front, swinging her handbag, then taking out the key and turning it in the lock. First left and then right!

I returned one day to find the neighbour's son eating food Ma had cooked. 'You love Indo food,' he informed me and it was just because of his English that he said 'you' instead of 'I'. Ma laughed and touched his cheek, her hand lingering on it and I sensed there'd been a joke between them that I had quite missed. It was something in the way Ma kept her hand on his cheek, perhaps for just a little too long, just with a bit more pressure than normal, that made me turn my eyes away. This is what happened then.

After the boy left, I said, 'Ma, it's the custom to bow here; you've seen how they do it.' Then I lapsed into an embarrassed silence.

What could I have said? How could I say to her now the things I'd never said before?

She had a way of taking me up on what I'd said and then proceeding to make quite something else of it that left me quite speechless. It was true I'd said to her, 'It's cold here, put away your sari and your nightie; you'll be more comfortable in my kurta and pajama.' That was for when she went to bed. Of course I didn't say as much, but that's what we'd been talking about, wasn't it? Ma, however, started wearing my kurta and pajama during the day as well, alone at first, and then in front of that boy too, who regularly turned up to guzzle Indo food. She shortened the length of my elegant silk kurtas and Aligarhi pajamas, and began to wear them with my woollen waistcoat on top.

'Going out?' I hadn't quite finished my question when Ma carefully arranged her Pashmina shawl over her kurta, my kurta, that is, and said as she went out of the door, 'I like this feeling of being free! It's good not to have anyone telling you what you can wear and what you can't.' She continued, 'Nobody here knows what my dress ought to be.'

Well, I knew. But there was no way I could have told her this, either.

Now I noticed Ma mugging up the names of all the stations as she wandered around Tokyo with me. She studied the maps. 'Oh, so there's only one exit here ... well, that's good, you can't get lost. "Deguchi" means exit,' she told me proudly. 'This is Nakano Shimbashi. "Sit here",' she continued, telling herself what she must do. 'Now comes Nakano Sakaue. "The doors on that side have opened, get down"', she said, by way of rehearsal again. 'The train for Shinjuku is standing right there ... just cross the platform and get in,' she informed me. 'And then, whether it's Yotsuya or Aka Saka Mitsuke, or Ginza or Tokyo or Otemachi or Ochanomizu ...'

She threw a challenge at me as she said this last word because she'd say Achonamazu in a hurry when she was trying to memorize the words and I'd pointed this out to her. But was I really rebuking her for her faulty Japanese pronunciation?

'You can go right up to the last station Ikebukuro if you like … that's great!' she exclaimed enthusiastically, as though this was something I'd asked her and she'd explained it all to me, there being nothing difficult about it at all. And she it was who told me, 'If you want to go to Shinjuku Gyoen or garden, you must get off not at Shinjuku, but two stops after that, at Shinjuku Gyoen Mae.'

'I'm going to Shinjuku Gyoen,' she called me at work one day. 'With the boy who came with me from India, don't worry.'

That got me worried, even more worried, that is. Where did Ma pick up all these boys? Why did she slap them gently? I felt my ears begin to burn. I shouldn't forget your age, that's what you tell me, Ma, I thought, bending over my papers.

We were almost into March.

One evening she informed me grandly, 'I've seen sakura buds.'

'What are you talking about?' I said irritably. 'It's too early for sakura.'

'How can sakura blossom just now?' she said, her voice holding more contempt than mine. And her eyes blazed, as though she'd have to go there first, pass this blaze of hers over the sakura trees; only then could they bloom!

'How did you get this obsession with sakura? Do you have sakura at home in Delhi too?' I laughed a little as I said this.

'I'm not at home, am I?' she laughed too. 'But there's only one sakura tree in all of this suburb of yours,' she told me. The neighbour's son had told her this and shown her the tree.

'Come on, let's go and see it,' she said. She broke into a laugh as she pressed the pedestrian switch at the traffic lights; 'I'm such a VIP, the lights will turn green just for me, and the traffic will come to a halt!' She pressed the button and scampered across the road like a rabbit. 'Let's at least see what sakura looks like!' she said, a little embarrassed when she saw the mood I was in. And we set off like children to inspect the only sakura tree in the suburb.

The month of March was upon us at last. The wind turned crazy. News broadcasts on television had details, in between other important news, of rustling in sakura branches, of buds restless to burst into bloom.

'They won't be able to bloom in Hokkaido yet. It's too cold.' Ma saw the pictures in the TV news eagerly, buds dancing in her eyes.

I laughed, 'You sound like you think sakura can't blossom if you're not there!' Ma threw back her head and stretched both her arms to the sky.

'I'd like to go everywhere, see everything. I want to go to Hokkaido too.' I had a feeling she was sorry for those buds that wouldn't be able to blossom if she didn't make it to Hokkaido.

'You're looking like a little girl, Amma,' I told her affectionately.

Her arms still stretched out in the same pose, Ma jerked her hands, 'I am seventy, son. What have I to be afraid of now?'

Her kurta sleeves slid down towards her shoulders as she jerked her hands, the loose flesh of her arms swinging.

My mother was seventy years old and my father had grown too fuzzy to notice if she was with him. So for the first time in her life, she'd left everything behind to come here, unimpeded.

'Have you come alone?' I scolded, taken aback at finding her outside my office.

I continued to tell her off in the subway, but she was busy cramming. At Harajuku she sprang up with youthful sprightliness from the silver seat reserved for senior citizens, grabbed hold of my hand and leapt towards the door that was just about to close. I had no time even to ask what she was up to and it was a miracle she didn't get out alone, leaving me inside, with both of our hands caught in the door. She pulled me along and stopped at the gate to Yoyogi Park.

'Right or left?' she muttered and then turned left.

'I know, I know,' the old man within me said, burying his head in his knees. 'She's been here before with one of those boys, maybe with more than one.'

Evening was drawing to a close. The sky was overcast and raindrops began to fall on the sakura trees in front of us. Ma looked at them, showing them to me. It was then that the buds must have started stirring. Sakura was just beginning to bloom on that evening of gentle rain, gleaming like rose-pink grains of sand in the moonlight. I opened out the umbrella and we stood under it for a while.

After that there was nothing I could have done; Ma slipped through my hands, just like the shining grains of sand. I didn't know how to explain when the family called from Delhi. I was at home, but where was Ma ...?

The month of March, as fleeting as only March can be, was already on its way out. And copying my mother, all of Tokyo grew crazy. Everyone started shouting 'Sakura, sakura!' just like her. 'Wait till next week ... just another four days ... Sakura's going to be in full bloom by Sunday!'

It's often been seen that those claiming to be balanced or prudent at the outset of events are unable to hold themselves in check once they find themselves in the midst of festivities. I, too, soon heard myself singing like Ma; carried away on the strains of the melody she'd struck all over Tokyo.

Sakura was in full bloom, surging like an ocean. My mother, like others in Tokyo, went about with head thrown back, eyes fixed above where only frothy white waves of fully-blown sakura were visible. She kept walking on and on. It is obvious that people will walk with uncertain steps if they look up. The euphoria of sakura swayed into our step as we walked and the joy born of sakura seeped into the food and bottles of sake kept under the trees.

There were as many people below as flowers above, in Chidorigafuchi Park. Ma had brought me here because there was something special about this park. The rest of Tokyo must be empty today, there were so many people here, and the sky must surely have stepped back for those masses of flowers. There were only flowers and people; people taking pictures closeup or painting, getting photos taken with an arm round a tree trunk, people singing, eating, frolicking, celebrating wholeheartedly. Ma walked and then stopped, started walking again only to stop once more.

On one side was the river with sakura along it, and buildings in the foreground.

'What's that?' Ma pointed to a building.

'Fairmont Hotel,' I replied.

Ma stopped and climbed up onto a sloping rock. A sakura branch bent down, close to her lips.

'I can kiss it,' Ma said. Maybe she did kiss it.

She stood there, resting a hand on an iron railing, an exhilarated white ocean frothing and foaming around her.

'I wish that was my home,' Ma said, pointing to a room at the top of the hotel. 'I could have lived there and gazed at sakura always, forever.'

It was then that something began to happen. Waves of bliss moved through the sakura branches; the ocean rippled. And I felt we weren't here at all, but had been lifted to the window of the hotel that was Ma's home, looking out upon this scene with Ma flying like a sakura petal.

I placed my hand beside Ma's wrinkled hand on the railing.

Someone in the ring of people behind us started karaoke and the dancing and singing began. I opened the lid of my hip flask and offered a cup of sake to Ma. She touched it to her lips. I raised my cup and looking into her eyes that were alight with sakura, I said 'Kampai, cheers!' and moved my other hand towards Ma. There was a burst of clapping and Ma's face glowed with the translucence of sakura. She took my hand in hers and began to dance. Sakura petals began to fly like butterflies.

And in Fairmont Hotel, a hotel no longer but Ma's home from another age, a window flew open and Ma, not seventy now but a young woman, gazed out upon us. She watched us as we danced and skipped, enraptured, beneath the sakura tree.

Translated from Hindi by Sara Rai

Vandana Singh

The Wife

In October Padma began to dream of the woods behind her house. In the dreams the woods came all the way up the slope of the backyard; there were branches poking through the bathroom window and leaves falling in the living room. She dreamed she was nibbling on unfamiliar fruits, swallowing the seeds whole, letting the wood take root inside her. And surely there was something – an animal, small, perhaps furry or feathery, and possibly lost – making a nest somewhere in the jungle of her mind ...

Once she dreamed that she was following the creature – refugee or interloper – through caverns where there were only the roots of trees overhead, tangled and interwoven like neurons. She caught glimpses of it in the twilight of the passageways, among the withered, dendritic limbs of ancient roots; at times it looked like a rat or a mole, with a long, prehensile tail, but sometimes it was a bird with pale, delicate wings like banners. After a breathless chase she caught up with the animal; she threw the free, trailing end of her sari over it and grabbed it swiftly through the cloth. On her knees she gathered the thing to her and it stopped struggling. It began to dissolve into the folds of her sari, leaving behind the hint of a shape, the outline of a face she knew or had known – and she woke. She lay in the big bed in the pre-dawn gloom, trying to bring the moment back, but she could not remember whose face it was that she had recognized.

After Keshav left – it had only been five weeks, although it seemed considerably longer than that – after he left her she took to walking in the woods. In the woods was the silence that precedes the first snow of a New England winter – a silence of waiting, broken only by sudden gusts of chill wind that made the skeletal tree-limbs rattle. She had the feeling that the dream-creature she was seeking was here, somewhere, roaming among the pines and elms and birches, rooting in the undergrowth. But all she found were old birds' nests caught in the branches of bare trees. And once a pair of battered boots covered with mud, by the side of a small stream, which made her wonder whether somebody had once tried to drown himself in one foot of water. But then, what had become of the body? The clothes? The ring he wore, if he wore a ring? It occurred to her that the wood held many stories and mysteries, not just her own, and that perhaps there were other people wandering about in it, following threads of dream or the trails of booted feet. Sometimes she would be filled with a breathtaking certainty that around the next corner, among the foreign trees, she would find the ruins of her grandmother's house, the shell of the mango tree that overshadowed it, cocooned in the heat of an Indian summer. Or that a silhouette in the distance would turn out to be the idiot uncle who babbled and made animal noises, who had died of a fall when she had been eight. But the paths she found through the wood never led to any places she had known before, nor did she meet anybody, except, once, an athletic young woman in sweatpants and parka, out for a hike. Once she came upon a clearing where she startled a stag that stood frozen in surprise for a brief moment. Then it flung its antlered head back, flaring its nostrils at her, and crashed out of sight. Another time she found the remains of a barbed wire fence and a sign half-buried in the mud, which must have hung from it once; it said 'Private Property'. There was nobody there but a squirrel on the tree above, looking at her and scolding.

*

There were twenty-seven cardboard boxes in the living room. Some were empty and some were already packed and labelled. She had a roll of labelling paper on which she had written their names separately for the first time: 'Keshav', then 'Padma', and so on; these labels she would affix to the boxes that were packed. Under the boxes labelled 'Padma' she would add 'Salvation Army donation' or 'Send to Sarita, LA'. Once a week Keshav would drive down from his apartment on campus to pick up his boxes. During his visits she would take her car and drive aimlessly up and down the empty country roads for an hour, to give him enough time to leave before she returned.

Next week he would come for the last time. After that she would no longer be what she had been for twenty-three years: a wife. All the fuss and bother of the wedding negotiations, the smoke of the sacred fire, the smell of ghee and flowers, the leave-taking when she left India to join Keshav in America, the weeks and months and years in a country of strangers, learning to adjust and adapt, the visits home, brief and increasingly infrequent, the deaths of her parents, the two children now grown and living away from them – all that was over. What was left felt like a sinkful of unwashed dishes the morning after a half-remembered party: the old house, the inevitability of solitude – and her face growing increasingly alien to her day by day.

Everything in the bedroom had been sorted already. The children's things she could keep, Keshav had said. She need only put aside some of the furniture for him, pack his books, his clothes, his memorabilia, the golf-clubs, the cocktail glasses. He would take care of the things he kept in the basement and his tools in the shed. Some days she sat on the sofa or the kitchen chair in a kind of trance or daze, letting memories jostle about in the attic of her mind – the faint, milky, talcum smell of her babies, the way Keshav's breathing used to fill their room at night, the texture of his skin, his beard, the musky odour of his sweat after he came home from the gym ... The way he had of probing at things, people or phenomena that he found interesting, like a dog worrying a bone, until he could capture their essence in words.

That reminded her of their first fight, after those rumours reached her about Keshav and his famous new colleague, Professor Marya Somebody, the one who had travelled through war zones and written a monumental novel based on her experiences. When she'd confronted Keshav he had been rather annoyed.

'How conventional can you get,' he'd said to her, his tone slightly mocking. 'I could have slept with her, you know, but I did not. What I want from her is an intimacy beyond the merely physical ... Don't you see, I am not interested in this woman as a *woman*. What I want to do is find the words – make a box from metaphor and symbol, meaning and simile, and put her in it ...'

She had wept a lot, wanting to believe him although she did not understand him, and he had held her and soothed her and sighed. Then he had lifted her chin with one hand and looked into her face.

'I do this with everyone, you know,' he'd said. 'Including you. I ask the question, who is she? How do I find the words that mean Padma? Who are you, Padma?'

'Your wife,' she had said with tremulous dignity, and he had shaken his head and smiled.

No, it hadn't started then, the rift between them. But why couldn't she remember that precise moment when he had first begun to close the door to her in his mind? She had come to know only gradually that she had disappointed him, like that time – the time she could never remember without a prick of anger, even after all these years. One night she had come home from the bookstore where she used to work, to find the house silent, with only the hall light burning. Her older son had been six then; his tennis shoes lay at the bottom of the stairs, soaked with blood. There were bloody footprints all over the floor and the stairs. Padma's bag had fallen from her grasp; she had flown up the stairs, calling for Keshav, for her sons, but the boys were peacefully asleep in their room. When she turned around, Keshav was standing in the doorway, watching her with an amused, rather satisfied expression on his face.

'An experiment,' he explained as she stared at him in disbelief. 'One I am going to conduct tomorrow in class, to demonstrate to my verbose young first-year students the importance of *brevity*. Isn't it amazing how much the human mind can make of a pair of tennis shoes, half a bottle of ketchup and a suitable setting?'

He had drawn her into his arms, apologizing, smiling.

'Do you realize how all our conclusions about the world are based on purely circumstantial evidence? What is real, and what is not real – all the universe gives us is raw *data*. We make realities out of *words*, Padma, words in our minds and on the page. Do you see?'

He was talking like he did at faculty parties. He had not understood her anger – he had thought that after the first shock she would laugh with him. But despite a Bachelor's degree in sociology – now gone to waste, like everything else – she was not sophisticated enough, she could not appreciate his cleverness. All the time she had been bringing up the boys, supplementing the family income with a series of small jobs, cooking and cleaning, reading her mystery novels, she had been unaware that she was, in a subtle way, a failure. At university functions she stood selfconsciously in her silk sari, feeling overdressed and out of place, while talk and champagne flowed around her in torrents. Faculty wives sent her glances full of curiosity and pity; professors talked around her as though she were a museum exhibit, the exotic bride of that brilliant, if unpredictable Keshav Malik.

Over the years he had stopped teasing her; he had periods of black depression, weeks at a time when he left her to the children and the house to brood in his study or the basement, alone. Slowly he had uprooted himself from her. She could have forgiven him for his flirtations, for the way he turned everything into a game, but she could not understand or forgive his retreat from her. The thin fissure that had opened between them slowly widened over the years, bridged occasionally by shared moments like the serious illness of the older son or the death of Keshav's mother, a woman they had both loved.

When her boys were young, she had no idea of the fragility of the world; it all seemed written in stone: her marriage, homework with the boys in the evenings, the rituals of cooking, sewing, making love. Now the past came to her in disconnected pieces. Fragments without context or meaning, like the time Keshav and the boys had caught butterflies in their nets and released them into the living room ... Her elder son, eleven at the time, had dragged her from the kitchen, breathless with laughter, saying 'Ma, come, look!' The butterflies fluttered in and out of sunbeams like miniature magic carpets. They alighted on the stereo. They flew into reproductions of landscape paintings on the walls. Keshav, opening a book, began to identify them. 'That one's a cabbage white. Look, a swallowtail, a sulphur ...' Suddenly she couldn't bear it. She tugged open the window, knocked out the insect screen. Keshav gave her a long, speculative look, then laughed. They joined her in chivvying the crazy butterflies out of the room and into the brightness outside. When the window was closed again Padma saw a couple of corpses on the speaker and on the coffee table. One was yellow and the other was orange and black. There was a dusting like pollen on the shelves and the furniture.

'There's one trapped,' she said wildly. 'In the picture. Behind the glass.'

It was an orange butterfly. She thought she saw its wings tremble against the glass.

'It's painted on, silly,' Keshav was behind her, pointing with an indulgent finger, stroking her hair with his other hand. And she saw it was so.

*

As she sat brooding over the recent past – trying to find without success some hint, some foreshadowing of how she had ended up like this – a thread of remembrance would take her inevitably into the deeper antiquity of her childhood in India. The big, untidy house with four generations living in the warren-like rooms: bright flocks of aunts chattering like mynahs, the milkman's cow at the gate every morning, the swish of milk in the pail. The mango tree, her favourite haunt and refuge – an old tree, a dark, multi-armed goddess with its labyrinthian trunks branching off into the sky, its long, green, waxy leaves murmuring like priestesses. A sparrow's-nestful of naked fledglings, their yellow mouths open, crying. Lying on a broad branch, the bark rough against her cheek, she had looked down onto the flat roof of the house, with the flower pots on the low wall that ran around it, and the clothes flapping on the line like little coloured flags. A view of her grandmother picking wild jasmine in the tangled garden at the back, looking up at Padma, smiling and shaking her head and calling her a monkey. But always, like a pariah kite circling, her mind came back to that one afternoon when time had stopped.

From her tree that bright, cloudless summer day, she had seen the idiot uncle come up onto the roof. She had watched him with interest, wondering what a grown-up with the mind of a three-year-old – a reliable source of entertainment for her small tribe of siblings and cousins – would do on the rooftop, a place that was strictly out of bounds for him. He had a way of assuming the identity of things other than himself. Once he had sat for hours on the floor of the drawing room, pretending to be – or thinking himself – a chair. Another time he had decided he was a muskrat – he'd run along the walls of the house, out into the back, where he had dug and snuffled among the bushes. He was not supposed to be on the roof, Padma knew – her grandmother lived with the fear that one day her youngest son would take on the identity of a bird. But that afternoon was golden, so filled with light and air and ease, that she had no presentiment of disaster. At first her uncle had simply wandered in circles, moving with the disjointed, disproportionate grace of a giraffe, patting the flowerpots, the clothes on the line, with his kindly, octopus-like hands. It had occurred to the eight-year-old Padma that she should perhaps call to somebody to tell them that Chotey-Mamu was up here alone, but watching him was too interesting. She had been debating whether or not to throw twigs or leaves down at him to see what he would do, when he began to climb up to the roof over the stairwell.

The stairwell roof was about fifteen feet above the rest of the rooftop. Her uncle hauled himself up using the spaces between the bricks as footholds. The child watching him began at last to comprehend that he was in danger, that she should tell someone. But her voice seemed to have died in her throat. Her uncle stood up on the stairwell roof, spreading his arms wide, a breeze filling his white cotton shirt and pajamas. Below him was a sheer drop to the paved floor of the courtyard. He leaped.

After all these years, when she shut her eyes she could still see him. He was aloft in the hot blue sky, his arms flapping, suspended a few feet above the stairwell roof. A wordless shout of ecstasy burst from his lips. He was flying, he was lighter than a cottonseed. For an eternity he swam in the air, his wild, unruly hair blowing behind him.

Then there was just the empty sky. She heard the sound of a fall, but did not immediately connect it with his absence.

The child Padma had stayed in the tree, watching as the house filled with neighbours; the doctor's car drove up, and a curious throng gathered about the front gate of the compound. As dark fell she saw lights spring up in the house and in neighbouring houses. She could hear the wailing of women and other voices in the rooms below and in the courtyard, but nobody came calling for her. Not her mother or grandmother. She lay on the branch of the mango tree, getting sleepier and hungrier, but nothing would make her come down by herself. She would stay there forever ...

Then she heard someone calling to her from the darkness below, and she had climbed down at last, slowly and sleepily, following the voice as it led her through the undergrowth, deeper and deeper into the wilderness at the back of the garden. She could not remember whose voice it had been, whether it was Chotey-Mamu himself or her grandmother, or a koel-bird calling in deep, flute-like tones from some hidden arboreal grotto. But there was clearly a path through the jungle, a narrow thread of moonlight woven through the darkness of trees and shrubs. Stumbling, scratching herself on thorny bushes, she had come at last to a warm, soft place and curled herself up to sleep, feeling comforted, forgiven, thinking how good it was to be home, to be safe.

The next thing she remembered was bright daylight. She was standing by herself under the mango tree. There was blood on her lips and some of it had stained her cotton frock. She felt neither hungry nor thirsty, only as though she had just emerged from deep sleep. In the house a woman was crying loudly. Abruptly the door in the wall of the courtyard opened. It was her father, standing looking about. He hadn't combed his hair and his shirt was all crumpled. He saw her, stared, then ran to her, calling her name, gathering her in his arms. Inside there was a smell of death and disinfectant. The strange woman with dishevelled hair and reddened eyes who enveloped her in the folds of her tear-stained sari was her mother. Her fingers had combed through the tangle of Padma's hair, brushing the leaves from it. 'Where were you, you wicked child? We looked for you all night ... in the garden and the park and everywhere ...'

She wanted to tell them that she had seen Chotey-Mamu fly, but the words would not come. All day they had asked her the same unanswerable question: where had you been?

Thirty-seven years later, sitting alone in a house full of boxes, she still did not have the answer.

As she mused, the room would fill with evening shadows, a

still-life in shades of grey, and she would get the feeling that the wood was waiting for her just outside the window of the room, that the trees were pressing on the walls of the house, whispering. In the ornamental mirror hanging from the dining-room wall, her reflection would look back at her like a wild animal from its lair: unruly hair framing a face gouged with shadows, the nose like a bird's beak, the eyes huge, nocturnal, like lemurs' eyes. She would shudder and shake her head to clear it of fancies and get up with a little sigh. Turning on the lights, she would fix herself a chutney sandwich or a roti wrap, and eat it absent-mindedly in the kitchen. Then she would get to work.

For days she drifted through the house like a moth blinded by the light, sorting, packing, labelling, until the rooms lost their dreadful familiarity. She took breaks in the afternoons to walk aimlessly in the woods. She tried to think of practical things, like what she should do next. Her elder son, who was working in California, wanted her to sell the house and move closer to him. Her friend Usha in India kept writing, asking her to come home, to start a new life.

Home. Her parents were dead. Her brother and two sisters had their own families. Her grandmother's house had fallen into ruin. Where was she to go?

Sometimes she got lost walking in the woods. There were no trails, no landmarks, and if she were not paying attention the trees in their wintry nakedness would begin to look the same, and the only sounds to guide her would be her own footfalls crunching on dead leaves. She would walk for miles until something in the landscape began to look familiar, and then quite abruptly she would come across her house sitting atop the slope. She never took the same paths through the wood, or so she believed.

*

Finally the day came when the boxes were all done – everything separated, sorted and labelled. Tomorrow he would come for the last

time. Only the wedding pictures defeated her – at last she decided
to put them in a box in the basement until she could make up her
mind. Keshav would not want them, of this she was certain.

At first she couldn't find the basement key. She had not been
down there for so long, it had not occurred to her to wonder until
now why Keshav had kept the basement locked. There were boxes
there that were university stuff, he had told her, some records from
the English department. She looked for the key in all the usual
places: the cupboard in his study, the little embroidered bag hanging
on a nail in the kitchen where she kept her own keys. Finally she
found it at the back of a drawer in his desk. It looked shiny and
unused, probably a spare. The door did not yield at first, although
she put her whole weight against it; then she saw in the half-light
(it was evening) that there was a bolt also. She had forgotten about
it. She drew the bolt and the door opened, creaking. The air below
came slowly up into her lungs: still, and faintly musty. She had a
sudden feeling of dread. But there was no going back. She took a
deep breath, stretched out her hand and turned on the light.

The stairs creaked a little as she went down, holding the banister.
At last she stood on the cold cement floor, gazing about her a little
fearfully. There was nothing there but the old oil furnace with its
pipes and dials, and dusty boxes stacked on the shelves. She realized
she had left the wedding pictures upstairs after all. She began to walk
around the basement, turning on the lights as she went. All was in
order. It was just that the air smelled a bit stale. No wonder she
had never felt like coming down here into the depths. No need for
Keshav to have told her not to. But in the middle of the basement,
suddenly, she smelled the wood. A tendril of fresh air that smelled
of cold earth, bark, moisture, animal droppings. She looked around
her apprehensively, but there was no place for anything to hide –
no rats, not even a cockroach. The windows were high in the wall,
narrow little slits opaque with age; they had been shut for years.
Nothing could have got in. But the forest scent – how to explain
that?

One end of the basement had been finished – it had a linoleum floor, bookshelves, a desk, and a wooden· partition separating it from the rest of the basement. Keshav kept odds and ends here, old theses of various students, yellowing articles, obscure travel records. She remembered this vaguely from the last time she had been down here – was it two years ago, or three? She went into the partitioned area. The forest smell was much stronger now, but it was dark in this corner. She remembered the light turned on with the pull of a string – she searched the air before her until she felt the cold chain touch her hand. When the light came on, she saw a wooden cage on the desk, its door broken open, and tiny droppings and urine stains over pages of notes in Keshav's tiny, fastidious hand. On the shelves there were jars containing a variety of unidentifiable substances, a pile of delicate pencil drawings of a half-dozen impossible creatures, and a number of old books with peeling spines. But what finally held her gaze was the open window above the shelf: something had clawed at the catch, leaving dark stains on the wooden frame, until the window had tilted open just enough to let out whatever had been trapped here.

At first she simply stood there, breathing hard in her anger, reminded of ketchup-stained tennis shoes long ago. This was Keshav's parting gift to her, another set-up, a trick to remind her of the old days. But why? What did he mean by it? Leaning forward she saw that some of the stains on the pages were still moist. Keshav had last been here a week ago. She didn't know what to think.

She stood very still. Suddenly everything became clear to her. She felt as though she had, at last, wandered offstage; she was the stranger looking into the lit windows of her own house. All these years she had thought it was her home, her refuge from the world, but after all it was only a *sarai*, a temporary stop on the way to the other place. The path lay before her like that silver thread of moonlight all those years ago, leading her to sanctuary: a single current of cool air, the forest's breath, the lifeline of dreams.

URMILA PAWAR

Mother

The afternoon meal was done and I was washing the dishes in the backyard. Aaye sat in the front of the house under the mango tree weaving bamboo baskets. She was in a hurry to finish all her orders. Her thin fingers holding the bamboo strip flew over the basket frame. Two of my younger siblings were playing on the verandah while Krishna, my younger brother, who came right after me, was asleep in the house because his body felt warm to the touch and he was feeling sick.

All of a sudden, I heard my mother crying. I wondered who had come by in the middle of the afternoon while the sun was so hot. I craned my neck to see what I could from my sitting position. Our uncle from the village and a couple of his acquaintances stood there.

I got up in a hurry, quickly wiped the pitcher I had just washed, filled it with cool water from the large water-barrel and took it out to the visitors. I was happy to see my Tatya. But before I could say anything to him I noticed the buwa next to him and was taken aback. His busy hair looked as if he had hairy caterpillars on his head. His face was dark and mysterious.

Tatya gave this man the water pitcher I had brought. Then he looked inside our door and said, 'Aga, Vahini, will you stop crying? What problem can you solve with crying?' After a short pause, he continued, 'It is true, schoolmistress (my father was a schoolmaster so she was called schoolmistress), the one who has to go has gone forever. Will he come back because of your crying?'

'Yes,' agreed the villagers who had come with him, 'Isn't that the truth! He is gone, his life has now turned to gold-dust. But what about all his children whom he left behind? Their lives should now be our concern.'

Just a month ago my father died because he had dropsy. At the age of thirty-five. Since then, everyone who came to visit us said the same things. Aaye cried every time someone came to visit and talked through her tears. But her hands stayed busy with her basket-weaving. My poor mother didn't even have the time to grieve in peace. She had four mouths to feed and she hadn't a coin in the knot of the sari tied round her waist.

Now that Tatya was here, she came inside and cried. Except that, today, her tone was somewhat different. She sounded like she was resisting something. As if reciting ovis, she threw instructions at me while she cried. 'Shantay, go light the stove, ga baaye ... Go make some bhakri for your uncle, ga baaye ... Serve him some bhakri with salt, ga baaye ...'

My mother's crying made my throat ache with a sob. I got up, shedding tears. Using all the flour we had in the bin, I made four bhakris. From the flat hanging basket I took out some dried salt shrimp and tossed them on the embers of the fire. The salty grilled smell went through the entire one-room house. I served two dishes with bhakri and invited Tatya in. The villagers and the buwa all came in to eat. Two men ate from one dish. My younger siblings had just finished eating but they were staring at the dishes anyway.

'Aga, why is Krishna sleeping today?' asked Tatya.

'He has a fever, he isn't well,' I replied.

Tatya raised his eyebrows and exchanged glances with the buwa, who nodded gravely. After they were done eating, the villagers and the buwa went to the verandah to eat paan. Tatya sat concerned near Krishna and said to my mother, 'Vahini, do you see what state the poor boy is in? You want to save your son's life, don't you?'

'Bhavji, why are you talking about it this way?' she said angrily. She had never taken that tone with him before. For the first time in my life of fourteen years, I heard her talk back in anger this way.

'Aga, what do you mean? When Arjun died, I told you to let this house in town go and move in with us in our family home in the village. We have a small house but there is some farmland and four mango and jackfruit trees.'

'Bhavji, but how will the children get an education in the village?'

'Why not, is there no school in the village? You think children in villages don't go to school?'

'Yes, they do, but that is no education. We are here in town. Here, our children go to school with children from other Brahmin and trading communities. They will learn to speak like them and be like them.'

'Do you think there are no traders in the village? Don't they send their children to the same schools? Vahini, let me tell you something, your children will be discriminated against badly in town because of their caste.'

'Caste troubles are in the village too. As a matter of fact, caste discrimination is much worse in the village.'

'Yes, it is true, but we have a whole neighbourhood behind us when that happens. Who will you ask for support here in town?'

'Aha, my husband always told us that Babasaheb Ambedkar told us to leave our villages and move to towns.'

'Yes, yes. Don't preach to me about all that. Go to towns and then eat what? Mud? What will you feed the kids here?'

'I'll work, I'll use my hands, I'll make baskets and sifting fans. I have that skill.'

'You can do that in the village too, can't you?'

'Sure, I can, but no one buys readymade baskets in the village for money. I am not going to leave this place. My husband gave blood like it was water for this hovel.'

'Yes, and that is why his blood turned into water and he died of dropsy. When all is said and done, Vahini, this is not a rational decision. There is something evil in this land.'

Aaye and Tatya argued about this for a long time. Tatya wanted us all to go to the village and Aaye wouldn't hear of it. Tatya was getting angry and frustrated. But he tried to talk as calmly as he could.

'Vahini, I knew you wouldn't believe me, and that's why I brought Someskar buwa along with me. He is very wise. He knows the past and the future. He will tell you about the quality of this land. Then, do me a favour and take your children and come home with me.' Tatya raised his voice a little and walked out to the verandah. Aaye went back to her work.

I was angry with my mother too. Why was she being so headstrong? Tatya would never give us bad advice. Besides, the village is really quite nice. We get mangoes and jackfruit to eat. We can find all sorts of berries in the hills. Different kinds of cucumbers and melons are always around the house. It's fun to bathe in the river. She wants to let all that go and shred her poor hands on the basket weaving instead. Of course, even though I was angry with her, I didn't have the courage to say anything to her.

At dusk, Aaye came in, dusting all the bamboo peels off her sari. She lit the lamp. Then she placed her hand on Krishna's forehead to check his fever. She said, 'Shantay, Bawa's body is really hot now. Will you rub some orris-root with water to make a paste for him?'

Tatya heard her as he walked in and he said, 'Aga, what is orris-root going to do? His fever is not a simple fever. Shantay, is there a fowl in the house?'

I had just caught a screaming fowl and was shoving it under a basket. I couldn't deny its existence. Aaye, however, tried to warn me with her eyes, imploring me to keep quiet. Tatya called the buwa inside, got Krishna to sit up and made preparations for the healing sacrifice. Aaye was watching all this quietly, alarmed. Her drawn face without her kumkum looked even more distraught in the lamplight. My younger siblings looked scared and clung to her.

The buwa slapped three dried stems with mango leaves on the floor and muttered to himself, 'Give to the right, now to the left.' I wondered what was falling to the right and the left. He jerked his neck every so often as if it was a rooster's chopped-off neck. Then he slapped the leaves some more. Tatya watched him gravely. The villagers who had come with him were nowhere to be seen.

Tatya pulled the fowl from under the basket and sat opposite Krishna with the fowl in his hands. Buwa sprinkled some vermillion powder in front of him. Tatya made the offering by saying, 'Hey, landowner, we will leave your land. I place this offering before you. Please accept it and let your son be healthy again, maharaja.' He applied ashes to Krishna's body and then dragged the fowl all over his body. Both Buwa and he disappeared into the darkness outside after that.

When they returned, the villagers came back with them and they had the fowl all cut up. Tatya handed the fowl to me, saying, 'Shantay, cook this offering and feed everyone.' Tatya's voice sounded heavy, it was clear they were all drunk. 'Vah ... Vahini,' he spoke, stuttering, 'don't worry about the expense. I'll take care of that, but I will show you the intent of this land after all.'

That night we all ate chicken curry and rice and the visitors set about their next business. They took lemons pricked with needles, ashes, vermillion, coconut, rice, incense, camphor and a small lamp in a flat basket. Tatya passed the basket to the buwa and said, 'Vahini, take everyone outside while I sit near Krishna for a while.'

We followed the buwa out into the darkness. He stopped after a while and said in a hoarse voice, 'There is something right here.' The sight of the buwa's mysterious eyes and his bushy hair in that pale lamplight, an awareness of his hoarse voice and the idea that something was underfoot, brought all our hearts into our throats.

All the kids were frightened, that was certain. Who knows how the adults fared?

The buwa sat down and watched the earth with keen eyes. He cleared a small area of seven inches square and settled the dust there with dung-water. There he placed the ashes, vermillion and some flowers. He burned the camphor there and started digging the ground under a rock next to it with a pick-axe. After he'd dug a hole about a foot deep, he put his hand in and suddenly he began to scream, 'Look here, look here!' He brought his hand up and showed us all the fresh blood that was dripping from it.

'Look, schoolmistress ... this is the sacrificial blood! This land is on a border where the town's calumny brings pain. This land needs more blood.' Buwa then prayed once again, 'Hey, landowner, we will leave your land. Forgive your innocent children this one time. Now we know you. You have shown us your power, maharaja. We have brought a small petal as an offering to you, not a whole flower.' As he said this, he broke the coconut open and before the sound died in the darkness, we heard Tatya's voice screaming from inside the house.

'Vahini, aga Vahini, come quick, run ... look at what Krishna is doing.' Our remaining courage left us as we heard this voice cutting through the darkness around us. Somehow, we managed to reach the house with Aaye.

Krishna was convulsing and foaming at the mouth. Aaye lost all control, 'Arre, look what happened to my son ... arre baba, my son ... look everyone ...' she cried out aloud. All of us children seemed to have lost our voices altogether.

'Look, Vahini, the land has shown us its intent hasn't it? That's what I was trying to tell you: if you had listened to me this could have been avoided. At least open your eyes now,' Tatya continued to badger her despite the state she was in.

The buwa applied ashes to Krishna's body and he slowly came around.

'Aaye, we are going to the village with Tatya tomorrow, you can stay here if you like,' I registered my angry opinion finally. I didn't want to stay here anymore and Tatya wanted the same thing.

'Shantay,' he said, 'pack your belongings. We will leave tomorrow. I'll educate you all. I am quite capable of doing that.'

That night had brought so much fear to our minds that sleep was almost impossible. My younger siblings held Aaye's sari tightly in their fists and went to sleep. In the verandah, the villagers were snoring while Aaye sat and pressed wet cloths dipped in salt water to Krishna's forehead. Very early in the morning, my eyes became heavy with sleep and through a haze, I heard Krishna's voice as if from a distance, 'Aaye, at night, after you all went out, Tatya gave me some medicine to drink and then I don't know what happened.'

Later I woke up with a start because Tatya was screaming. The villagers were ready to leave and Tatya was pacing furiously. Aaye sat outside calmly weaving her basket. Her face was no longer drawn and tired. She looked angry this morning.

'Shantay, wake the children. This is not your mother. She is your enemy from a past life, your enemy. She is ready to kill you all. She doesn't want a home. She wants to live in the town. She'll only be satisfied after she sends you all to your deaths. Come on, wake the children up.' Tatya said this as he walked in, stomping his feet.

Outside, Aaye started her wailing and again started speaking as if she was reciting ovis. 'My dear husband … my master … my love … you left your children behind and you are gone. You told me not to trust your brother, Tatya. You were right, my raja. He poisoned your son at night, raja. He made him unconscious. All the crows have gathered like birds of prey, arre. They are waiting to sell your land. Now what should I do … oh God!'

Aaye's words hit Tatya's core motive directly and he was shocked. Suddenly he lost all his courage and slipped out of the house like a cat. When he came to the verandah, he walked away as fast as he could without so much as glancing at Aaye!

Translated from Marathi by Veena Deo

A Large Girl

She watches *Devdas*, remote in hand, so the magic of instant access to any moment in its 184 minutes of sequinned shimmer is hers. She is a large girl. I knew her in school. She was there in school as early as Standard II, she tells me. But I didn't see her till maybe VII or VIII. Overnight, she came to our attention because she grew boobs and kept popping her buttons. Then she did the long jump on Sports Day and her skirt did that thing cheap umbrellas do, spine buckling and bowl upturning to heaven. There she landed, and she was so pink, I thought: tulip.

Everyone else was laughing. But there were some things I knew even then, maybe about the world, maybe about me. In any case, the last thing I wanted to do was laugh. What I wanted was to slip my hands down those trunk-like legs. My own were so inadequate. What must it be like, I thought, to have so much?

In Class VIII, she brought in a biography of Marilyn Monroe. Held between desk and knee it circulated down the row, across the aisle, down row two, and so on through the class: girls in one half, boys in the other. We flipped to the marked 'hot' pages, to the forty or so pictures in black and white, there to give some meat to the printed word, which in any case we ignored. Unlike the black-market-quality pages with their bleed-through words elsewhere in the book, these thicker glossy pages in the middle were adequate for the task of delineating each angled thigh's unsubtle and tight press to hide – what? Nipples pulled oblong by raised arms floated free in what was already let loose – levitating fruit – front and centre of head thrown back and wide, arched smile inviting – what?

Pushpa, the idiot-mouse of our class, burst into tears. She was necessary comic relief; the sacrificial victim of our collective misgivings. What had we seen and how would this act now mark us? There was a sense of Class VIII's free period having been turned, in Sridevi Nair the teacher's absence and with the aid of Janet's wicked pinkness, into a communal orgy. 'Quick, let's forget.'

She was there till Class XII, and I knew her as the nun's charity-case, the unclothed girl to steer clear of. The nuns would punish girls whose hems rode above their knees. How they allowed hers to creep up and up and stay there so that we were, I was, forced to obviate her – well, that's a question between the nuns and their gods. Obviate her, I did. There are no other incidents to recount till we reached Class XII – just the buttons, the jump that tuliped her, and Marilyn Monroe.

Our last day in school, the girls wore saris, the boys wore suits, and we prepared to dance – girls with girls and boys with boys. The school's Annual Day that year had revolved around a historical play, set in the colonial period, written by a team of nuns and credited to the Head Boy and Girl. For the play we had rehearsed a waltz fifty times in a day: boys in suits were paired with girls whose mothers cut saris into some understanding of ball gowns. On the strength of this earlier experience, the nuns urged us the evening we danced our goodbyes to pair up, boys with girls. The Head Boy and Girl to their, and everyone else's, discomfort led the line-up and the rest of us, in one of those stray acts of shame-faced rebellion, refused to follow suit. And so it was I found myself in Janet's embrace and, for the five minutes our feet described a dip-rise-dip square on the floor, I examined anew the corkscrew self, the twisting slumbering worm of me that had longed for this. Her hands on my shoulders and mine at her waist, and before or during that last dip, hers travelled as did mine from there to here, and then very quickly there were samosas and autographs and true and false expressions of sorrow across the throng of 120-odd crying-smiling-unfeeling-anxious-about-to-die youngsters.

In school she was presented, whether by herself or by the nuns or somehow – as an orphan. But here's the story she tells me now: her father arranged her mother's death – murdered her. He was an electrician – stripped the insulation off the wire and lined it up so her mother would be the one to turn on the washing machine. He basically, as Janet puts, 'fried her'. I read a short story, Hitchcock's, once: same plot. Maybe her father read it too. But in his case the ending was different. Where Hitchcock's man kept his mouth shut and got away with it, Janet's father told his brother who turned him in. I have a brother and cannot imagine doing that – turning him in – no matter what the crime. Her father has been out of jail for some time. He's written to her, and she wants me to go with her to meet him. What kind of man would write to his daughter thirty years after murdering her mother and expect that she would want to meet him?

Her favourite story – she reads it out loud to me, in her favourite reading position, lying full length on top of me, her belly smashed into mine, book propped on pillow above my head – is *Kabulliwallah*. She is addicted to my stomach. She likes that I am the one who has given birth and worked my way back to flat, whereas she ... Well, I like her large and soft. She weeps in the reading. Every time. But how am I to weep when this is the fifteenth reading, and with every turn of the page, she must shift her weight and belly must renew acquaintance with belly with that sweaty, burp-cheer sound I find so funny? She weeps some more. Then she gets angry and says: 'You don't understand me.' And even on those occasions when I accept this as truth – and there are more of these occasions than not – she still must push on to the inevitable: 'How can you understand me? You are the little Miss Richie Rich who ignored me all through school.'

Here's what I tell her. Here's what I say that mollifies her: 'God, give me another life so that I can do it right next time. Another life, so I can appreciate you and love you as you deserve to be.' I deliver this without rolling my eyes. I don't shrug my shoulders or in any other way temper the fact that I mean this with all my heart. This life has not been enough and will continue to not be enough to love Janet. And it's not because her hunger is so beyond the pale. It just is the case that the love she wants is not in my means to give.

Here's another story from the past that Janet's father's recent resurrection has laid to rest. For the longest time there was a rumour in school that she was not a complete orphan; that her father was alive, even if her mother was dead; that he was alive and – get this – sailing the seas, an Australian sea captain. Why Australian? Don't ask me. She likes her stories sequinned. She likes them to shimmer. So she embroiders. Some of us embroider, and others of us will briefly hold in our hands a particularly fine piece of embroidery, so we can admire the journey the needle has taken.

We did not believe this story in school, although it would have accounted for Janet's name, her fairness, the breadth of her shoulders, her large bones. But she was not the first Anglo-Indian the rest of us had encountered, and her Australian–captain father only made the class titter. I know now where she got the story from. My daughter is eight and addicted to a character in a book series – Pippi Longstocking – an enormously self-sufficient orphan girl whose missing sea captain father she claims is still alive: a Cannibal King marooned on an island.

My own father, mother, brother, daughter and husband are alive and well. My marriage has been a good one for nearly fourteen years. It was an early marriage. I agreed to marriage because I lacked the imagination then to see how else a girl might make a life. My imagination, Janet believes, has continued to be lacklustre, and so she attempts obligingly to fill in where she senses inadequacy.

When I loan her money for the one-plus-one in the Shahpur Jat area, she immediately has us moving in, not just my bed and dresser set, which she admires, and the cut crystal in the dining room display, which is a wedding present from Mohan's parents, but also my daughter Rohini, and even Mohan's newest pup, Chetan. The thing about Janet's claim to gifts of imagination is that this imagination of hers too conveniently, it seems to me, skirts the truth.

We go through a phase where she questions me endlessly about Mohan – his likes, dislikes. Yes, the likes and dislikes of our lovemaking are uppermost in her thinking. I never feel it necessary to answer these questions. But I have told her what I thought of him when I first saw him. We met at my house with the parents around, his and mine. I don't count that as a first meeting. I never really saw him that day. No, the first time it was just the two of us was at the club near his parents' home in Anand Niketan. He had more or less grown up in that area, and he met me at the club entrance with this certain assurance, and we went inside this room and talked. We passed through the topic of exes quickly, and I teased him some and asked him what qualities in him had attracted these other girls. He looked so terribly pleased as he said, 'You'll have to ask them.'

Then there was some fumbling when the waiter came, and he ordered club sandwiches for both of us. He apologized to me for not doing better with the waiter and told me then that this was his first time in The Room. The Room, being the room we were in, a room in which children were not permitted, a room meant For Adults Only. He had celebrated Diwali in childhood at this club and spent summers swimming in the pool and I suppose had become an adult and moved away before he could take advantage of adult privilege. He was feeling grown up that day and so was I. So in the end I married, I think, because it was the grown-up thing to do and right that I should do it with this grown-up that I was becoming fond of.

Janet refuses to understand this story. 'Yeah, so you are fond of him. But tell me you have the hots for him and I promise I will believe you.' She doesn't really want my answer. 'You can't say it, can you? Yes to hots? No? No hots.' She thinks she is taunting me.

Or lying next to me, when I turn inviting her to spoon me, she will peel back instead and run her hand from my shoulder to my butt and slap me there and ask, 'What's his favorite part?' If I remain silent she will pinch or poke at me. 'Is it here, your butt? Men always like a woman's ass. They never think to like her elbows or her toes. Or maybe he has a foot fetish? Does he? Maybe he sucks your toes, heh princess?' It's no good keeping my back turned. She will move on from favourite body parts to favourite positions. I turn to her and busy myself nibbling her front.

She keeps a picture of Rohini, and one of Chetan with Rohini, along with the many others of me in her room. She would no doubt have a perfectly imaginative tale with which to dress up the addition of Mohan's picture to this tableau. I can't imagine what this would be. In any case, I tell her, 'No, it will make me uncomfortable', and refuse her the picture when she asks. With Janet, the truth, if inconvenient, is something to be ignored. I can't live that way.

Janet and I first run into each other in the parking lot outside my gym. She is coming out of a shop in the same complex. It turns out to be a beauty parlour, and she turns out to be working there. We light up, standing between the cars; breaking my big rule about public smoking. It would take any busybody in that gym, to whom Mohan is known, seeing me smoking, for me to get into a lot of trouble. For all that Mohan is a chain smoker, I am not permitted to smoke. On the rare occasion, say if we are good and soused, on an anniversary, at Buzz, or better still at The Imperial, and if I beg and nag, then, maybe then, he'll light me one and hand it over.

But my girlfriends and I always smoke when we get together. We do it on the roof. I keep a mat rolled up on the stairs. We take it up with us when we go. Ours is a rented place, and I have done nothing by way of plants and things to beautify the roof. The mat serves to soften the crumbling concrete on which we have to crouch to prevent nearby tenants from invading our privacy. The mat is where Janet and I first kiss.

The first time we kiss, she lights a cigarette and passes it to me, and then she lights another one. We are talking, but not easily. After the cigarette in the parking lot, and the exchange of phone numbers, a month passes before I realize she will not be the one to call. I call. She comes over. There is all the awkwardness of her taking in the toys scattered throughout the house – most of them Mohan's, I explain to her. I am not the gadget freak, and the endless updating is his way of flexing his muscles.

She is subdued downstairs, but loud enough on the roof, so I am relieved when finally we sit quietly, leaning back on the short wall. I wish for time to get the clothes cleared from the line before they get infected with our smoke. But it is also strangely peaceful as they stir, combing their shade-fingers of coolness over us with each breeze. My shoulder is touching hers and she slides down and rests her head on my lap and from there squints up at me. She is still as she was in school – large hands and long legs. I am still as I was – content to keep within myself; my inner curve yearning, in its own circular fashion, itself. So then why am I unfurling as she reaches for my face, her one hand doing the bidding and the other still locked onto the cigarette? A second passes, her hand is on my cheek, and I follow her example, my free hand cradling her cheek, so we are both leading and following together into that first kiss.

It is not a kiss to get lost in – we are each of us balancing, one half engaged in not accidentally burning the other. She flicks her cigarette away and with both hands pulls my head to hers. But I don't have her sophistication or just plain old ease. I am still balancing as she searches my mouth – her tongue acrid, like Mohan's.

I take to leaving her. After the first, second, third, fourth time, she stops mourning and starts instead to throw me out. I leave and the leaving is unbearable to me. For a day or two I remain gone from her. My last memory of her is of a graceless shrug of dismissal; the slam of her eyes shutting me out.

I leave her for many reasons. The first time – when Rohini comes up the stairs to the roof one afternoon, and the metal stairs, instead of clattering as I had expected, absorb her Keds tread silently, and suddenly she is there – looking at us. 'Mummy,' she says. She is wearing a stricken smile. She is saying with her eyes, 'I don't see you with a cigarette in your hand.' She is saying, 'I don't see the pack placed square between you and aunty.' 'Mummy,' she says, breathless from the run up the stairs, shamefaced from the discovery she has made. 'Nina threw the Frisbee hard at Indrani, and now Indrani's nose is cut, and, and,' she says riveted by the competing drama of the story she has come to share and the story she has just discovered, 'Indrani's nose has sooo much blood coming out of it. It's everywhere.'

For the next two days, I try to tell Janet we shouldn't smoke together. I even tell Mohan the truth: 'Janet and I were on the roof, and you know she smokes. Well, she lit me one, and the next thing Rohini was up there, and I think she saw us.' Mohan does not get angry. 'Let's see if Ro says something. There is no need to bring it up if she doesn't.' After two days he and I agree Rohini had forgotten. But I remain frantic that Janet should understand why we can't smoke up on the roof. The more she turns her ears off, the more determined I become that I will not only stop our little smoking ritual, but also that I will never smoke anywhere, for any reason, ever again.

I am supposed to go to her place some days later. I don't. A week passes, and she texts me: 'talk?' I can't help myself. She greets me at the door, pulls me to her and kisses me on her side of the length of fabric she has hung in the doorway. My one hand automatically searches behind me for the wood beyond this cloth, till she imprisons my hand in hers, pulls it between us and slips something into it. Our foreheads are touching and we both look down to what our hands are doing – transferring fruit – light green and translucent, from hers to mine. Then, she looks straight into my eyes and hers are smiling. 'Amla,' she says. 'It will be the oral fix you need to quit cigarettes.' My mouth is already puckering. The fruit is sour and tense in taste, but leaves the mouth sweet and wet as if washed with rain. We kiss, and I forget about the door. She shuts it in the end, pushes me ahead of her into bed. But the amla is really only for me, and afterwards she lights up as always, ashing her sheets, pillows, my hair.

The fighting continues. It becomes about her father. She insists she needs me with her when she goes to see him for the first time. I tell her, 'Faridabad is too far away. How will I account for a whole morning, afternoon and evening?' She is stiff in anger: 'You spend the whole afternoon here. No problem.'

'But', I say, 'I am always there to pick Rohini up at 3:30.'

'Tell your husband to get her this once.'

'No, I can't. He doesn't like to interrupt his work like that.'

'This is important to me,' she says.

I don't believe her. Her neighbour has told me that her father has already been by to see Janet. I wonder if perhaps they have met more often than this once.

I don't say to Janet: 'You're a liar.' I wonder why she wants me to see him. She has not repaid me the loan, which I wheedled out of Mohan. I wonder if she is going to ask for more money; if, perhaps, her father needs money. I don't say: 'You're a liar.' Instead I say: 'No.' Then, 'The truth is I am a married woman. And a mother.'

She says, 'That's never been a problem. What's there in that?'

We are silent. I think about her father in her room. I wonder if he wondered what we – Rohini, I, and not to forget Chetan – are doing on Janet's walls. I wonder what story Janet concocted to explain us to him.

'Why do I have to meet your father?'

She regards me seriously. 'I just want him to know that I have a good life. And you are part of what makes my life good.'

But I feel stubborn. 'No,' I say. Mostly I am thinking, 'Why do I like her? She is so vulgar.'

I cautiously tell friends from school that I have run into Janet, and their reactions are uniformly similar. I think it is Shilpa who says, 'She must have had a hard life,' and I concur.

The last time we are together at her place, she meets me first at the bottom of the stairs leading up to her flat. She is four floors up, and the walls all along the climb are repulsive, stained with the spit-splat of paan. On the second floor landing someone has lined up some potted plants on either side of their front door, and above on the wall is a pencilled-and-taped-to-the-wall sign in Hindi: 'Spitting on Plants is Not Permitted'. On the flight up from the third floor landing she turns to me and says, 'You're having your period.' I nod, and she adds, 'I can hear your pad rustling.'

The very last time we are together, she kisses me under my stairs. She has thrown me out the week before when once again I refuse to accompany her to her father's. She says that he is asking to meet me. I am adamant in my refusal. At the end of a week's silence, she shows up and gestures to me from the service lane that fronts my place. I wave back to her from the upstairs balcony, more to reassure the flower-seller who is studying the proceedings, than to indicate any sort of welcome. But then she crosses the lane, comes in the gate to the front door, and I pull her in from there. She takes her hand out of her pocket and, glistening in her cupped palm, are two amlas. I rest a fingertip on one and gently rock it in her palm where it bumps repeatedly its sister-self. And again Janet and I are facing each other. She is my height, I realize: her largeness is all in her breadth. There is a way we line up – eye to eye – that feels like pleasure.

'Take it,' she indicates the amla with her chin. I take one, and she folds her hand shut over the other. 'You don't want us to continue?' she asks.

'No.' I am wooden. 'Janet, I don't want to be destructive in any way. In my life or yours. You have to understand that.'

'Tomorrow?' she asks, 'You won't change your mind?'

'No, Janet. Tomorrow, I won't change my mind.'

She kisses me before she leaves. This, our last kiss, is quick. It is a kiss of dismissal, but also sweet. In the lean of her face, I feel her eyelashes brushing mine, and her tongue has no anger to it; nor any persuasion.

A time will come – a time that is starting now – when I will no longer know her. I will attend the Jahan-e-Khushrau festival and, sitting in the last rows, I will be surprised to see Anju seated two seats away from me. We will press hands across people's laps, and I will be embarrassed as I tell her that I will come soon to pick up the tailoring I have left at her boutique some months before. She will laugh and say, 'I have kept it all together for you. It is ready.' Rohini will place her head in my lap and ease the mobile from my purse and proceed to play a game on silent mode. I will be irritated and will want to scold her to enjoy the music. Mohan will put a hand on my knee and will still me. We will together whisper and wonder who it is that owns the splendid house with lit banks of windows overlooking Humayun's tomb and the festival. 'They are so lucky, dining there on the rooftop,' we will think. The next day, I will meet at a party one of the diners from the night before. And I will exclaim: 'This is such a small city. I never thought ...'

At Café Turtle, I will overhear a man talking about Jhumpa Lahiri's *Interpreter of Maladies*, and the next day the same man will be at *Confluence*, with another woman this time. He will turn out to be an authority on steel sculpture. I will meet him, and he will talk shyly about his expertise. It will be on the tip of my tongue to say to him, 'What a small world we live in. Just yesterday ...' But he will break in and say much the same words to me.

I will stand one evening, in line, at the PVR in Saket and Mohan's attentiveness will leave me feeling cherished. He will agree to watch *Memoirs of a Geisha* not because it is the only movie showing at 5:15, but because he will know how much I will enjoy this movie. In the next line, we will see our old neighbours quarrelling and we will happily embrace them. It will have been years since they vacated from above us.

I will begin soon to live all the days ahead of me. In the afternoons, I will think: Do you miss me? Do you miss me? A thousand and one chances will come and go in this small city, in this small world. I will never see you again.

The Thief

Narayani wore a bright green sari with orange flowers, not unlike the African tulips that bloomed on the tree outside our neighbour's house. She stood on the street – our street, littered with tyre-crushed lilacs – speaking broken Malayalam from the black metal gate leading to our house.

'How much for sweeping and mopping?' Grandmother asked, drying her wet, freshly dyed hair with her fingers. 'Everyone here gives 125 rupees but because we have five bedrooms I'll give you 150.'

Narayani, not made uncomfortable by the mention of money, said, 'I'll cook and wash clothes, but I won't clean.'

Grandmother looked meaningfully at me. I was to her left, in our garden, sitting on one of the marble mushrooms Grandfather had installed under the frangipani. Grandfather said it was difficult to see any possibility of softness or colour – or did he say colour and life? – emerging from the frangipani at this time of year. To me, it seemed as if the tree was upside down, its dry roots spread in the air. I did not know what Grandmother meant by that look of hers so I imitated it in reply: I pursed my lips, widened my eyes, and raised my eyebrows. Grandmother needn't have asked Narayani why she wouldn't clean – everyone knew that some maids would not clean other people's houses, particularly their bathrooms; they even kept lower-caste maids to clean their own – but she did.

'No,' was all Narayani said in reply, shaking her head, smiling, hoping she hadn't embarrassed a potential employer. Grandmother ignored her reply.

'What kind of food do you make?'

'Kerala food, Punjabi food ...'

'We don't like Punjabi food.'

'I can make Chinese also. Gobi manchurian, vegetable spring roll, noodles.'

'Will you wash the dishes at least?'

After an hour of negotiating various chores and their reimbursements, it was arranged, and announced, that Narayani would cook lunch and dinner; buy groceries; wash dishes; attend to the door, the three phones, and to sundry errands for family members. She would also be responsible for making tea (with strictly designated quantities of sugar, water, milk and spices) for us and for those who visited the house. It is impossible to list all the people who came to our house in a day, but I read in one of Grandfather's articles, 'There is inherent nobility in every descriptive attempt, however inadequate.' (I'd never want Grandfather to know I read, much less remembered, something he'd written.) There were men who came to sell milk, coconuts, vegetables and fruit; the garbage man; the driver; the gardener; Grandfather's peon; at least a couple of relatives and friends, or a reader of Grandfather's columns who was 'just passing by and thought I'd drop in'. Then there were the people who came on a weekly basis: Grandmother's broker and her real estate agent; and on a monthly one: the broad-shouldered Kashmiri carpet and cloth sellers with fair faces and red lips; the cableman and the manager of the trash collecting service. I am sure I've missed some, like the people who came to collect funds for the parks, the tennis court, the street signs and the like; the odd-job men; relatives and friends of the maids; and the saleswomen in rubber slippers and long-sleeved blouses who sold washing powder and cook books.

Narayani lived twenty miles from the city in a one-room shack, which she cleaned, broomed, and wet-mopped first thing in the morning. Then she made lunch for her family; it was always sambar and rice, and, on a special day, an added spicy vegetable, all of which she mixed and packed in light steel boxes with rubber-coated hooks for her daughters to take to their English-medium school. 'Don't talk in class and listen to madam,' she said to them when they left the house, their hair tightly plaited with red nylon ribbons. Their father did not get up, if he was home, before one or two in the afternoon. Narayani took the 7.25 bus, which took about an hour to get to our part of town. From the bus stop, she went straight to the Old Lady from the North that lived across the street from us – it was she who sent Narayani to Grandmother when Terrible Birama left.

The Old Lady lived in a two-storied box-like house by herself. The building had been painted yellow once. She had sons and daughters who lived abroad and visited her when they were getting married or to show her their children. Three maids other than Narayani came to the Old Lady at different times of day. She told my Grandmother this was a wise thing to do: 'It keeps them reasonable; they don't think your world will collapse without them.'

The first thing Narayani did at the Old Lady's was make tea. She heated a cup of milk with a few spoons of sugar and poured it into a small china cup, whose edges had gathered unwashable lines of dirt. Then she put a Taj Mahal tea bag in the cup, and gave it to the Old Lady in a saucer on a large tray edged with cane. Narayani had her tea at our house; 'taste is not same,' she said, if tea was not boiled. While the Old Lady drank her tea, Narayani gathered the white saris that had been hung to dry on the first-floor balcony, and ironed them. The Old Lady insisted her underwear – also white (she was a widow) – was ironed as well. After the ironing, Narayani gave the woman a massage in a room that I imagined to be very dark because I never saw any electric light in the house, not even at night.

Narayani often spoke of the massage, and each time she did I tried to imagine the Old Lady naked. She had a strange body. Its shape was like an almond, tapering toward the ends and wide in the middle. Her face and neck had so many layers they reminded me of Sultan, our neighbour's boxer. Once, in the early evening, when Grandmother and I were playing badminton, she stepped outside her house to buy coconut water and I saw her in something other than a sari – a short-sleeved nightgown that reached just below her knees. Her ankles and wrists were small, and though there was hair visible everywhere, fair soft skin lay below it. When she turned, I caught a glimpse of her back. She did not seem to be wearing underwear: two masses of flesh hung some distance below her waist, not far above the back of her knees, and the dress stuck to her as if it was wet. Narayani did not like to massage her because the Old Lady wanted her to go on and on. Sometimes the massage would take a couple of hours. By then, Narayani's hands would become erratic, lose all sense of rhythm and touch. The Old Lady would let another few minutes pass, after which she would say, 'Bas.'

The slam of the kitchen door – enough to scare the koels off the avocado tree – at 10.30 meant Narayani had come. She entered by the back door because Grandmother had asked her not to ring the bell. Grandfather's study was near the front door, adjoining the garden, and he did not like 'frivolous diversions' and 'unnecessary distractions'. He had spent more than forty years of his life working for the government, in the Research and Analysis Wing. It had been a few years since he retired; now he wrote articles on India's intelligence failures for the national newspapers. From the kitchen, Narayani walked into the hallway and called to each of us in turn, declaring her presence with customized greetings.

'Amma, what we making today?'

'Baby, you want noodles?'

'Akka, tea for you?'

She knew the answers to all these questions, but she never stopped asking them. The vegetables were rotated weekly between beans, cabbage, lady's finger, long gourd, and green brinjal. We made only three or four types of curries: coconut curry with shrimp and the puli Grandmother grew in the garden; sambar with carrots and drumsticks; curd curry; rasam with as much garlic as tomatoes. There were two kinds of breads: chapatis without ghee, and oily parathas; and two kinds of rice: white and brown Kerala rice, which I did not eat because Grandmother, at every meal, said, 'It is *very* good for you, *full* of vitamin B and potassium.' Narayani also knew I liked Superhit Kishen noodles, which Grandfather called 'poison food', for breakfast during the holidays; I was promised this daily treat by Father if I passed Maths. If I didn't, I would have to resume the three-hour daily tutorials with the teacher who called me by no other word but 'idiot'. Mother, whom Narayani called her elder sister, liked her tea black, without sugar, boiled with a few seeds of cardamom and a thumb-long piece of ginger. Narayani poured three cups into a flask that Mother took to work. Father left home before Narayani arrived.

Because of Grandfather's cholesterol levels Grandmother put almost no oil or salt in the food. Often, I made myself a mayonnaise sandwich with white bread, not Grandfather's organic wholegrain that was also '*very* good for you'.

Narayani didn't like it when I didn't eat her food. She would wait for Grandmother to step out of the kitchen, which didn't happen very often, then add the forbidden condiments to the food. Grandmother would tell us, and our guests, 'We put no oil or salt in our food and it is still *so* tasty!'

In the kitchen, I liked to stir the vegetables, and fry fish and potato chips. Narayani would grate coconut halves over a serrated steel knife attached to a wooden stand, sitting with her knees raised on either side, or she would cut onions, her eyes pouring forth. At first, she spoke to me in Malayalam and Tamil, and I mixed some of that into my English. Then I started to speak only in English because she was good at getting the gist of what I said. In months, she learnt to understand and speak comprehensible, even if erratic, English.

It was inevitable: all of us spoke the language except Grandmother who insisted on talking in Malayalam, even to those who did not understand it, like our poor Kannadiga gardener. Grandfather said how shameful it was that a great language was dying and though he said it to no one in particular, or everyone at once, say in the car on our way back from a dinner, after he had had his customary two rums, I knew his accusation was pointed at me. I was sure Narayani was the only maid in our neighbourhood who said 'You're welcome,' when you said thanks, and who said 'Esscuse me,' when she sneezed, even if there was no one around.

It was spring, almost six months after Narayani came to work for us. That season, each day, Grandfather took me for a drive to look at the laburnums. They bore flowers for only two weeks of the year, he told me. I liked the yellow, bell-like flowers that looked as if they might all fall at once if one were to shake the tree ever so lightly. This was the time of year that Grandmother vacuumed the house. Once a year, she liked to clean the carpets, which were swept daily by the cleaning maid, a thin, fair woman with dreamy eyes and clean skin who, unlike her colleague, was reserved in her speech: she replied to everything with a nod or by shaking her head. On a Sunday afternoon, when the rest of us were taking a nap, Grandmother walked into the garage. The vacuum cleaner wasn't there.

It had to be Narayani, Grandmother told me. She was the only one who went into the garage to use the tandoor when we had guests for dinner (every weekend). By this time, Grandmother had become quite used to Narayani, a situation that was not at odds with her constant complaining about her; if something was wrong with the cooking: 'This Narayani has not learnt *anything*,' and if someone praised it: '*I* put the masala'. Having Narayani around meant Grandmother could go to the weekly meetings and activities of the Ladies' Club of Bangalore; she could watch her favorite show in the morning, even if she watched it with an overpowering restlessness, going into the kitchen during commercials, answering doorbells and phone calls. For some reason, when she watched TV, she was more attentive than ever to what was going on in the house.

'Narayani, I can't find the vacuum cleaner.' They were in the kitchen making lemon rice and fish curry. Narayani was not unfamiliar with Grandmother's effortful, innocent turn of tone.

'Where did you keep it, Amma?'

'In the garage.'

'It's not there?'

'No. I want to clean the carpets. It's always been right there next to the Maruti.'

'Did you look properly?'

'Yes, Narayani.'

'I'll go look for it.'

'Not now, first finish cooking.'

Grandmother did not think Narayani was lying, though who else could have done it? The other maid never went into the garage. She entered and left by the main door, and she had often returned the limp rupee notes she found in our clothes. The peon that came to help Grandfather was like family. He ate lunch with us and helped Grandmother in her garden: feeding the ever hungry fish in the lotus tank, turning the soil, picking the papayas and coconuts, watering the lawn, fixing the solar lamps. Even if he had gone up to her and confessed to the crime, say, she would have laughed, slapped him on the back, and said, 'Poda!'

Grandmother wondered whether she should fire Narayani over a superfluous vacuum cleaner. Unlike other big cities, Bangalore – I heard her telling Mother who was about to fire her driver once – did not have a ready supply of unskilled labour: 'Maids, drivers, gardeners, watchmen are not easy to find.' That must have been why we kept that driver who showed up bloody-eyed, unshaven, unwashed, wearing the same brown pants and dirty white T-shirt for three or four days in a row. He insisted on being paid by the day, and his grandmother in a distant village was sick at least every other week. Once found, the workers were hard to keep; they demanded many things other than their salaries. Take the Terrible Birama whom we had to sack. She had demanded a steady supply of brightly coloured gel toothpaste, Parachute coconut hair oil, medium-strength Colgate toothbrushes, and Lux beauty soap. Grandmother drew the line at Fair & Lovely. Birama liked to sleep till seven, which was the time Grandfather liked his breakfast of idli, upma or putta, and she watched TV in the dining room, with the volume up loud, compounded by her laughing and talking back to the characters on the screen. On a day when Grandmother was out and Birama was watching a movie, we asked her to make a prawn curry. She nodded her coconut-oiled head and when we came down two hours later, she was still watching the movie. On her return, after being briefed by us on this outrageous behaviour, Grandmother said, 'This will not do, Birama, you find another place.'

'I was going to leave anyway,' Birama said. 'You people shout too much.'

Grandmother looked intently at the frying pan. She asked Narayani to put more turmeric in the rice and, next time, not to use so much oil for the fish. Before leaving the kitchen, she told Narayani that no one liked the biryani she had made the day before because there were far too many chillies in it. That evening Grandmother asked all of us to lock our valuables away and not leave money lying around. No one except she and I knew about the stolen vacuum cleaner. (Later, when I told my parents about it, they did not seem to care.) No point in telling Grandfather; he would say, 'Why do you always talk of trivial things? When I was your age, I was reading James and discussing Spinoza.' I didn't make the mistake of asking him who these people were.

The month after the vacuum cleaner incident the cleaning maid quit. Two of my shirts were found missing. Naturally, we, that is, Grandmother, questioned the maid since she was in charge of washing, drying, folding, and delivering the clothes to our rooms. She didn't say a word, just shook her head. The next day she arrived with a large white plastic bag, so stuffed one couldn't hold its ends together. It contained everything we had given her as gifts for Diwali and Christmas over the years. She left a week later, insisting on working out the full month even after Grandmother, feeling betrayed, angry and guilty, had agreed to pay her anyway.

None of us suspected Narayani of taking the shirts. We were too used to her to imagine not having her around. I liked the hour or so that I spent talking to her in the kitchen. Grandmother did not like it because Narayani worked slower when she talked. If she got excited about something, she would drop what she was doing altogether and speak in an English that was as wild as her gesticulations: 'Tell me, baby, what I do with him? I tell him to get out my house but he is not go.'

Soon after the other maid quit, Narayani lost her job at the Old Lady's. One of her younger, unmarried sons had returned from the US to find a wife. One day, he saw Narayani massaging his mother and asked her to do the same for him. She was massaging his legs and arms when he took her hand and put it into his shorts, smiling kindly at her. Narayani went straight to the Old Lady and said, 'Give me money for this month. I don't want to work here.' The Old Lady asked her why and Narayani said, 'Your son behave badly with me.' The Old Lady from the North became very angry, more so because Narayani was speaking in English. She told her never to show her 'dirty black face in this house again'. Narayani lost a monthly income of 300 rupees. Grandmother told her she would add the amount to her salary if she cleaned our house. Narayani agreed, saying, 'You are like my family. Is okay to clean your house.'

It was summer, but this time I wasn't allowed to eat noodles – I had done badly in the exams. I was reading *The Princess Diaries* when Grandmother came in, as always without knocking. She asked if I had given Narayani a key chain Father got me for my birthday.

'Why?'

'Did you give it to her or not?'

The key chain was attached to a smooth, red, glass heart with watery yellow and blue ribbons inside it. I saw it in a store where

Father was buying the weekly race guide and I said I wanted it. He gave it to me as a surprise for my birthday. After using it for a couple of months I put it away. Surprised at my quick understanding, I realized Narayani must have picked it up from one of the dumps in my room, the TV room, or my parents' room.

'I don't remember, why?'

'What do you mean you don't remember? How can you forget such a thing? You people ...'

'I gave it to her. Now can you leave me alone?'

'If you gave it to her how can you forget and then *suddenly* remember? And this is no way to speak to your grandmother.'

It was easy to lie to Grandmother. If she considered most people untrustworthy, she thought her own family incapable of hiding the truth from her. She told me not to give anything to Narayani without asking her and left the room. Mother told me later that Grandmother had seen a bunch of keys hanging off Narayani's waist. The keychain was tucked inside the skirt of her sari and attached to a hook with steel hearts painted gold. Grandmother's eagle eyes noticed the polished hearts gleaming in the late morning light in the kitchen.

'Narayani, where did you get that keychain?' Grandmother asked.

'Baby gave it to me,' Narayani said without blinking.

I started going to school again and I didn't see much of Narayani until the Diwali holidays, when she wore new saris every day. On Bhaiduj, she invited her brother home for lunch and served him three vegetables, two curries, rice and papad, and rice pudding; at the end of the meal she touched his feet and he gave her fifty-one rupees. On Laxmi Puja, Narayani wore a red sari printed with flowers of a darker red; she pinned a few strings of jasmine in her hair. Narayani had dark, unblemished skin that glowed after she washed it with a thick paste of gram flour and milk cream. Her forehead was small, and from a distance it looked like her eyebrows weren't separated. Her eyes were as dark as her hair, and her unusually long lashes made her look much younger than her twenty-eight years. The pink of her lips had faded around the edges. With her high cheekbones, small breasts, slim waist and strong, lean hands, Narayani looked like a new college student aiming for a degree in Zoology. She wore enough gold to show off her caste: dangling earrings, a mangalsutra – paid for by her, not her husband, a daily reminder of the financial indignity of her marriage – that hung loosely around her neck, another necklace, thicker and tighter, with small red and green stones, studs in her upper ears, glass bangles that matched her sari, two anklets, which composed different melodies depending on the work she performed, and two or three toe rings. For all four days of Diwali, she wore on her forehead an uneven blot of red powder mixed with a few grains of rice. One day she arrived long after noon. She had given lunch to the girls in her neighbourhood, she said.

'Five girls who are not married, I give them lunch. Before they leave I give one steel bowl, one jasmine gajra, one blouse piece.'

'Did you do that also for your husband?'

Narayani missed lunch on Tuesday for her husband's health and avoided meat on Friday so God would find her husband a job.

'No, this is for my daughters so they get a good husband.'

'Like yours,' I teased her.

'No, not like my husband, baby, why you say like that?'

There was only a month to Christmas. Grandmother had begun preparations: shopping for the ingredients that went into her famous plum cake; assembling the tree and its decorations; buying gifts for those who would attend our annual party and cards for relatives who lived abroad. At this time of year, Grandfather's work seemed to increase, and at night he listened with practised disinterest to Grandmother's updates. He would be in charge of the bar at the Christmas party. He always took great care to mix the exact proportions of water, tonic, soda or fruit juice with the various liquors. He never used lemons: 'Only people who don't know anything about drinking use lemons.' He stocked imported stuffed olives and cocktail mixes; three cabinets in the living room stood ready with glassware that he used only for the Christmas dinner.

It was a week before the party when Grandmother walked into the kitchen and asked Narayani to come to her bedroom. I was helping her stir-fry vegetables and she was telling me about the TV her mother's employer had given the family. It had been lying unused for months, Narayani said, because her mother could not afford the monthly cable fee of 250 rupees. Her neighbours were planning to chip in so the women could watch their favourite soaps, and the men, cricket. When she reappeared from the bedroom a few minutes later, it was with a preoccupied expression on her face. But she continued to work, her eyes giving nothing away.

'So are you going to pay too?'

'Ya.'

'How much?'

'Ten rupees.'

After that she wouldn't say a word. I ran to Grandmother. Grandfather's pink diamond ring was missing. Great Grandmother had given the ring to him on his twenty-fifth wedding anniversary. She had taken the ring to the church at Velankanni, where it was 'blessed by Mother Mary for peace and prosperity in marriage'. Grandmother told this story to whoever praised the ring. It was a rectangular diamond with four thin gold claws. Around it, on a circular frame, also gold, were twenty-one minute white diamonds (I counted them). Grandfather's mother had died a few months after their anniversary, so the ring bore added value. Grandfather wore it along with his engagement and wedding rings, and another white stone ring that was given to him when he was very young to shape his temper.

Grandfather was in the habit of placing the ring on the counter of the washbasin each time he used it. The day before Grandmother found it missing, he had forgotten to put the ring back on. He remembered it only that night. Grandmother was in the kitchen, rinsing and stacking the dinner dishes. When she came into the bedroom she noticed he was more talkative than usual. For the first time in many months, he asked if she was tired.

'Oh, of course not. It is *nothing*. Sweet of you to ask! How was your work today?'

'It was OK.'

She took a sleeping pill – she had been taking them for as long as I could remember – and they went to bed. He waited for her to fall asleep. This took a long time: she didn't hear him snore so she wondered what was bothering him. Hours after they had occupied their ends of the bed, Grandfather called out Grandmother's name, first softly, then boldly. He got up and looked for the ring in the bathroom, in the closet, in the kitchen – where he had gone to get custard apple ice cream, which he didn't eat for dinner because he was scolding me for having only chocolate ice-cream for my meal – in his car, and even in the garage, where he never went. He wondered how to break the news to his wife. He knew, like the rest of us, that a lost item became for Grandmother a call for an entrenched battle with the perceived perpetrator of the crime. The announcement of the loss was followed by hours, sometimes days, of recrimination at the carelessness of the loser. The whole house was put on alert, the servants ruthlessly questioned; and threats of contacting the police were made.

This time the maid under investigation was Narayani. By now the areas of comfort that she provided Grandmother had increased considerably. She gave her the massage that Grandmother had always envied the Old Lady from the North, as well as a head rub and hot towel treatment three times a week. Still, Grandmother was quite upset about the ring, and it was out of the question to overlook it like she had the vacuum cleaner, the shirts, or the keychain, which by now she was convinced had also been stolen. She considered going to the police but could not bear the thought of them entering Narayani's house while her daughters were present. Once, when I was away, Narayani had brought her younger daughter to meet Grandmother. She took a liking to the girl who 'had beautiful eyes.

Must have got them from her *father*.' Grandmother also liked the fact that the girl refused everything she was offered: chocolates, biscuits, chips, my ragged Barbie dolls, even the chance to watch TV in my room. '*Such* a nice girl!'

For the next few days Grandmother was unusually quiet, though she continued to supervise arrangements for the party. We had been anticipating a hullabaloo of the most unpleasant kind but it had been a few days and she had said nothing. She told me not to spend time in the kitchen anymore. On one of those days, Narayani came in to clean my room. I was studying for a moral science exam. The frangipanis were finally in bloom and through my windows I could see several clusters of bright flowers, diffused yellow and pink, hanging at the very end of the branch. Grandfather always asked me to wash my hands after I plucked a frangipani flower: the thin white fluid was poisonous; 'That is why no birds come to this tree.' I couldn't help asking Narayani how she was doing. She said her husband told her he was leaving her.

'He go to another woman. She give him more money. I give him hundred every week. She will give him one fifty rupees.' I asked her why she was unhappy at losing a husband who beat her and her daughters. 'You not understand, baby,' she said, and left the room.

Later that day, over lunch, I heard Grandmother talking to Narayani in the kitchen – their first conversation in many days.

'You know, Narayani, that ring we lost some days ago? It brings good luck *only* to the person it is given to. If someone else wears it, that person's marriage is destroyed. I pray to god that *nothing* bad happens to whoever has the ring.' I couldn't hear Narayani's reply. Maybe she said nothing. She had begun to look different. Her eyes were dull. She tied her hair in a way that made her look much older. Many times her blouse or bangles didn't match her sari. She had also put on weight around her stomach. The day after Grandmother's talk, Narayani looked as if she had been crying. Her eyes were an ill mix of red and yellow. She said her husband had left her and taken their eldest daughter with him. When I went into the kitchen, I saw

Grandmother rubbing Narayani's back as she wept. Later, Narayani made tea for everyone, then lunch – okra curry, dry spinach with cumin and garlic, and fried mackerel.

The next morning, when Grandmother was teaching me subsets, we heard a shout: 'Amma, look what I found.' Grandmother calmly put her pen down and left the room. In her bedroom, a shiny piece of metal lay on the lower mattress of the bed, near the wooden footboard. Narayani was holding up the mattress with both her hands, her face engaged in an effort to show extreme surprise and elation. The afternoon sunlight that filtered through the cotton curtains split the pink diamond into several hundred pieces, and in it I could see traces of striking blue and purple.

TISHANI DOSHI

_____

Spartacus and the Dancing Man

Spartacus was born with three holes in his heart. When he came into the world, Bean and I were put on trains to different cities to stay with different aunts. We came back only when the doctors had fixed up Spartacus and his grape-sized heart. Everyone called him the miracle baby. Charlie and Love held him as though he really were a miracle baby.

What was it like having Spartacus to grow up with?
Hard and soft, hard and soft.

We lived in a house of ghosts at the time. They were everywhere. Bean and I used to catch them in our sleep at night. We used to chase them out of closets, listen for the sound of anklets on their heavy feet, wait for them at the doorway of our dreams. During the day they'd hang from the flame of the forest tree in the front yard with long ropes of twisted hair and gauzy gowns, their feet turned backwards at the ankles. When they saw us coming they'd stick their tongues out of their heads and roll their eyes about madly. Nan told us all about them. She used to put us up, one on each knee, and tell us which ones to watch out for.

There was the midget, Mary Jane, who lived in the pantry guarding tins of biscuits, who spat and hissed and cursed if you disturbed her sleep. There was Lady Cassandra who liked to chase cars after midnight, her face at the driver's window, streaming black hair behind her. There was the *churrel* Helen, who slept in Spartacus's baby cradle. A *churrel* is the ghost of a woman who loses her life in child-birth. *Churrels* are the saddest ghosts of them all.

Nan said that ghosts only stay in places where there's no feeling of shame, no faith in religion, no sense of discipline, no inclination for forgiveness, no patience and no knowledge. The ghosts in our house were ignorant, dark and foolish, she said. They remember their previous births and are neither humble nor wild. They know nothing.

But the ghost that knew everything was the dancing man. He used to climb down from the toy shelf every night like a dark island against the walls of the room that Bean and I shared. Sometimes he would slide all the way across the floor and teeter at the edge of our bed sheets. Once, when Bean was fast asleep, I thought I heard him whisper, *I'm going to tell you a love story*, in a voice that sounded like the night wind caught in a gust of leaves.

Charlie used to say that the beginning of love starts at the beginning of a space in time. And a space in time can be as big as a football field or as small as the opening at the top of your throat. Spartacus, coming the way he did with his twenty-four-ounce body and his arteries no thicker than the tip of a ball-point pen, found the tiniest space in our family to come rushing in and save us: he lifted us up and threw us crashing down. So even though I love Charlie and Love and Bean, and most times I love Nan, I love Spartacus like nothing else.

When Bean and I were little we used to hold Spartacus down and tickle him. She used to get his legs and I used to get his arms. He had a thin brown stomach then, with a bumpy pink scar that ran down the middle of it. His bellybutton hung out of its hole like an ear, an extra flap of flesh. We used to tickle him in the ribs because we didn't want to open any of the stitches that held him together. *Be careful of his ven-tree-culls*, Bean used to say. He used to laugh till tears came choking out of his eyes. Nan would hear us from the kitchen and yell at us to leave him be. When Charlie and Love went out at night, we'd dress Spartacus up like a girl so we could be three sisters instead of two. Bean trained him to say naughty things to Nan, and, in secret, we both used to try to get him to love us best.

In our family, Bean was the imagination and I was the memory. She used to spend hours inventing identities for herself, making trips to foreign cities, wandering through their chaotic bazaars, bargaining for trinkets in their tapered streets. She charted routes across continents, discovered new islands, flew around in her biplane, hitchhiked from town to town with cowboys and troubadours. She did this long before I knew that a world existed outside our home, long before I understood what it meant to have a longing to leave.

Spartacus learned to walk when he was three. He was four when he learned to run. When he was twelve he had his first accident. By then he'd been running for years, waiting for a chance when we were asleep or distracted to find an opening in the gate or door. He'd run down the road, tearing down it like a wild animal, looking back every few seconds to see if we were following, laughing himself silly. At the corner, he'd wait for Charlie or Love or Bean or me to come and get him. If no one came, he'd dance around and dart about from one end to the other until we did. Once, he ran right across the road at the end of the street and a scooter knocked him down. The neighbour's maid, who was buying vegetables, saw the whole thing and came running back with waterfalls streaming down her face, telling Nan how Spartacus just lay there on the road still as anything, not even crying. Bean and I didn't cry, but we were thinking the same thing: Spartacus was surely going to die. Nobody survived accidents like this; we were sure of it. Charlie told Bean to get into the rickshaw with her to the hospital, but Bean refused. She stood there with the tears frozen in her eyes and refused to move. *I won't do it, I won't do it*, she kept saying over and over again.

Finally, I got into the rickshaw with Charlie. All the way to the hospital I wondered what kind of a ghost Spartacus would become if he died, and if he'd continue to live in our house. I prayed Spartacus wouldn't die. I prayed to all the gods I knew; Charlie's god and Love's god, because they were different. When we got to the Emergency Room Spartacus was sitting up in bed, blinking. He'd grazed the tops and bottoms of his teeth, elbows and knees. Charlie held him to her chest and wept. When Love got to the hospital he held Charlie and Spartacus for a long time. I stood at the corner of the bed watching them. I thought it must have been like this when he was getting patched up to become the miracle baby, when Bean and I were in different cities. It would have been nice to have Bean stand with me in the room watching Spartacus not die. On the way home in Love's car, Charlie held Spartacus like a baby in her lap. A twelve-year-old baby.

At home, Bean and Nan were waiting with dinner-plate eyes. Love went over and picked her up and told her not to look like a watermelon face. It was okay, he said. *Isn't it good to see Spartacus is okay?* I asked Bean that night why she wouldn't go to the hospital with Charlie. I remember Bean turning to face me with her two long plaits hanging down the sides of her head, her tiny eyes opening and closing quickly. She said if Spartacus were to die there'd be a hole in our family bigger than the three holes in Spartacus's heart and no one would be able to patch us up. She said we'd have to walk around with fleshy bellybuttons and bumpy pink scars down our chests for the rest of our lives.

There were no noises the night we brought Spartacus back alive. Nothing moved. All the ghosts seemed to be sleeping out in the tree keeping a sacred silence. I didn't hear the cats mating on the neighbour's wall, or the dancing man climb down from the toy shelf. I didn't even hear Dick Whittington on his way to becoming Mayor of London tapping his staff at the door to Charlie and

Love's bedroom. Bean and I got up in the middle of the night in our matching pyjamas and crept into their bedroom. Spartacus lay between them with bandages on his legs and arms. Bean got into Charlie's side and I got into Love's. We lay like that for a whole night; a family in troubled times, sleeping in a house of ghosts. It's a feeling I still go looking for when I go looking for love.

*

Here is Charlie. Here is Love. This is what they call each other.

Sometimes it seems like they came into the world the way they are now. Charlie in her embroidered maxis and trumpet-sleeved tops; Love in his wide ties and bell-bottom pants. Charlie's real name means snow, and Love's real name means light. It's hard to think of Charlie as mother. She is mother, she is all that is mother. Her skin is white, her eyes are green, her hair is tinged with golden lights, her stomach is white, her breasts are white, and everything about her is soft. Where Charlie comes from they call everyone Love, and that's how our father came to be called Love. In their letters to each other, Charlie used to call him, *My darling love*. Now she just calls him Love. But when she's angry she calls him by his real name.

The story of how Charlie and Love fell in love is the most romantic story I know. When they were very young, Charlie and Love went far away from their homes. They hadn't decided to meet that way, but it was in a country of snow and light. We don't know how they met; if it was at a party or walking down the street, or if they bumped into each other at a library, but we know that Charlie followed Love all the way back here and they travelled all over this country taking pictures and labelling them with captions. *Nakhi Lake – Nakhi Lake means nail lake. Boating in Nakhi Lake – Me trying my hand at it – A legend tells of a man digging out the lake overnight with the nail of his thumb in order to marry a princess.*

There's a picture of them at the Taj Mahal, which is the most romantic building I know because a man made it for his dead queen. She's a *churrel* now because she died giving birth to the king's fourteenth child. He emptied out the state treasury to complete the mausoleum for her and cut off the hands of hundreds of workers so they'd never be able to make another thing like it again. Later in his life, he was captured by his own son and thrown into a cell facing the Taj, forced to see the white spires from his window for eight long years until he died.

In this picture, Love is wearing a brown tweed suit with an orange flower in his buttonhole, his brown arm around Charlie, his unruly hair moving sideways in the wind. Charlie's in a green silk sari with a pink ribbon in her hair. Her blouse sleeves are so short, her thin girly arms poke out of them like broomsticks. The Taj behind them is gleaming like their teeth: marble, white, gleaming love. I used to carry that picture with me everywhere to remind me of love, what it was like to be separated from it, and, also, to remind me that Charlie and Love were once so incredibly young, like two people we didn't know. They were so young they could hold everything in their hands; everything belonged to them. Nothing slipped through their fingers.

Of course it was Bean who found the letters. When we found them we didn't need to be told anything. We found out how Charlie and Love wanted to live in their country of snow and light and have a family of their own; how their parents didn't want them to be together so they grew angry and ill and silent and walked around with heavy tumours in their chests. Love went home to his ill mother and Charlie went home to hers. They waited to see if it would go away, if love would leave them in peace. They wrote every day; six months of Charlie's aerogrammes – her thin, blue, upright handwriting; six months of Love's craggy bound books – untidy and unending. They put everything in those letters. They wrote about us even though we weren't even there yet. In Charlie's letter: *My mother asked if we'd even thought about having children, and the shame of it. Of course we'll have children darling, three of them, and they'll be so beautiful.* Bean and Spartacus and me.

We figured that it was because they didn't come from the same country or colour or God that no one wanted them to be together or have us. But in the end, like Charlie said, love finds an opening in space or time. In the end, their families let them go. When Bean and I were born, the family were quiet, but when Spartacus came they tried to say, *We told you so*. Charlie always said that what happened with Spartacus was that there was too much love, they'd choked him with it when he was in her; that if everyone had just let her alone she wouldn't have had to hold herself so hard.

When Charlie followed Love here, she left something behind. We don't know what it was, but nowadays she goes searching for it. Bean and I watch her talking to herself when she's dusting the lampshades, setting the table, wiping the dishes, hooking up the sagging curtain. All the time her hands are moving, her lips are moving too. We can't figure out what she's trying to say. When we ask, she looks at us and says it's nothing. But Bean and I know it has to be something. We know because we're older now and we've started doing the same things: murmuring, talking in our sleep, stopping midway in a room to straighten something.

We think it might have something to do with growing sick for a home. How it must be to leave everything you ever knew to start a new family. To have only one Love on your side. Sometimes we think it might be Spartacus weighing down upon her. Perhaps she worries what will happen to him. She's scared he'll forget who we are, or go crazy, but she doesn't say anything about it. This is the way it is with our family. We feel everything but say nothing. Love taught us to be that way because in his family they used to say too much, and once things are out in the open you can't put them away. When Charlie came to stay with Love at our grandfather's house, the family talked so much about her, in whispers and out loud, that Charlie and Love had to leave and make their own house. You can't put words back into drawers; they won't fold up neatly, or fit where you want them to. Bean and I worry about Spartacus too. How he'll never be able to look after himself.

I think of where we go to feel safe at nights. To our rooms, our houses, our beds. How these may not be the safest places in the world because when the darkness comes, the walls and seams that seem to hold us up can easily be undone. Dangers can enter like wild fires or killer waves at twilight or dusk, soundless and high, sweeping away the foundations of our lives as though they were specks of foam. I've seen pictures of families standing on the roofs of their houses, caught up in floods and tornadoes and earthquakes. Families in countries of war, living among the ruins of their old houses, hoping to one day rebuild brick and stone so their children won't have to sit outside with bloodied faces and hearts. I think what it must mean to lose a home and a family and a country all at once, like Charlie. I think of Spartacus dying and making a hole in our family. Of nobody being able to fill it up with love.

*

Everything seems shut up now. The windows, the doors, the small flights of stairs. The wooden banister of our grandfather's house. We are whooshing down now, Bean and I. Our skirts flying up behind us. We need the skirts to cover our bottoms, to make them slippy so we can slide down.

I want to tell Bean about the darkness, how it has come again. How it feels like the dancing man has come down from the wall after Charlie and Love have put us to bed, and the snakes and dragons and Dick Whittington on his way to becoming Mayor of London are standing guard at their bedroom door. When Bean would dream of fairies and Ferris-wheels and I would hear the cats mating on the wall, their shrieks like babies dying. It has come again, the sound of babies dying.

What happened to me was something like a darkening. I want to tell Bean how I lay on a hospital bed, too young to know anything, so young that there were bones in my face that have since disappeared. How I walked out on jittery knees, collapsing on the floor of the elevator, trying to keep my eyes open, wanting to ask someone who knew, was it a boy or a girl? Was it like Spartacus? Could it have been?

Bean doesn't know anything about it and I can't tell her because she'll change the way she sees me. I can't tell Charlie or Love because they'll change the way they see me too. I have to fold it up and put it away. Could I tell Spartacus? Unblinking, smiling Spartacus?

When the man who pretends to love me comes, he lifts up the corner of my skirt, slides his hands across my shaved pubis and smiles. He's teetering at the edge of my bed-sheets. It's a secret we share. Isn't it fun? Oh, it has stopped being fun a long time ago. His hands don't melt on my skin anymore. They move like rough sandpaper over my body. I bend down and unzip his pants. He smiles again. Is this what he's waiting for? When it's over, he leaves. I make him go far away. He calls from a telephone booth saying things like *love* and *want*. I think about the letters that Charlie and Love wrote to one another filled with *darling* and *love* and *when we have children*. I know this is nothing close to it.

I want to tell Bean how he found his way into our room to sit in the wicker chair waiting patiently for me while Nan took her to piano lessons. I want to tell her that when I visit our house I can still see him sitting there, with his dark hair spread against the wall like an island. After all the wanderings, he's still sitting there, and he speaks. He doesn't know about the bucket at the side of the table with the lid covering the baby in it. He doesn't know about the nurse's eyes, their covered mouths, their green starchy uniforms.

What do you call the ghost of a baby who dies before it's born?

I have two permanent ghosts in my life. This is what I want to tell Bean.

Bean would say I'm wallowing in self-pity. She wouldn't believe me if I told her the dancing man really exists. How he climbs down like a shadow to creep in your bed and spread your legs. How he stays till morning, but by morning it's always too late; you've wet the bed, you've cried, you've heard the babies dying. Charlie will come and say, *Look what you've done. Not again!* Bean will sit up in her bed and smile, a perfect child in crisp white sheets, the sugar still at the corners of her lips, the fairground still whirring in her head. And I'll climb out with soggy evidence of shame between my legs. And Nan will say, *shame shame puppy shame.* Water won't cleanse it out: not water, not fire.

*

Bean comes back to me after all. She wants me to tell her things. I knew it would come to this. That I'd have to be the one to explain. We meet in the house where everything started, the house with the flame of the forest tree. We meet in our dreams, tossing in our beds like Love, moving our lips with worry like Charlie. We talk. We are silent. We hold hands and walk all around the house, looking behind curtains, in the cupboards, under the sofas, in the bathtub, any place where Spartacus might be. We must find him. For everything to be right again we must find him. We look in places where he might have rolled himself into something quite small, almost disappeared, waiting for us to find him, catch him, save him. Maybe he's waiting at the corner of some street in one of Bean's imagined cities. Maybe he's standing there with his sparkling eyes, laughing so hard he has to pee, holding his crotch, waiting for us to come and get him. We think if we could go back there we'd understand something we missed before; something Charlie and Love forgot to tell us.

Here is Spartacus sitting with a new family. He ran out from the gates of our grandfather's house down the road to where the slums are. He's sitting outside with the other children playing in the mud. We've just driven past him and we didn't even recognize him. Love says to turn around, turn around, we missed something. We reverse the car and see him, the air comes back into us. He's sitting with a smile. He's the happiest we've ever seen him. Nobody's bothered him at all. They don't care that he's sitting with their children making funny noises, playing in the dirt. They're sitting with their feet in the muck on the pavement of the streets outside their thatch houses with marbles for toys. Spartacus is happy. We pick him up and put him in the car. We shout and breathe and laugh all together. We drive back home and close the gates to our house, so no one can get out and no one can get in. We climb into our beds at night and try to sleep without saying the things we fear the most out loud. We gather up the sheets and fall into them. We walk about in our dreams trying to find out what it is we missed. We look for each other behind corners and what we find is only this: this house with its thin walls, emptied out, and turned inside out. We call out each other's names and they echo off the walls like smoke.

Aishwarya Subramanyam

Lotus

His eyes gulped her in without blinking, without thinking, fearful she wasn't real. She was a family of fireflies twinkling, laughing at him; she was swishes of mist draped on a blushing moon. No! She was sand, sifting through his fingers. Seashells for eyes, seaweed for hair, a mouth of water that held planets. Surely he didn't deserve her. His stomach was full to bursting, but he hadn't eaten. He thanked his god. Thank you, uncomprehendingly, thank you. Surely this was love.

He held her with tender terror, unable to stop himself touching. How could he stop? He watched as a lucky calloused finger – was that his finger, his hand, his hard dead tentacles? – traced the swell of her face. The skin a layer of malai on boiled milk, it might tear if he pressed into it with more force than that of breath on bubble. The nose a princess, an upturned triangle full of lost ships, pirates crazed with longing. Impossibly black eyes that shone with the wisdom of innocence, knowing all, knowing him. The pinkest of lips ... so, so pink ... parted. Was she about to say something? He shushed her, bringing the petals together with thumb and forefinger. There would be no talking. No words must come, he could not bear it.

She was a lesson in perfection. And she was his.

Carrying her to her new home, his eyes apologized. It wasn't much, but she mustn't mind. He was so poor, this was all he could give her. She shifted against his chest slightly, trying find a softer rib for her forehead to rest on. But she would be more comfortable here, happy here. There was the smell ... but she would get used to that. It was a warm home, and he could see that she was cold, although she didn't make a sound.

Wrapping her nakedness tighter into the swathe of cloth, he laid her down, his heart in his hand, a cushion. Oh, it was such a mess. He shooed away flies, moved some things out of the way. A half-eaten chapati, scrunched-up paper, banana peels. He found his breath again as he pulled back to look at her. She would redeem everything. She would be the lotus in the mud.

He must go now. He didn't want to leave her, but there were others waiting for him. Others like her. No, there was no one like her. But there were others he could not leave. He kissed the valley of her brow, and a slight shudder went through her at the cold of his cracked lips. He didn't trust himself to speak; words felt bulky on his tongue, difficult to balance. She understood, he knew she did. Now she would sleep. She yawned and her eyes began to close. As her head fell to one side, mouth open in an imitation of life, he waited for the breathing to steady so that he might leave her then.

A final drinking in, a final touch. He would never see her again. But every time he blinked she would form in the film on his eyes, draining away and reappearing at every whisper of a second. He shut the door quietly, and gripping his tatters about him, he walked into the night, death fog curling around his feet, coursing through his bones. The feet walked him home, and he broke the news to his three daughters. Their mother was dead. She had died in childbirth, the baby was stillborn. The wails of the orphaned girls sliced through mud walls. Who would take care of them now? Neighbours came, and joined in lamentation, an excuse to throw their own buckets of grief up to the heavens.

The poor man. How would he manage with four daughters? They had been trying for a son for years. His wife wanted to give him a boy, so much. She knew she was weak, she had miscarried several times, but despite his protests she had still wanted to try. She was the luckier one, now free of shackles. And it was better for the child to have been born dead. What was there in this life for her anyway? Where she had gone she would know no hunger.

The men of the slums gathered around him, smoking, saying nothing. And he sat at the threshold of his hut, blinking, breathing.

Two days later, policemen found the dead body of a newborn baby girl in a roadside garbage container. She was in rags, the icy night air had taken her breath away. She had died in the stench and the buzzing licking flies. They took her, a cold-blue lotus, from half-eaten chapatis, scrunched-up paper and rotting banana peels.

The Giantess

Thousands of years ago in far away India, which is so far away that anything is possible, before the advent of the inevitable Aryans, a giantess was in charge of a little kingdom. It was small by her standards, but perhaps not by our own. Three oceans converged on its triangular tip, and in the north there were mountains, the tallest in the world, which would perhaps account for this singular kingdom. It was not a kingdom, but the word has been lost and I could find no other. There wasn't any king. The giantess governed and there were no other women. The men were innocent and happy and carefree. If they were hurt, they were quickly consoled. For the giantess was kind, and would set them on her knee and tell them they were brave and strong and noble. And if they were hungry, the giantess would feed them. The milk from her breasts was sweeter than honey and more nutritious than mangoes. If they grew fractious, the giantess would sing, and they would clamber up her legs and onto her lap and sleep unruffled. They were a happy people and things might have gone on in this way forever, were it not for the fact that the giantess grew tired. Her knees felt more bony, her voice rasped, and on one or two occasions, she showed irritation.

They were greatly distressed. 'We love you,' they said to the tired giantess. 'Why don't you sing? Are you angry with us? What have we done?' 'You are dear little children,' the giantess replied, 'but I have grown very tired and it's time for me to go.' 'We will make you happy. Only please don't go.' 'Do you know what I want?' the giantess asked. They were silent for a bit. Then one of them said, 'We'll make you our queen.' And another one said, 'We'll write you a poem.' And a third one shouted (while turning cartwheels), 'We'll bring you many gifts of oysters and pearls and pebbles and stones.' 'No,' said the giantess, 'No.' She turned her back and crossed the mountains.

Biographical Notes

AMBAI is the pen-name of Tamil writer C. S. Lakshmi, who also writes in English. A prominent writer of short stories, she has also published literary criticism in English. Her writings include collections of short stories and two books of interviews with women singers and performers. Ambai is also a filmmaker and founder of the Sound and Picture Archives for Research on Women (SPARROW) based in Mumbai, India.

CHANDRIKA B., a writer of short stories in Malayalam, lives in Kerala where she is a university teacher. She is one of Kerala's best-known writers and has published a number of short-story collections.

SHAKTI BHATT's prize-winning short stories have appeared in anthologies and journals in the UK and India. She was working on three novels when she died unexpectedly in New Delhi in 2007. She was twenty-six.

MEENAL DAVE is a teacher and writer based in Gujarat.

MAHASHVETA DEVI, one of India's foremost writers, has a large number of novels and short stories to her credit. Published in several

Indian and foreign languages, Mahashveta Devi writes of the lives of tribals and ordinary men and women. She sees her writing as a political commitment to bettering the lives of those on the margins. Among her many awards are the Ramon Magasaysay Award, the Sahitya Akademi Award and the Jnanpith Award. She writes in Bengali.

TISHANI DOSHI was born in 1975 in Madras (now Chennai), India. She was educated at Queen's College and the Johns Hopkins University, USA, and is now a dancer, poet and novelist. She received an Eric Gregory Award for her poetry in 2001 while living in London. In 2005 she won the All India Poetry Competition and was also a finalist in the 2005 Outlook-Picador Non-Fiction Competition. Her first book of poems, *Countries of the Body*, won the Forward Prize in 2006, and her first novel, *The Pleasure Seekers*, is soon to be published by Bloomsbury.

ARUPA PATANGIA KALITA is one of Assam's leading award-winning novelists. She has more than ten novels and short-story collections to her credit. She teaches Literature in Assam.

MRIDULA KOSHY currently lives in New Delhi after an absence of two decades from the city she considers her true home. Much of her time is taken up being a mother to three children, and in what remains she writes, and plans to continue writing.

SUNITI NAMJOSHI was born in India in 1941 where she worked as an officer in the Indian Administrative Service. Subsequently she taught at the University of Toronto for many years. Her poems, fables and satires have been published and widely read. She lives and writes with Gillian Hanscombe in a small village in Devon, England.

MANJULA PADMANABHAN is an artist, illustrator, cartoonist,

playwright and novelist. Alienation and marginalization play a large role in her writings. *Harvest*, a play about the sale of body parts and exploitative relations between developed and developing countries, won the Onassis Award for Culture. She has a number of collections of short stories to her credit.

URMILA PAWAR is a well-known writer from Maharashtra. Author of several novels and short stories as well as a widely acclaimed autobiography, Urmila Pawar has won many awards for her work. She writes in Marathi.

BULBUL SHARMA is a writer, artist, nature lover and educationist. She has published several collections of short stories and a novel, *Banana Flower Dreams*. She works with children with special needs, holding painting workshops and also conducts nature walks. She lives in New Delhi and London. Her works have been translated into several languages.

GEETANJALI SHREE is a historian by training but now devotes her entire time to writing fiction. Author of several collections of short stories and four novels, Geetanjali lives and works in Delhi and writes in Hindi. She is also involved in a number of campaigns and issues that address fundamentalism and sectarianism in Indian society.

VANDANA SINGH was born and raised in New Delhi. An early interest in science and a steady diet of myth, legend and village lore provided by her mother and grandmother led her to appreciate the wonderful quirkiness of people, animals and the universe as a whole. As a teenager she also acquired a lifelong interest in peace and environmental issues. She obtained a doctoral degree in physics from the US, where she currently lives with her family, teaching college physics and writing fiction, including science fiction, and fantasy for children and adults.

MARIJA SRES was born in 1943 in Bratonci, Slovenia. In 1971 she went to Gujarat, India as a religious sister to work with rural women. She studied Gujarati literature and, for over thirty years, has worked with women of the Dungri Garasiya tribes. She has written several books of short stories and her work has been translated into several languages.

AISHWARYA SUBRAMANYAM has spent the last two years in the UK, where she finished a Master's in Film Studies at the University of East Anglia, Norwich. She has worked as a journalist and film set designer in Hyderabad. She lives and works in Delhi. She is twenty-five and getting older.

WAJIDA TABASSUM was born and brought up in Amravati, Hyderabad. She is author of twenty-seven books of fiction and poetry. Several of her stories have been translated into other languages and some have been made into films. Wajida Tabassum writes in Urdu.

Acknowledgements

Grateful thanks are due to:

Jeet Thayil for permission to reproduce 'The Thief'.

Anjum Katyal for the translation, and Seagull Books, Kolkata for permission to reproduce 'Rudali'.

Meenaxi Barkotoki for the translation, and Katha for permission to reproduce 'Numoli's Story'.

Zubaan for permission to reproduce 'A Large Girl', 'Lotus' and 'Spartacus and the Dancing Man'.

Vandana Singh for permission to reproduce 'The Wife'.

Marija Sres and Jivabhai M. Katara for permission to reproduce 'How Kava Deceived Kavi and Defeated Her'.

Veena Deo for the translation, and Zubaan for permission to reproduce 'Mother'.

Chandrika B. for the translation of her story and the Kerala Sahitya Akademi for permission to reproduce 'The Story of a Poem'.

Lakshmi Holmstrom for the translation, and Kalavachudu and Oxford University Press for permission to reproduce 'A Movement, A Folder, Some Tears'.

Kali for Women for permission to reproduce 'Teaser' and 'Cast-offs'.

Sara Rai for the translation, and the author for permission to reproduce 'March, Ma and Sakura'.

Penguin Books India for permission to reproduce 'Mayadevi's London Yatra'.

'The Giantess' published in Feminist Fables. Melbourne. Australia. Spinifex Press, pp 29-30.